I0731266

DOUBLE BACKED MAGIC

RISE OF MAGIC
BOOK 6

STEFON MEARS

Thousand
Faces
Publishing

Also by Stefon Mears

Published by Thousand Faces Publishing, Portland, Oregon

http://1kfaces.com

ISBN: 978-1-948490-19-1

The year is 2028
Six decades after the Rise of Magic

1

For a man about to meet the president of the United North American States, Donal Cuthbert felt surprisingly calm.

True, the surroundings might have helped. The west wing of the White House, near the president's office, held an atrium that was the envy of the entire Washington DC area, if not the whole eastern seaboard. Scores of varieties of flowers, arranged in rows among the soft grass, resplendent in the afternoon sunlight that filtered in through the glass ceiling.

All the official flowers of every state in the Union, from Newfoundland to Alaska to Chiapas. Each with a little plaque, describing the flower and where it came from.

Such a disparate variety of plants from vastly different ecosystems.

Beautiful as they all were, Donal was more interested in the little magics used by earth elementals to keep every one of them in bloom year round, despite the DC climate.

He'd noticed the four elementals first thing, of course. The gnome variety popular in the western part of the world. Donal had spotted them as soon as secret service agents had seated him on this stone bench and retired to posts still within sight, though not close enough to be considered threatening.

A year ago, the presence of armed guards might have felt threatening to Donal anyway. They were clearly watching him, and for all he knew they were licensed to do him a great deal of harm if he did anything he wasn't supposed to.

But then, a year ago, even the act of waiting to meet President Gutierrez would have tied Donal's guts in knots of tension. He would have sunk deeply into meditation to minimize his anxiety, but it wouldn't have been enough. By the time he would have been called in to the meeting, he would have been a nervous, sweaty mess.

A lot had changed in the past year.

Between Donal's graduate studies in Thaumaturgy, the time he'd spent with his patron, interplanetary business magnate Donatello Mancuso, and the pure insanity of Donal's past year, just meeting the president no longer felt intimidating.

Really, it came down to this — after a man has had to negotiate with the Fae Queens of both Summer and Winter at the same time, very little feels quite so frightening.

So Donal kept his mind clear with light meditation while maintaining enough of his attention on his surroundings to note the movements of the earth elementals as they did little things to aid the surrounding plants and keep them vital.

He was just considering a deeper study of the techniques they used when a man approached across the grass, from Donal's right.

The man was in his early twenties, like Donal, and about the same middling height, but the similarities ended there. This man was tanned where Donal was pale, blonde where Donal's hair was black.

And he wore a suit of dark blue silk with a red tie, which could not begin to compare with the pale blue airsilk suit Donal wore, with a tie of the blue and black tartan designed just for him.

An aide, no doubt.

"Mr. Ambassador," the aide said, "the president is ready for you."

"Thank you..." Donal said, as he stood and straightened clothes that didn't need straightening.

"Jefferson, sir. Randal Jefferson."

"Thank you, Mr. Jefferson," Donal said, noting the name and remembering it, the way Mr. Mancuso had taught him.

The secret service agents fell into step, pacing Donal and Jefferson without getting too close as they crossed the atrium to the heavily enchanted oaken double-door that led into the president's office.

Donal had to struggle not to shift awareness and study the enchantments layered on and around those doors. Fascinating as the study would have been, though, he knew he couldn't risk getting caught up and losing track of where he was and what he was *supposed* to be doing.

Donal smiled, imagining how his familiar, Fionn, would be proud of his restraint. Fionn, of course, waited right now in the silver faun pendant around Donal's neck. Donal had been told in no uncertain terms that he was not to have his familiar present when meeting the president.

Mr. Jefferson knocked twice, then opened the door.

Donal felt the wards as he crossed them — detection wards, looking for threats and contraband, mixed in among more general sorts of protection wards.

The round office, itself, looked much the way it was presented in the news shadowcasts. Rich blue carpeting, featuring the UNAS seal. Large, ornate wooden desk, likely the same one used by presidents since before the Rise of Magic, back when there were only fifty states — one of them Hawai'i — Puerto Rico was still a territory, and Canada and Mexico were separate countries.

A pair of ficuses flanked the desk. Huge windows behind it showed the lawn beyond. Paintings on the walls of past presidents. Busts of Washington and Lincoln.

And, of course, the president himself, seated behind the desk, between the twin flags — one representing the UNAS, and the other the office of the presidency.

All men should age as gracefully as President Diego Gutierrez. Said to be only fifty years old when he took office two years ago, he remained as fit and vibrant as a man half his age. About a half-dozen centimeters taller than Donal when he stood to greet his guest, and the only graying to his black hair had been gentle and at the temples.

Even his skin. Apart from a few mild laugh lines, it was smooth and dark as polished teak.

And the black airsilk suit he wore fit him perfectly.

The two secret service guards took up positions near the door behind Donal. The only other occupant of the room was a small sylph, currently invisible, who would record and witness all conversations for the official state records.

And, likely, send for help if anything ... *untoward* were to happen.

"Sorry to keep you waiting," President Gutierrez said, smiling as he shook Donal's hand with a trustworthy grip.

"To be honest," Donal said, taking the seat the president offered with a gesture, "I'm surprised you wanted to see me at all."

"Are you?" And there was the quizzical smile Donal had seen in interviews whenever President Gutierrez was asked a question he felt had an obvious answer. "You're a UNAS citizen, but somehow you're the *human* ambassador representing not one, but *both* Fae Courts. You don't think that sounds like someone I should meet?"

"Well," Donal said, drawing a deep breath, "that depends. Am I here to talk with you as president of the UNAS? Or in your role as a member of the United Terran Government Security Council?"

Donal made a show of looking about at the absence of a UTG flag, or anything bearing the planetary logo.

"My interest is in both capacities," President Gutierrez said. "But at the moment, my primary interest is in the UNAS."

"Then what can I do for you, Mr. President?"

"Does it have to be straight to business? You've had quite an exciting year, so far, I understand. It's only May, but even though you're at the top of your doctoral cohort at CalThaum San Luis Obispo, you've had time for ... how many? Four ambassadorial trips to Luna?"

Donal had made five trips to Luna, to meet with representatives from the Du Mak and the Courts' newly resurgent ancient enemy, the *Fomhóraigh*. Not that any of those talks had been productive so far.

All of which, Donal had no doubt the president knew.

He drew a deep breath while he considered how Mr. Mancuso would handle this situation.

"You've had a busy year so far yourself, sir. The embargo on Terran goods to Luna has to be hurting the American economy. And it can't be easy holding the line against the planetary draft, when Russia, Japan and China are all pushing for it. Is it true you've started discussing the possibility of acknowledging Mars' independence if they aid you in bringing Luna back into the Terran fold?"

President Gutierrez chuckled. "You sound like a politician, not a magician."

"Believe me," Donal said, with perfect honesty. "Right this moment I'd rather be studying the techniques used in the wards that protect this room, not to mention investigating the enchantments on your desk and your person."

"Well as a magician, what do you think of the Machado Proposal?"

The Machado Proposal, put forth by Magister Ronaldo Machado, would improve space charts and navigation by binding lacunas — space elementals — into cubes of carterite at fixed locations throughout known space.

"Honestly?" Donal said, surprised at the question. "I think binding creatures whose existence is movement into fixed locations sounds cruel. I think there has to be a better way."

"Cruel?" Both of President Gutierrez's eyebrows shot up in surprise. "Interesting choice of words."

"I believe all spirits deserve respect and consideration, regardless of whether or not they possess physical form."

"An unusual perspective for a magician, I believe."

Donal shrugged. "I am not responsible for the ethical views of others."

"Still, as I understand it," President Gutierrez said, "every helioship engine and scanner array includes at least one bound lacuna. How would the Machado Proposal be different?"

"Lacunas are often bound to ships, but those ships rarely stay still long." Donal stopped himself short of entering lecture mode. Shook his head. "But you didn't invite me here as a magician, sir. You invited me as an ambassador. And I still don't know why."

"You are in an unusual position, Donal — may I call you Donal?"

Donal nodded.

"Thank you," President Gutierrez said, notably not offering Donal the same privilege. "You're in an unusual position, Donal. You're not only a Terran citizen, but a UNAS citizen. And yet, you have been afforded an ambassadorial position, not to mention diplomatic immunity, by a foreign power that operates on Terran soil."

"The Fae Courts are allowed such, under the terms of the agreement they negotiated with the Terran government long before they asked me to work for them."

"But where do your loyalties truly lie? My God, man, you're *human*. Will you really put Fae interests ahead of your own people?"

"You were born in Puerto Rico, Mr. President," Donal said. "Do you put that state's interests ahead of your country's? You serve on the United Terran Government Security Council — do you put Earth interests ahead of American interests?"

"I could argue that what is good for the planet is good for America, and that what is good for America is good for Puerto Rico."

Donal shrugged. "And I could argue that what is good for the Fae Courts is good for Earth. And like your argument, sometimes it would be true, and sometimes it wouldn't."

"Hardly the same thing."

"Perhaps." Donal shrugged again, trying to make the movement a statement and knowing he didn't quite pull it off. "Is that what you asked me here to discuss?"

President Gutierrez's eyes darkened a shade, and between his sculpted eyebrows, a frown line of disapproval showed itself.

"Very well. I'd been hoping this meeting could be more cordial, but... I've heard rumors that the Fae Courts and the *Fomhóraigh* are preparing for war. Can you confirm this?"

"I have been given no information that would confirm or deny that." True words, and what he had to say officially, even though Donal personally had every reason to think it was true.

President Gutierrez sighed. "You're not making this easy, Donal."

Donal's instinct was to apologize, but Mr. Mancuso had driven home the point over and over again that his job in any negotiation — and Donal was pretty sure this counted — was *not* to make the other side's job easier.

Apologizing would be giving the other side a leg up, after the president had already claimed a superior position through making Donal wait, holding the meeting in his own office. Not to mention his little name game.

The president's nostrils tightened in a quick breath.

"Well," he said, "as the Fae Courts of Earth—"

"The Fae Courts," Donal corrected. "The Courts recognize no constraints on their domain, and will not be referred to as the Fae Courts of only Earth."

"Fine," President Gutierrez said impatiently. "If you won't even give me that much." He frowned, as though he'd expected Donal to be easier to push around. "The *Fae Courts* are allies of the United Terran Government, which includes all of its member nations. Do you agree to that much?"

"It is my understanding that the agreement between the United Terran Government and the Fae Courts encompasses all the nations of Earth," Donal said. "So in that sense, yes, but in the sense of the courts being allies of any one nation against another nation, definitely not."

"That's fine," President Gutierrez said, smiling again. "I have no interest in asking our Fae allies for aid against any other country, on behalf of the UNAS."

"All right," Donal said, suspiciously.

"However, as things stand, the Du Mak steadfastly refuse to

consider negotiating any kind of alliance with Earth. They appear to harbor a grudge over the events on Ganymede."

"They were kept in pens like animals, for experimentation."

"None of which was known of or approved of by the United North American States," President Gutierrez said, smiling and raising an index finger as he made his point.

Donal didn't believe that for a moment. Not with the UNAS on the Security Council. Still, he had to admit...

"I have no information that refutes that."

"As such," President Gutierrez said, smiling wider, "would you be willing, in your capacity as ambassador for a UNAS ally, to introduce a UNAS envoy to the Du Mak people? With a goal of fostering a greater understanding between our peoples and opening talks toward a possible alliance?"

Donal frowned. "An alliance with just the United North American States? Not the United Terran Government? Does the UTG charter allow member nations to negotiate outside alliances?"

"When the UTG charter was formed, there was no one else to ally *with*. So nothing in the charter forbids it."

"And if the Du Mak people ally themselves with the UNAS, but end up at odds with the UTG? What then?"

"Such an unfortunate situation would be a matter either between us and the Du Mak, or of internal Earth politics," President Gutierrez said with a smug smile. "Either way it would not be the concern of the Fae Courts."

"You understand," Donal said, "asking this is asking a favor from the Fae Courts."

"It's a reasonable request from an ally," President Gutierrez said, smiling. "And favors are the currency of politics."

Oh, the arrogance. President Gutierrez clearly didn't understand or didn't believe what it meant to owe a favor to a fae, much less to the Fae Courts.

By contract, during his service to the Courts, Donal himself could not owe or be owed favors from any fae. But when he acted on behalf of the Courts, any favor he granted was as good as one granted by the queens themselves.

Both queens.

Donal wanted to warn President Gutierrez. But by contract, he had to represent the interests of the Fae Courts to the best of his ability. And breaking that contract could get him into far deeper trouble than any single favor.

Still, he had to say something.

"You're playing a very dangerous game, Mr. President."

"As are you, Donal."

"Don't I know it," Donal said, standing. "All right. It's a fair request, and a favor the Courts can grant. I'm due to go to Luna again next week—"

"Actually," President Gutierrez said, smiling even wider, "I have something else in mind..."

———

OF ALL THE PLACES ON LUNA THAT EDIK BARSHAI COULD HAVE BEEN right now, the estate of Rasputin Pajari might not have been his *last* choice, but it was close.

Very close.

Gaudy. Absolutely gaudy. It was one thing to have the kind of money that all the great families of Luna seemed to have. It was something else entirely to shove the facts of that money down the throats of their guests.

And hard as Edik found this to believe, even he had to admit he was present as an invited guest.

The mansion was ludicrous. Four stories tall. Two wings branching off of the main house. Dozens of chimneys — as though anyone actually needed to burn *wood* for heat — and a design that otherwise would have done Mother Russia proud at the turn of the twentieth century.

The roof was spiked around a couple of towers, and had that onion shape in other spots. The windows were arched, and the back patio where Edik waited — not to mention the stairs down onto the vast green lawn — were all done in gray-white stone imported from somewhere outside Moscow.

The décor of the patio was done in harsh-looking wrought iron furniture, but every bit of it enchanted for maximum comfort.

Hell, even the table in front of Edik was keeping his coffee hot inside the fancy, delicate cup, etched with images of Cossacks on horseback.

Of course they were Cossacks. The Pajari family, like all the lunar great families, liked to imagine themselves boyars before the fall of the tsars. Pajari himself probably wished he had an army of his own Cossacks to send against his enemies.

Past the lawn, a forest of evergreens. Past the forest, the curved yellow wall of Pajari's Barrier, separating his estate from the otherwise uninhabitable lunar surface around it.

The great families always had the best Barriers. The most modern. In Kennedy, the spells that made Earth's moon inhabitable left little telltales, because they were some of the first of their kind established anywhere. The kinks hadn't been worked out yet, leaving little ways that the air and water were just ... off.

But here, here the air smelled the way Edik remembered the air of Earth. And the no doubt the water was just as pure and perfect. The sky above was a strong, royal blue, and the afternoon sun looked the kind of yellow that felt right in Edik's bones.

Money. Plain and simple. Money that let Pajari keep a private forest for his own pleasure.

A forest that, from the look of it, was likely composed of the same varieties of evergreens Edik used to see as a child, camping with his father near St. Petersburg, back on Earth. Pines and firs, by Edik's guess.

Pajari was somewhere in that forest right now, hunting foxes with his eldest son. *Despite* being late for a meeting *he* called.

"It's a power play, pure and simple," Edik said to Dola, who was sitting in his catly-cat pose — body tall, paws together, tail wrapped neatly around his paws.

Dola looked like a slightly translucent, meter-tall shaggy gray cat. In truth, though, he was Edik's familiar and the best friend he'd ever had.

"Steady," Dola said, in tones that only Edik could hear. "Someone is listening."

"Of course someone is listening," Edik said in plain English. "And the other great families are probably spying on Pajari's spies. They all play their great games, while Luna suffers."

"Steady," Dola said again, keeping his words just for Edik. "Don't give Pajari the satisfaction of getting to you."

"To hell with him," Edik said, standing up, drawing a shocked look from Dola. "I'm not here trying to drum up business. He wants to meet about the Du Mak, let's meet. But if he thinks he can—"

A horn blew in the distance.

Edik frowned and tried counting to ten through a deep breath. Didn't help. He still wanted to draw the saber at his side and...

No. That was no good either.

Two horses approached from the woods, riding swiftly. Pajari on one, his son on the other.

"Hold!" Pajari called as they closed on the patio. "Hold, Edik! We come!"

The nerve of the man, assuming familiarity. No doubt taking it as the "right of his position."

Well, at least he wasn't acting so familiar as to call him *Edyoga* or something along those lines.

Edik sighed and sat. If the meeting was happening, it might be worth having.

Pajari and his son tied off their horses to the post at the bottom of the stairs, both smiling as they ascended.

Rasputin Pajari was not a tall man, but he made up what he lacked in height with muscles. His black hair met in a high widow's peak, much like his taller son's. Both of them had downright ruddy complexions, even when they weren't sweating the way they were now, when compared with the near translucent paleness of most of the great families.

They were both dressed for riding. Those pants that bowed outward at the thigh. Black leather boots that reached the knee. Pajari in a black shirt, and his son in deep forest green.

Even their hunting clothes were probably airsilks or something equally expensive.

Maximilian Pajari differed from his father in more than height. He had a Journeyman's aura of power about him. Much more impressive than anything a mere Initiate like Edik could manage.

"Ah, Edik," Pajari said, rubbing his hands together. "Settling for coffee? At this hour?" He turned toward the house and called, "Beer! And cigars!"

"You will smoke with us, will you not, Edik?" Pajari smiled as though they were best friends while he and his son took their seats.

"Never developed the habit," Edik said. He never developed the habit of afternoon drinking either, but declined to point that out.

"You come with your familiar out and a sword at your side," Pajari's son said. "Are you expecting trouble, Captain Barshai?"

"Dola goes everywhere with me," Edik said simply, "and I'm merely accustomed to wearing the sword."

True, but he wouldn't go disarmed around Pajari anyway.

Pajari's son shook his head. "Bad habit, relying too much on your familiar. You really must learn to keep it in its place, or—"

"When I want your opinion about familiar relations, I'll ask."

Maximilian Pajari's eyes narrowed and his brow lowered. Clearly unused to a "peasant" talking back to him. But Edik would be damned before he'd let a punk like that talk down to Dola. Journeyman or not.

Pajari laughed, clapping his son on the back.

"You see?" he said. "Edik here, he is a man of strong opinions. This, *this* is why I like him."

A serving girl brought the beer and cigars out then, and Edik immediately felt sorry for the poor thing. She had the misfortune of being attractive, blonde and young — hardly more than eighteen, making her about a decade younger than Edik or Maximilian.

Working in a place like this Edik had no doubt those attributes had made her life harder.

Most lunar great families kept their servants dressed in conservative, traditional attire. But if this poor woman was any example, Pajari preferred his ... on display. Her blouse was cut low enough that Edik doubted she'd dare attempting to take stairs with any kind of speed for fear of bouncing right out. And her skirt fell no lower than mid-thigh.

Edik looked her only in the eye as he took his beer, and he thanked her politely before turning back to his ... hosts. Who simply took in the view as their due while accepting their drinks and cigars.

At least they didn't touch her.

"So, Rasputin," Edik began, but Pajari's son cut in.

"Mr. Pajari."

"No, no," Pajari said, waving his hand as though holding his son back, though the glint in his eyes said he was no happier than his son about the familiarity.

Well to hell with him. He'd started that.

"We are all friends here, *da*?" Pajari continued. "Of course Edik may call me Rasputin."

Edik smiled back with nothing like friendship. True, he had to deal with Pajari. Each of them acted as an intermediary for a different faction of the Du Mak. Edik, the faction led by Artissatass (formerly known to Edik as Cinnamon) and Pajari, the faction led by Hrissapkuss.

Though how Pajari had gotten his role, Edik still didn't know.

"As I was saying, Rasputin," Edik said, and he must have hit the name a little hard because he got a warning glance from Dola, "since you called this meeting, I assume you must have news?"

"Straight to business?" Pajari clucked his tongue. "Come, come. We may be men of very different backgrounds, but I always find that work goes better between friends."

Edik bit down his first three responses and made a show of sipping his beer. It was too heavy, too hoppy, and the bitterness of its aftertaste lingered.

Admittedly, some of that opinion might have had more to do with Edik's company than the beer itself.

"Good, *da*?" Pajari said with a smile. "Brewed by a man of mine here on the estate. Finest beer outside of Russia."

To make his point, Pajari downed about half his glass in a gulp.

"I have heard," Pajari's son said after downing about a third of his own beer, "that Lukyanov has overextended himself this time. His move for Lunar independence is failing. This Terran blockade."

Dola put a paw on Edik's foot to steady him. Edik might not have cared for Alexei Lukyanov, but Lukyanov's daughter Anna was one of Edik's best friends, as well as the liaison for those *Fomhóraigh*.

"And with Natalia Romanova so much on Mars of late," Pajari said, raising his glass as a toast, "I think we will soon see the ascendancy of the Pajari family to the top."

"I'm more concerned," Edik said, in the most diplomatic tones he could manage — which meant Dola only gave him a *slight* warning with his claws — "about getting Hrissapkuss and Artissatass on the same page, diplomatically. Where does Hrissapkuss stand on—"

"Edik, Edik, Edik," Pajari said, shaking his head slowly. "Too much you are among these spacers with their hurry hurry hurry mentality."

"I'm the captain of a helioship," Edik said. "I *am* a spacer. And honestly, I'm more at home out at Kennedy Spaceport than in a place like this."

"Obviously," Pajari's son said, looking over Edik's clothes with distaste.

Edik had nothing to be ashamed of. His fine, multi-pocketed black pants had a stylish red stripe down the side, all the way into his high, polished black boots. His pale shirt matched the stripe, and the jacket hanging off the back of his chair matched the pants, right down to the number of pockets.

Combined with the saber, his trim blonde hair and his Van Dyke, Edik felt himself on the very cutting edge of spacer fashion.

"But you are no mere pilot now," Pajari said, as though his words weren't insulting. "You are a diplomat. You must begin dressing for the role."

"Edik..." Dola warned, still keeping his words pitched just for Edik.

"Artissatass still objects to the Lunar offer," Edik said, "finding Luna too small and the terrain not to his liking. He still favors Mars for both reasons, though he doesn't like the Martian offer any better."

"Very well," Pajar said, heaving a great sigh and finishing his beer.

Not that he began to speak again just yet. Oh, no. No, he had to pick up his cigar, cut off the end with a boot knife, and hold it to his lips. His son mirrored the movements.

When both cigars were ready, Pajari's son called a fire elemental out of ... something on his right wrist, concealed under his shirt.

Both cigars lit, and both men inhaled deeply, sighing with pleasure as they sent their smoke skywards.

"Ahhh," Pajari said with a great smile. "You deny yourself too many of the little pleasures in life, Edik."

Edik said nothing. Took another sip of his beer and forced a smile.

"Hrissapkuss," Pajari said at last, "favors the Martian offer. He feels the request for military aid is reasonable, and the ... thaumaturgical aspects of the deal could be renegotiated to Du Mak benefit."

"Mars won't let go of the magic," Edik said, shaking his head. "They're counting on Du Mak magic to help them stay independent. And as for the military requirements..."

Edik let his words trail away, because Pajari was smiling again. But this time, the smile had implications.

"What?"

"I do not like the Mars idea myself. That would move the Du Mak too close to the Mars corporations. Worse, it might be playing into the hands of Natalia Romanova."

"Well..." Edik began as Pajari puffed his cigar, but Pajari waved him to silence while savoring his tobacco.

"It has occurred to me," Pajari finally said, "that perhaps there is a third alternative we have not been considering."

"Earth? They're allies of the Fae Courts, and Artissatass definitely wants to stay out of any Fae-*Fomhóraigh* conflict."

Pajari held that smug smile as he puffed his cigar.

"Stay for dinner. We will talk."

Edik wanted to say no, but knew he couldn't. Not if he was going to help the level-headed faction of the Du Mak people avoid the predations of the likes of Pajari. Or worse, Romanova.

Edik fought down a sigh as he sipped his beer and prepared himself for a wasted afternoon, followed by a proposal he was sure he didn't want to hear.

ANNA LUKYANOVA SAT IN AN IMPOSSIBLE PLACE, SURROUNDED BY impossibly beautiful people.

The place was the surface of Luna — outside of any Barrier.

Here in the center of this great crater, the stone and dirt were grayish, with just a hint of green. As were the curving walls of the crater in the distance and the nearby benches, tables and gazebos. Even the divan she reclined upon had, like the half-dozen others around her, been raised directly out of the lunar surface by magic.

Surprising, how comfortable it was.

The sky above was blacker than night back at the Lukyanov estate, and full of stars. Not a comforting sight though. One of those stars walked among the others as a giant — the sun — and the Earth itself loomed nearby as though ready to come squash this foolish rebellion by size and weight alone.

Anna should not have been able to breathe, let alone talk. All of her school instruction in both History and Introductory Thaumaturgy had emphasized that only a brilliant combination of thaumaturgy and alchemy had rendered sections of Luna habitable for human and animal life.

Terrain outside the Barriers, like space itself, was said to be lethal to all human and animal life.

But her *Fomhóraigh* hosts had used their arts to make this place safe for her, without the need for any Barrier.

Her *Fomhóraigh* hosts.

As a daughter of one of the most prominent of the great families of Luna, Anna had been raised to think of herself as beautiful. Slender and poised with sleek blonde hair and flawless skin, even Anna's older sister Radya claimed jealousy of Anna's face and figure.

Add to that the elegant dress Anna wore today, the color of fine, pale sapphires to match her eyes, and the antique cameo she wore on a thin gold chain about her neck to suit her station as an ambassador, and she would have stood out in nearly any room.

But here among these *Fomhóraigh*, Anna felt positively plain. A lump of molten steel among the finest works of Rodin.

The half-dozen around her now, for example. Their skin was golden. Their faces, hair, bodies — all the very definition of perfection. Perfection they emphasized at the moment by wearing nothing more than what appeared to be sharkskin loincloths, both the men and the women.

In truth, the magnificence of even one of these *Fomhóraigh* would have been all but too much for Anna — for any mortal — to bear for very long, were she not wearing the fine mirrored pin prepared for her by Hierophant Nicholas Mason.

Mason's enchanted pin made their overwhelming beauty ... tolerable. Dimmed their brilliance. Allowed Anna to maintain coherent thought around them, as well as her dignity.

Very important, for the person who served as their ambassador.

Hierophant Mason also recommended thaumaturgic training, to develop Anna's mind in ways that would render the pin unnecessary — or at least *less* necessary.

Privately, Anna doubted the training would help. Her tutors had always claimed she possessed no talent for thaumaturgy.

Besides, where would she find the time?

"The offer from the Lunar government—" She began, but the *Fomhóraigh* directly across from her — Nalacha, their leader — interrupted.

"We are not interested in their offer."

"You should at least hear them out," she said patiently. "They regard the whole of this moon as theirs. I know you disagree, but—"

"It was the children of Danu who drove us from the Emerald Isle, so long ago," Nalacha said, idly gazing up at Earth. "Humans could never have done it. And they will not drive us from here if we decide to stay."

Anna considered the things she might say. The threat of fireballs from Terran Naval ships. The shooting war with Earth. The Terran embargo, and its impact on Lunar society...

"If you stay, they will be your neighbors. Isn't it better to get along?"

"So they can call us 'good neighbors' and pretend we're the children of Danu?" He shook his head, one slow, smooth motion while his deep green eyes held Anna's...

She had to look away and steady her breathing. And when had her pulse started racing?

"Humans track all comings and goings," Anna said. "Whether it's from Kennedy to King or Tubman to Newton here on Luna, or from San Francisco on Earth to New Leningrad on Mars, all travelers are expected to carry passports and register with customs. Without some kind of agreement—"

"Their laws do not apply to us."

Anna tried to remember whether or not the fae required passports when traveling, but could not recall. If, indeed, she'd ever known. She would have to ask Donal Cuthbert when next she saw him ... or perhaps that MacPherson woman.

All things considered, Anna knew she would much rather speak to Donal Cuthbert.

Anna sighed. Not because she felt the physical urge, but to make a point. It was a calculated sigh, not too deep, not too shallow, and left her with her eyebrows slightly raised and her attention on Nalacha without gazing into his eyes.

"Every time you speak of the children of Danu," she said, "hatred fills your voice *and* your aspect. The mere mention of them provokes a similar reaction from your companions."

Nalacha raised one immaculate eyebrow. "I assume you mention this for a reason other than provoking this reaction."

"Of course," she said, leaning forward just the slightest amount. "My concern is that you might be letting your hatred for them cloud your judgment. You last faced them at war, where they bested you. Am I wrong in thinking you might desire a rematch?"

Nalacha said nothing, but his eyes burned a little brighter.

"And you do not believe such a conflict would require allies?"

"We know what allies we wish." Nalacha leaned back slightly. "We require no others."

"Ah, yes, the Du Mak," Anna said, as though the notion still held some novelty, rather than having remained an open question these last five months. "And I will meet with their representatives again soon enough. But Earth already stands in alliance with your enemies."

"An alliance Earth likely regrets," Nalacha said with a smile. "They must have been certain that their new allies had no living enemies who could pose a threat."

"Many enter into alliances foolishly," Anna said, lifting one casual shoulder. "Yet the fact remains that the alliance exists. And the children of Danu are positioned in ways to hurt Earth should they attempt to abrogate their responsibilities in the event of war. Do you disagree?"

Nalacha said nothing. If he was even breathing, Anna could not tell.

"Then would the *Fomhóraigh* not stand to benefit from an alliance? Luna and Mars would both be willing to ally with you, if terms could be reached."

"Terms entirely to their benefit."

"Yet if you go to war with your ancient enemy, and Earth brings their warships to the fight, what warships of yours will oppose them?"

"We need no warships," Nalacha said with a small, secret smile.

"So you say," Anna said, allowing just the smallest amount of her impatience to ease into her voice. "And so you have said before. Though you have yet to tell me what resources you possess that could counter warships."

"That is true," Nalacha said. "I have not."

And now the other *Fomhóraigh* around him all smiled at Anna as well.

"You make it very difficult to act as your ambassador."

"Not at all," Nalacha said. "You know what matters, and yet you do not know enough to be dangerous to us, should they use magic to steal secrets from you."

"I've told you," she said. "That is forbidden by interplanetary law."

"And I suppose humans have abandoned espionage?"

Anna hated it when Nalacha mocked her. True he was thousands of years old, but that did not mean he had to treat her as a child.

"Of course not. But the rules plainly exempt ambassadors from magic that probes or controls the mind. Not only do we have ways to test for it, but those rules form the underpinnings of interplanetary relations. If they were violated, we could never have peace talks again. Never hold serious business negotiations. There would be no trust. Everything would break down. Our societies. Our governments. Everything."

"Ah," Nalacha said, arching one eyebrow again, "but all that need happen would be for one side to break all the rules once, decisively, at the right time."

Nalacha brought one hand down in a chopping motion. "There would never again be an opposing side to make war."

Anna had a counterpoint ready, but saw her arguments on this topic would again gain no foothold.

"So you will not tell me how you could counter the Terran warships."

"I will not."

"And yet despite these unrevealed resources, you still wish an ally against your ancient enemy?"

"Do not underestimate the children of Danu."

"By that logic, that the children of Danu see benefit in an alliance with Earth should indicate some value in a similar alliance for you."

"Whatever they gain from that alliance, they did not seek it for aid against us. They did not expect our return."

Anna tightened her stomach to brave what she had to say next.

"Are you certain *you* are not the one underestimating your ancient enemy?"

Silence from Nalacha and his companions, but the weight of their gazes felt oppressive. Threatening.

A subject change then.

"So you will not hear the Lunar offer?"

"No."

Anna sighed again, a little deeper this time. Actual impatience bleeding through. She would have to watch that. Natalia Romanova would never have allowed it, not unless she did it to make a point.

"You listened before. Even sent back responses."

"We have been away from humans for quite some time," Nalacha said, gazing once more toward Earth. "These offers from Luna and Mars, they have been most instructive in the ways that humans have changed, and the ways they have not."

"So that implies that you named me your ambassador to have an individual human to study as well?"

No response from Nalacha. Not that Anna really expected one.

"I take it this means you will not hear the Mars offer either."

Nalacha shook his head once more, slowly, and a single time.

"So the only reason I *remain* your ambassador is to improve relations with the Du Mak? Even though you know your enemy seeks alliance with them as well?"

"No, you must return to the humans from Mars and from this place and tell them we are considering their offers. Find some point to dispute in each offer, and raise objections to it on our behalf. The details don't matter, so long as they must go away and reconsider their offer."

"I don't see the point."

"Nor must you," Nalacha said. "Although no doubt you will

discern it when I tell you I also wish to know the status of the Du Mak negotiations with Luna and Mars."

"I presume you wish me to discover this without allowing anyone to know I'm interested?"

"Of course."

"That will be all then?"

"Not quite. There is one more matter we wish you to attend to."

2

DONAL PAUSED OUTSIDE THE STAINED MAHOGANY DOOR TO HIS SUITE ON the sixteenth floor at the Washington Arms. Like the hallway around him, the door was a study in simple elegance.

Donal could smell wood oil on the air, and a hint of coffee from down the hall. Someone must have left their door open. He could even hear someone moving about a room down there somewhere, which wasn't possible from the hallways when the doors were closed.

Subtle work of air elementals kept the late spring air from making the hall too warm or too muggy.

All important information.

Donal noted it, and excluded every one of these details from his attention within the span of a normal breath.

He focused down now into the wards he'd lain on the room when he checked in. The hotel's resident magician had objected, as expected, but Donal asserted ambassadorial privilege.

Wards against attack, theft and intrusion, of course, as well as alarms should anything manage to get through without his permission.

Those were fairly standard for Donal. An improved version of the type he'd done since he was a freshman in the dorms at U.C. Santa

Cruz. And even those had been an improvement over the ones he'd
cast on his bedroom back in high school.

Donal had come a long way since then.

And given the nature of his work, the wards he used now
included defenses against scrying of all sorts. Intricate traps that
would capture as much information as possible about any such
attempts.

As a whole, the wards were designed to look less precise and
organized than they were, to make puzzling through them a little
trickier. And all the countermeasures and detections were hidden
behind more aggressive sections of shielding.

Overkill? Perhaps. But though mind magic used directly against
an ambassador was forbidden, scrying was simply considered part of
"the game."

Donal slipped his tuning fork out of his sleeve. He tapped it
against his wrist, and waved it past the wards to check the response.

He listened not only for how the tuning fork harmonized with the
sounds of his own magic, but for discordances created by the signatures of other magicians, trying to get past his wards.

Eighteen attempts, just since he checked in ... noon was it? Yes,
that sounded right. About three attempts an hour then...

No attacks. That was good. No spirits sent to carve through the
wards and lie in wait, either. Better and better.

In fact...

Yes, from the tones of the discordant notes, all the attempts had
been scrying. Nearly half of them by the same magician...

Esme?

Esmeralda Villaseñor, the girl Donal had been dating before
December turned their lives around. Esme had been tied with Donal
at the top of their cohort, but she was awarded an internship with the
First Magician of the United North American States.

It was supposed to be a winter break thing, with her rejoining her
cohort for the spring semester. But apparently she did too well.
Hierophant N'Kembe offered her the chance to stay on for a year
under his private tutelage, in addition to her duties.

Of course, she'd jumped at the chance. Who wouldn't have? A year of apprenticeship to Hierophant N'Kembe?

Donal hadn't seen her since. But then, they'd both been busy...

Donal chuckled and slipped his tuning fork up his sleeve. He touched the wards with a soft flare of his own signature for identification, then took his old-fashioned brass hotel key, unlocked the door, and slipped inside.

The room was nice, but not too nice. Over the last couple of years, Donal had spent time in hotel rooms, ship cabins, and private residences that individually probably cost more to assemble and maintain than any two floors of this hotel.

But that he could appreciate the simple elegance of this hotel suite told Donal that he hadn't gotten jaded. Yet.

The furniture here was all handmade, by local craftsmen. The mahogany bar near the half-bath to the left. The matching desk near the window wall. To the right, the fine cherry coffee table between the firm but comfortable matching dark blue sofas.

Beyond those, the bedroom, just as finely appointed.

True, the chocolate brown carpeting wasn't to Donal's taste, but it was comfortable underfoot, and went well with the gold-colored curtains and the textured, cream-colored walls.

Donal got himself a glass of clean tap water from the bar, and called Fionn forth from his pendant.

The *cú sidhe* resembled a meter-tall, slightly translucent, emerald green deerhound, with eyes that blazed with courage. He spoke with an accent that wasn't quite Scottish and wasn't quite Irish, but definitely Celtic.

"All is well?"

"Esme's been playing the wards game today," Donal said, smiling without really meaning to. "Like we did at school."

Fionn cocked his head to one side. Raised an ear. "Did she succeed in penetrating your wards?"

"Check for yourself," Donal said. "And while you're at it, check out the signatures of the other magicians who tried to scry on me today. See what you can figure out from them."

"Of course, master," Fionn said in approving tones, and turned and zipped inside the wards.

Donal was fixing himself a snack of guava, pineapple and apple slices when Fionn returned to stand in front of Donal at the bar.

"It is my opinion," Fionn said, "that Journeyman Esmeralda Villaseñor made no serious attempt to breech the wards. She prodded several different places, apparently with the goal of letting you know she knew you were in the area. Perhaps a way of saying hello."

Donal chuckled. "And the others?"

"Will you be contacting her before you leave?"

"Not sure I should," Donal said, frowning despite the tang of fresh guava on his tongue. "Technically she works for the UNAS and I'm an ambassador for a foreign power."

"You would describe the Courts thus?"

"They represent a government that is not part of the UNAS or UTG." Donal shrugged. "They qualify. What about those other signatures?"

"Ambassadors are allowed their own lives as well," Fionn said. "I daresay the queens would encourage you to see her."

"That may be," Donal said, "but the queens play a long and deep game. They might be cooking up some advantage a decade from now, based on something Esme and I might discuss at dinner tonight."

"Do not let their theoretical machinations ruin your potential for happiness. Her internship will end about the same time as your contract with the Courts."

"Assuming one or both don't get extended," Donal said. "The signatures?"

A ripple of displeasure worked its way down Fionn's fur in a way that let Donal know this part of the conversation would return.

"Four were connected with news agencies, attempting to determine if you were present. They failed. Three were from offices of American senators, attempting the same, also failing. One was from the office of the president of the United Terran Government, purpose unknown, but failure likely. The last—"

"Whoa," Donal said, raising a hand. "Tell me more about that one."

"The signature belongs to Journeyman Carmella DiGregorio, registered attaché to President Fong Xi Wang."

"And you can't tell what she wanted?"

"I cannot be certain," Fionn said. "The scrying attempt happened during the time frame of your meeting with President Diego Gutierrez. It did not seem so much to attempt to penetrate your wards, as to simply observe them."

"Hah," Donal said, slapping a hand down on the bar. "They were worried that I was using a memory circle variant to record information from the meeting without use of an elemental."

"So the attempt was merely to watch for incoming spells carrying your signature." Fionn twitched his ears appreciatively.

"But why the UTG? That seems like something the UNAS would..." Donal sighed. "Esme."

"It is true that several of the attempts by Journeyman Esmeralda Villaseñor took place during your meeting with President Diego Gutierrez."

Fionn didn't sound any happier saying that than Donal was hearing it.

"So she was doing the same thing, but in a way she hoped I'd miss."

"Perhaps," Fionn said. "Or perhaps she was required to check by her position, but did so in a way to let you know she still thinks of you fondly."

"Not sure I can take that chance."

"Would it not be better to invite her to dinner tonight? See her in person and assess the truth of the situation?"

Donal frowned. "What were you saying about the last signature?"

"The last was from your brother."

"Bran?" Donal felt his shoulders and jaw tense, and consciously relaxed them. "Come on. How could I possibly have missed *Bran's* signature?"

"You did not. There was no spellwork to the attempt from which you could track a signature."

"Doesn't make sense anyway," Donal said, not quite processing Fionn's words as he thought about his brother. "I'm pretty sure he's out at space somewhere right now, on his way back to Ganymede. I mean, if it *was* him, what could he possibly have wanted?"

"I have no way to be certain. I know only that the attempt was done through his familiar, Res, who—"

"What?" Donal dropped his apple slice and crouched down to eye-level with Fionn. "Res flew all the way here?"

"I have said so," Fionn said, apparently less impressed at a familiar traveling hundreds of decans through space to deliver a message than Donal was. "Res prodded at the wards in five spots, then left."

"Cardinal points and the center of the top?" Donal asked as understanding spread a wave of cold down through him.

Fionn tilted his head in a way Donal had come to think of as a nod.

"It's a warning," Donal said. "Trouble incoming. A way of telling me to stay vigilant." Donal smiled wistfully. "Part of a code we worked out in high school, long before I summoned you."

Donal shook his head. "Bran couldn't risk a link, which means someone's watching him."

"Your brother has achieved quite a bit of fame. And now that your name is commonly spoken in powerful circles as well, it is only natural that some might wish to recruit him for his connection to you, if not for his own sake."

Donal laughed in disbelief. The great Bran Cuthbert? The man who successfully challenged for the Magister's license without first completing a Master's of Thaumaturgy? The savior of Ganymede? The...

Well the list of Bran's achievements went on for far longer than Donal wanted to consider.

But the idea of *Bran* being sought for his association with *Donal*, that just sounded nigh impossible to believe.

Still, a warning was a warning.

"Settles it," Donal said. "I'm taking dinner in the room tonight. We have an early flight tomorrow, and it's not the one you're expecting."

Before Donal could explain, someone tapped lightly three times on the door to his room.

It seemed to Donal sometimes that he was not permitted even a single moment's peace.

That had to be an exaggeration. He knew it.

But it certainly felt that way. He'd finally gotten a little time to himself. Was he allowed to enjoy it?

Of course not.

The triple-knock door of Donal's suite was repeated. An urge to sigh welled within him.

He felt as though he should be tired. He'd flown in just that morning from California. Spent the afternoon at the White House, playing politics. Now, to find out that Bran was worried enough about Donal to send Res all the way from somewhere at space just to use their old code as a warning?

Surely all that should have left Donal feeling exhausted. Drained.

And yet, he still had energy. His training had seen to that. Even the nervous tension of a few minutes ago had already eased out of his muscles, again thanks to habits built through his intensive, advanced thaumaturgical training at graduate school.

The truth was, whatever problem awaited Donal on the other side of that door, he was probably ready for it. Or at least as ready as he could be.

He just didn't want to be.

All he wanted to do right then was order room service and watch shadow plays in the en suite entertainment system for a while, before having a more serious chat with Fionn, meditating, and going to sleep.

But Donal had the distinct feeling in his gut that even this simple plan was to be denied him.

Fionn looked at Donal, expectation all through those fiery eyes.

"See who it is," Donal said through the sigh he'd been fighting. "But send them away unless it's very, very important."

"Even if it's Esmeralda Villaseñor?"

"No. If it's her, I'll see her," Donal said shaking his head and feeling certain that he should have said *yes, send her away*. That would probably have been the proper, professional answer.

No matter how much he personally wanted to see Esme again. Even just to talk. Laugh a bit, maybe.

Was that wrong, for a man in his position meeting a woman in Esme's position? Would the fact of their preexisting personal relationship make it right?

Half a second of thought, and Donal was already once more at the crux of what had bothered him so often over the last several months.

How was Donal supposed to know what the right course of action even *was*?

Most of the time he felt like he was making this stuff up as he went.

Ambassadorial work was clearly every bit as intricate as advanced thaumaturgy, in its own ways, and yet Donal hadn't had any classes to prepare him for it.

Well, to be fair, his many talks with Donatello Mancuso had certainly helped...

Donal took the rest of his little fruit plate over to a couch, easing down on the soft cushions as he tried to enjoy a bite of pineapple.

Focused attention. Now *there* was something he understood. The yield of ripe pineapple flesh between his teeth. The sweet bite of the juices on his tongue even as he savored the scent.

Delicious.

Fionn returned before Donal even had a chance to swallow.

"Rowan MacPherson awaits without." Fionn's voice had that tone that reserved judgment, while still making clear his own opinion.

Donal wished he knew how the fae hound managed that. "Do you wish her sent away?"

"No," Donal said, tossing the rest of that piece of pineapple down his throat and standing over the protest of his legs. "Why would you even ask that right now?"

Fionn trotted beside Donal on his way to the door. "I had no specific instructions regarding—"

"Fionn," Donal said. "We haven't seen or heard from her since that big meeting in Faerie, months ago. Yes, I want to talk to her."

As Donal opened the door, he made a pass with his hand to key the wards to his next movement.

There she stood, on his doorstep. Rowan MacPherson.

If there were a poster girl for Irish beauty, that girl would dream of looking like Rowan MacPherson. Not just her smooth, creamy skin or the way she filled out her cerulean blue dress. No, her eyes were emerald, and flecked with gold. Her long hair was crimson, with golden highlights when the light hit it just right, as late afternoon sunlight from Donal's windows did now.

If Donal's mother could have designed a woman for him, that woman would have looked like Rowan MacPherson.

Of course, unlike Rowan MacPherson, a woman Donal's mother designed would *not* have had fae blood.

Donal still wasn't sure what exactly she was. Rowan called herself a changeling. In Faerie, she'd looked much like one of the *Daoine sidhe*. But Donal knew there was more to her story than that.

"Rowan," Donal said, smiling as he took her hand, both to shake it and to ease her through the wards without lowering them. "I'm so glad to see you up and about."

When last he'd seen her, Rowan was in danger of ... severe repercussions from the queens of Faerie over actions she'd taken in their name, while hosting a meeting of humans, fae, Du Mak and what turned out to be those legendary enemies of the Fae Courts, the *Fomhóraigh*.

Of course, those actions had prevented a brawl that would have prematurely ended important negotiations...

"I have you to thank for it," she said, moving in to hug Donal while he closed the door. "Your words that pressured the Courts into publicly calling what I did a good thing. In front of allied and enemy witnesses."

He stiffened a bit as her arms wove about him, but returned the hug all the same. She smelled of heather and spring air, and Donal tried not to think about how good she felt in his arms.

Donal wasn't certain that he and Rowan were friends, but they were most definitely allies. One a human, one at least raised by humans, and both trying to survive working with the Fae Courts.

The truth was, he was glad to see her. He just wished he knew how far he could trust her.

"Come," he said, slipping from the hug and gesturing toward the couches. "Sit. Have something to eat. What have you been doing these last months?"

"Much as I wish I could," Rowan said, her eyes tracking around the room as she spoke, "I was hoping you would come have dinner with me."

"With all the things we need to discuss?" Donal asked, letting the shock show on his face. "I'm pretty sure we want to be behind my wards for this conversation."

"For *that* conversation," she said smiling, "most certainly. But tonight there's a dinner I must take as a Fae ambassador. Present a united front with me?"

Her expression turned hopeful, and from Rowan that meant more than it did for most people. The way she explained it once to Donal — when pressed — one of the gifts of her nature was that she could communicate intricate levels of information through pose and gesture. Information that viewers would understand on a deep level, even if they couldn't explain it consciously.

So where most people might shine with hope in a moment like this, Donal felt Rowan's hope as he might feel the presence of a spirit.

This was unusual, though. She wasn't in the habit of playing that kind of game with Donal.

"Rowan," he said, in a warning voice.

"Oh!" she said quickly, shaking her head and letting her hopes retreat to just her eyes. "Sorry. I'm just nervous. This meeting is important, and their majesties still have me feeling like my next mistake *will* be my last."

Fionn started to clear his throat, but Donal waved him to silence. He gave one last longing thought to a quiet evening alone, then set that thought aside.

"Who are we meeting with?"

Donal's phrasing made Rowan smile. And not just with her lips or her eyes, but her whole aspect. As though she smiled from the core of her person to the outermost reaches of her aura.

It wasn't manipulation. Donal wasn't sure how he knew, but he knew. It was just a moment of pure happiness that she clearly needed.

"It's complicated," she said. "I'll explain on the way."

A WHOLE AFTERNOON OF PUTTING UP WITH PAJARI. EDIK REALLY deserved some kind of medal for this.

At least he hadn't had to be in the man's presence *all* day. He *had* gotten a small break after finishing his beer. Pajari and his son invited Edik to come riding, but Edik hadn't been on a horse in years, and wasn't all that eager to repeat the experience.

Runners were a much better way to get around. They had cabins for comfort, and their gait was generally smoother than a horse's.

Also, horses, as living animals, were far more likely to have their own opinions about speed, direction, and so forth.

Given his own free choice in the matter, Edik would simply have returned to the *Third Son* and waited for dinner. Maybe had something to wash out the bitter aftertaste of that heavy, hoppy beer.

Well, by preference he would have left *the estate* in the *Third Son* and *returned* for dinner.

But Dola had insisted that Pajari would take such behavior as an insult.

So instead of being anywhere Edik could have been happy, comfortable, and unwatched, Edik settled for pacing the "garden" while his hosts went riding.

Edik's understanding of gardens was that they involved plants. Maybe edible, maybe just pretty, but definitely not trees.

Put a bunch of trees together and the result was supposed to be a grove or an orchard or something.

Apparently Pajari used a different dictionary. Not a surprise. Edik wouldn't be surprised to find out the man redefined a good number of words, just to see the shock on guests' faces when confronted with the discrepancies.

Pajari's "garden" was composed of fruit trees. Lemon trees, orange, grapefruit, cherry, apple, pear... Edik had stopped counting or caring. They were all in bloom, not yet bearing fruit, and the sights and smells of the various colored blossoms were by far the most enjoyable thing about Edik's afternoon at the Pajari estate.

Dola even added to the entertainment by chasing birds and squirrels that he had no intention of catching.

It was a silly thing, but it always made Edik laugh.

Edik would have been only too happy — relatively speaking — to have spent the afternoon wandering among the fruit trees and chatting and playing with Dola.

But no.

Whether a short ride was always Pajari's intention or whether Edik's decision not to join in the "fun" got the ride cut short, Edik had gotten a mere twenty minutes in the "garden" before a serving man came to fetch him.

That was how the man put it, too. "Mr. Pajari has sent me to fetch you, Captain Barshai. You are awaited in the billiard parlor."

The serving man had been only a little older than the girl who'd brought the beer and cigars, but he was dressed in the kind of formal livery Edik expected from servants of a great family. The way the older serving man had been, when he'd first admitted Edik and brought him out to the patio.

Black pants. White shirt. White jacket. Shiny black leather belt and shoes. All of it crisp and covering.

No doubt about it, then. Pajari was a pig.

But Edik had to go play pool with this pig. In a room with white walls and a predominantly blue floor, all designed to look as though the game were played in the sky.

Turned out it wasn't pool Pajari played. It was billiards. No pockets, only three balls including the cue ball, and a whole lot of bank shots.

So Edik spent the afternoon getting trounced at a game he'd never played before, while his host rebuffed any and all attempts to discuss anything of actual importance.

Lunar politics, business, sports, these were the things Pajari was willing to discuss while murdering his guest on the billiard table and getting served cognac and cigars by that same poor blonde serving girl.

Edik hoped she wasn't Pajari's favorite. That just sounded like a cursed position to be in. Edik didn't even feel safe asking her name, for fear that Pajari would mistake politeness for sexual interest.

Edik didn't want to know what would have happened then.

So by the time Pajari was finally willing to put his cue away and have dinner, Edik's mood was foul. Only Dola's nonstop calming voice — still pitching his words so Edik alone could hear them — kept Edik from doing something ... inadvisable.

Dinner was taken on the veranda, outside the third floor art gallery.

Had Edik known about the art gallery, he might have asked to see it while he'd been killing time. It was full of paintings and statues that looked over a hundred years old. They might have been original works of the likes of Levitan, Repin, Serov, Kandinsky, Antokolsky, Shupin, Kobro and others.

Mixed in, of course, was a tapestry of the Pajari family tree going back to the days of the tsars, and Pajari family portraits were mixed in among the works of masters as though they belonged there.

Still. This was a room Edik could have spent time in quite pleasantly. And now all he got to do was pass through it on his way to the whitewashed veranda under the burning sky of sunset.

The view of the setting sun above Pajari's forest was, admittedly, spectacular. Edik spent so much time in the spaceport or airborne aboard the *Third Son* outside of Barriers that he'd forgotten how breathtaking the sight of a sunset could be.

The interplays of reds and oranges, contrasting against the darkening blues and purples of the sky.

Absolutely stunning.

Dinner was to be at a single, small round table. Scarcely big enough for four place settings, and only set for two.

Crystal plates with silverware that looked like real, polished silver. Crystal goblets for water and red wine. A wooden buffet set off to one side covered in closed chafing dishes, with a chef standing behind it, and the blonde serving girl holding a silver platter like a shield, with her eyes downcast as she waited for orders.

This was too much.

Edik knew magicians who could communicate telepathically with their familiars as easily as they could speak their native languages. Donal Cuthbert, for example, or that Hierophant, Nicholas Mason.

Edik, though, was nowhere near their skill level. Especially burning with anger the way he was right then.

Took all the focus Edik could muster to send a quick instruction to Dola.

Find a moment when you can talk to that poor girl alone. Tell her if she wants a job where she can wear actual clothing, I'll be happy to help her find it.

Edik felt the smile Dola didn't let show.

"You are well?" Pajari asked, casually pointing. "Sweat on your brow."

"Just..." Edik drew a deep breath. Let it out slowly. "Just a long day."

Pajari scoffed, took his seat, and gestured as he talked.

"You make stress for yourself too easily, Edik. Come. Sit. Eat.

Enjoy. Life brings us many stresses. Do not add to your own list needlessly."

"That..." Dola said, in English to Edik's lament, "was good advice."

"Try not to sound so surprised," Pajari said, laughing. "I am the head of a great family. I know stress. But I also know *pleasure.*"

Edik fought hard not to let his eyes get drawn to the poor blonde girl as he sat. That last word had practically been a leer.

"So," he said, desperate for a change of subject, "your son will not be joining us?"

"Maximilian is at his meditations. He will dine later." Pajari shrugged. "I did not think you would mind."

Edik nodded, cautiously.

Pajari laughed. "Even now, you worry you will insult me by admitting what is obvious. You and Maximilian do not like each other. But have no fear. I do not insult so easily. Believe me when I tell you, Edik, of all the heads of great houses, I am the easiest to get along with."

Edik wouldn't touch that one with North's airship.

"Well," Edik said. "You had something you wanted—"

"No, no," Pajari said, waving off the topic as though it were distasteful. "After we dine."

Edik sighed.

Dinner, at least, was good. All right, it was better than just "good," if Edik was being honest.

The steaks tasted like choice cuts of actual Terran beef. Prime, juicy, spiced just right and cooked to a gentle medium rare. To go with the steaks, asparagus with the best hollandaise sauce Edik had ever tasted, and fresh-baked pumpernickel bread, still warm from the oven.

Edik didn't recognize the vintage of the wine, but it must have been picked out by the chef, not his host. For the wine not only went perfectly with the steak, it was also subtle. Which his host most definitely was not.

A slice of rich, frosted chocolate cake — which also went well with the wine — rounded out the meal.

Edik tried to start right in on the topic at hand just as soon as the last bite of cake was eaten.

Pajari, of course, would not hear of business until after his cigar.

Pajari was still smoking as the last of the sun vanished behind those trees, and a pair of serving men lit candles along the veranda. White pillar candles that must have been made with alchemy, because they seemed to cast much more light than Edik would have expected. A level of light that was downright comfortable.

Pajari was smiling at Edik as the power of the candles became apparent. Clearly expecting Edik to ask.

Edik had a more important question in mind.

"So," he said, "the Terran embargo on beef hasn't affected you yet?"

Pajari scoffed. "Surely you couldn't believe a silly thing as a political embargo could affect one such as I."

Edik sighed, certain he'd been baited into asking.

Pajari laughed. Waved dismissively.

"You are too easy, Edik. Teasing you is no challenge. To business then, ah?"

"Sounds good to me."

"So eager you sound." Pajari blinked. "And where is your Dola? I thought you kept him near today, to help keep your temper in check when dealing with one of us impossible *boyars*."

"Just checking on the ship for me," Edik lied. "Letting the elementals know we'll be leaving soon."

"Not so soon as that," Pajari objected.

Edik got as far as a drawn breath before Pajari cracked a smile and laughed aloud.

"Too easy, Edik. Too easy." He chuckled again while Edik fought not to reach out and slap the man.

"Now," Pajari said, rubbing his hands together. "The Du Mak. No more of your distractions."

Edik didn't rise to that one, but Pajari chuckled anyway.

"Yes," Edik said. "You had a third option beyond Mars and Luna that didn't involve Earth?"

"Only the obvious choice," Pajari said, smiling. "Venus."

Edik's turn to scoff. "They'll never go for it. First settlers made it clear, they don't want visitors. They don't want tourists. They went there to be left alone. If the Du Mak settle there—"

"They must have a spaceport anyway, *da*? Venus is nowhere near ready for independence. They cannot avoid all traffic from Earth and survive. And anyway, Earth would not let them."

"But the Du Mak—"

"The Du Mak can settle apart from the humans. In exchange, maybe they share some of their magic to keep visitors away from the private, settler areas, without committing to any military efforts."

"Artissatass might go for that," Edik had to admit. "If Venus agrees to it."

"As would Hrissapkuss. You see. I told you we would find them common ground. And Venus, they would be fools not to go along with it."

"Still," Edik said, frowning. "As an Earth colony, can Venus even *make* an agreement like this?"

"They negotiate on their own for goods and services," Pajari said, smiling even wider. "I had my people verify that just this afternoon. And all we discuss is an exchange of goods and services. Not any kind of military alliance that would anger your Artissatass."

Edik didn't think of Artissatass as *his* in any way, and he didn't like hearing Pajari say otherwise. Implied bad things about Pajari's own view of himself, in regard to the Du Mak.

"So," Pajari said, "you and I, we will make Venus see the genius of our idea. *Da*?"

Pajari wanted to share credit for this idea? Or would it be sharing blame? Either way, Edik wasn't sure how he felt about that.

Still, the idea had to be pitched.

"I suppose there's no harm in talking to a representative of Venus," Edik said slowly. "Do they even have anyone here on Luna we can talk to?"

"*Nyet*," Pajari said, his smile widening to show teeth. "We must go to Venus. You will fly with me?"

"If I'm flying to Venus," Edik said quickly, "I'm taking the *Third Son*. You'd be welcome to fly with me, of course—"

Pajari scoffed. "A worthy offer and a worthy ship, my friend, but I fly only in perfect comfort. I will take my own ship. But are you certain you do not wish one of my fine cabins for your ease?"

"And miss piloting the voyage myself? When would I ever get the excuse to fly to Venus again?"

"If we do our job right," Pajari said, spreading his arms, "perhaps all the time."

Thoughts of taking that flight were certainly happy ones — especially if Pajari was flying separately — but one thing still bothered Edik.

"I'm still worried though, that we're going to get there and get shut down by Earth."

Pajari's smile got downright predatory. "Between just us" — Pajari blinked, likely realizing that Dola was beside Edik again — "and your fine familiar, of course, I can assure you that I have taken steps in that direction."

A sense of cold dread descended on Edik's guts.

"What steps?"

"You will see, my friend," Pajari said. "You will see."

THE FINEST RESTAURANT IN WASHINGTON DC WAS SAID TO BE *La Petite Coupure*, and Donal could understand why.

It began with elegantly done décor. From the outside, illusions made the single story building look like an elegant French chateau, seen from a slight distance. What appeared to be the front gate, leading onto rolling green lawns decorated with intricate topiary arranged from colorful flowering bushes, was actually the front door of the restaurant itself.

Inside, the chateau theme continued. High ceilings (illusion), old, warm wood for the walls, covered in wallpaper that mimicked the court of Louis XIV (real wood, though aged and papered through more deception magic).

It smelled of a welcoming fireplace, gentle floral perfumes, baking breads, roasting meats and marvelous, intricate sauces. But all those aromas formed only gentle greetings. None assailed the nostrils, merely seeped into one's consciousness slowly.

The main dining room even had the light, airy feel of a ballroom. Not too warm, but not too cool.

More illusions made the diners at other tables appear to be denizens of King Louis' court, in style, dress, manner — and language. Privacy at *La Petite Coupure* was assured through spells that made the speakers at other tables sound as though they spoke archaic French. Even the waitstaff had to touch each table to take orders, answer questions, and recite the specials.

Admittedly, Donal himself couldn't tell modern from archaic French. The *maître d'*, however, had cheerfully explained that detail when Donal had asked while being led to his table.

Apparently the words of other diners were not translated, but replaced with discussions that might have been germane to the court of the Sun King.

Marvelous bit of craft, those illusions. At least the work of a Magister, though to know more Donal would have had to take time to study the spells. Alas, that would not only have been rude to his dinner companions, it would have been frowned upon by management.

Anyone who puzzled through their spells might figure out how to eavesdrop, after all.

The individual tables continued the Louis XIV theme as well. The table Donal sat at had an antique ivory finish, hand-trimmed with gold, and matching chairs upholstered with silk. All quite real, and possibly actual antiques.

The food, of course, was exquisite.

Donal had chosen the *confit de canard*, and was delighted. The combination of the salt, garlic and thyme in the marinate with the agonizingly slow-cooked meat of the duck had all but melted on his tongue.

Beside Donal, Rowan had chosen *salade niçoise*, though her mind seemed to be more on the conversation to come than on her food. She didn't look nervous, though she did look curious. But then, Donal might only have been able to tell because he had come to know her.

Still. Another lesson Donal had learned from Mr. Mancuso. If your guests will not discuss business until after dinner, eat slowly and savor your meal. This will show confidence, as well as give you time to read the behavior of the other diners.

And the two other diners at the table would not discuss business until dinner was finished.

Andre Dos Santos sat directly across from Donal in a fine dark silk suit that would have fit in well anywhere in Washington, though he wore it with a soft-looking pale green shirt with a yellow tie for a look that Donal could never have pulled off. But the devilishly handsome man made the combination work. But then, he'd likely been putting combinations like that one together longer than Donal had been alive.

Still. If Donal hadn't been wearing airsilk, he might have felt underdressed.

Mr. Dos Santos was an ambassador from Brazil, which was interesting. Brazil was said to be leading an effort to unite the continent of South America — some said all the countries as far north as Guatemala — to form a negotiating body that might be able to compete for trade with the UNAS.

Beside Mr. Dos Santos and across from Rowan sat Matsuo Etsu, ambassador from Japan. Ms. Matsuo wore a black airsilk suit with touches of jade at the cuffs and tie tack, as well as jade clips that held her graying black hair back from her smooth, seemingly ageless face.

Neither ambassador gave anything away as they ate, but in light of Donal's earlier conversation with President Gutierrez, he suspected he knew the reason for this dinner.

Nevertheless, when Donal finished he savored the rest of his glass of Riesling, rather than attempt to begin conversation. Rowan, as they discussed in the runner cab, followed his lead.

Rowan had a great deal more experience than Donal at backroom deals and espionage, but she had never undergone the kind of casual training Donal had from that master of negotiation himself — Donatello Mancuso.

The Riesling was light, and went perfectly with the duck.

It was Mr. Dos Santos who finally smiled, stretched, and spoke.

"I must thank you for meeting with us on such short notice. Ms. MacPherson. Mr. Cuthbert."

"No thanks are necessary, Mr. Dos Santos," Donal said, attempting to share a smile and knowing his effort was nowhere near the standard set by his mentor. "We all at this table know that we are on duty every hour of the day and night. Opportunities do not wait for appointments."

"True," Ms. Matsuo said. "Nevertheless, you are kind to meet with us tonight."

They began their pitch then. The topic was exactly what Donal expected — both Brazil and Japan wanted Donal and Rowan to provide their envoys with an introduction to the Du Mak. Same request President Gutierrez had made.

The United Terran Government might not have been able to come to terms with the Du Mak, but Donal was starting to think that every country on Earth thought it had the right to form its own alliances.

Donal almost — *almost* — lost time wondering whether or not the "united" part of the United Terran Government was beginning to unravel. But he kept his focus on the conversation.

Donal watched the way Ms. Matsuo and Mr. Dos Santos worked together to make their points. Oh, they didn't trade off while speaking, or anything so obvious. But they supported each other's points in subtle ways, and each avoided saying anything that could undercut the other.

Clearly they had been preparing for this meeting, even if they pretended otherwise.

This meant that Brazil and Japan must have come to some sort of understanding. Either that, or each believed that the other would only help them achieve an alliance with the Du Mak.

They were playing a deeper game here, but Donal lacked enough information to even guess what it could be.

Donal raised the concern about the UTG charter and member nations making outside alliances. Apparently both Japan and Brazil interpreted the charter in the same way as the UNAS.

When they finished, both Ms. Matsuo and Mr. Dos Santos were looking at Donal. But Donal turned to Rowan.

"What do you think?"

"I'm not sure it's a good idea," Rowan said, as they had planned in the runner on the way over. "The Du Mak are not allies of the Courts at this time. Introducing one ally to another, that's standard diplomacy. But introducing one ally to a foreign power with whom we do not have an established formal relationship…"

She shook her head, just enough to keep her hair from bouncing on her shoulders.

"That could undercut our own diplomatic efforts, as well as hampering yours. You might do better without us."

Ms. Matsuo confined her reaction to a stoic blink, but Mr. Dos Santos' shock spread across his face.

Donal waited for one or both — both, as it happened — to open their mouths before he raised a hand for silence.

"Your points are well taken, Rowan, as always," Donal said, before turning his attention across the table. "It might hamper our own efforts with the Du Mak. But there is also a possibility that it might *aid* our efforts, if we are able to spin it properly."

"Just so," Ms. Matsuo said. "And, of course, our representatives would speak only well of you in our own talks with the Du Mak."

Donal nodded. Drew a deep breath.

"It is within the power of the Fae Courts to grant this request. But realize, even with your envoys speaking well of Rowan, myself, and the Courts, providing this introduction may work against the efforts of the Courts."

Donal raised a hand again, before they could object.

"I wish you both to understand that this means the Fae Courts would be doing a favor for Japan and Brazil."

Mr. Dos Santos smiled and started making noises about favors as the currency of diplomacy and such, but not Ms. Matsuo. Ms. Matsuo seemed to actually hear what Donal was saying. And what it *meant*.

"Perhaps you are right," she said carefully. "The Fae Courts are important allies of the United Terran Government, and through that organization, allies of the government of Japan. It is not in the best interests of Japan to risk inhibiting the efforts of the Fae Courts."

Mr. Dos Santos had stopped talking now, and turned to stare wide-eyed at Ms. Matsuo.

But she continued speaking.

"As such, Japan withdraws its request. If Japan is to meet with the Du Mak, we will approach them ourselves."

Mr. Dos Santos tried to say something, but Ms. Matsuo spoke over him.

"And Japan strongly recommends that Brazil do the same." She had his attention now, and gentled her voice as she finished. "An alliance with the Du Mak may prove important for both our countries. But *this is not the way*."

"Forgive me," Mr. Dos Santos said to both Rowan and Donal. "Would you excuse us both a moment?"

"Certainly," Donal said, and before he could finish his sentence, Ms. Matsuo and Mr. Dos Santos were up and moving, their rapid words sounding like French even before the restaurant's deception magic shifted their outfits and hair to styles of that old French court.

"Well," Rowan said with a shake of her head, "I think that relationship is doomed."

"Relationship?"

"They're lovers," Rowan said as though it were the most obvious thing in the world. "You couldn't tell?"

Donal shook his head.

Rowan gave him an affectionate smile and patted his wrist. "So observant in so many ways, but you do have your blind spots, Donal."

"Don't we all," Donal said, nodding toward the departing ambassadors.

"Too true. At least one of them's been paying attention," Rowan said, irritation in her voice. "Honestly. Asking for a favor. You'd think they'd do as much research on their Fae allies as they do on each other."

"You'd think," Donal said, shaking his head. "But if you'll excuse me, I'm going to take advantage of this opportunity."

Donal went to use the facilities.

———

THERE WERE NO GROUP RESTROOMS AT *LA PETITE COUPURE*. NO, EACH customer who needed to use the facilities got to do so in the privacy of his or her own room, surrounded by wooden surfaces finished in antique ivory and trimmed with gold filigree.

Nor were customers confined into something so small as a stall. The restroom Donal stood in had to have measured a good three meters wide, and four long.

Even the ceramics of the toilet and sink looked authentic enough that Donal might almost have been convinced that the court of Louis XIV had modern indoor plumbing.

Then again, perhaps it did. Donal didn't know.

The gentle scent of roses pervaded the room. Small antique paintings and what appeared to be an authentic antique mirror completed the appointments.

Elementals even kept the sink water on the toasty side of warm.

This was just the sort of restaurant Donal had once believed would be beyond his means for most of his life. That he had dined in such places with increasing frequency over the last couple of years still made him marvel from time to time.

In fact, he was marveling over just that fact as he dried his hands on a soft, warm towel when someone tried to kill him.

The assassin melted out of the shadows and struck from behind. A single thrust with a knife, aimed for Donal's throat.

But Donal had been playing awareness games with Fionn since someone had tried to blow him up on Mars, not so very long ago.

"Field work," Li Hua had called it, after rescuing Donal from that explosion, and Donal had taken the idea to heart. Practiced the idea of needing thaumaturgy at a moment's notice, even in the field, through those games with Fionn.

In those games, Donal had pretended to be a spy, whose survival depended on spotting threats in the crowds around him. He had learned to stay casually aware of his surroundings at all times.

So when the assassin melted out of the shadows, Donal spotted the movement reflected in the mirror, out of the corner of his eye.

He ducked and spun away from the strike, throwing his towel at the assassin, who smacked it aside with a free hand.

Shadows yet clung to the assassin. Donal could not tell if his assailant was male or female, tall or short, lean or muscled, clothed or armored, or any real details at all.

Only the steel of the single-edged knife could be seen clearly.

The magic of the shadows was the only thaumaturgy about the assassin. Not a magician then, but someone enchanted for a task.

Donal's heart pounded in his chest. His mouth dried. His mind whirled, but for the life of him, he could not remember how to produce the Jenkins Flash.

Thaumaturgy was not an explosive art. Donal could not summon balls of fire, nor shoot bolts of lightning from his eyes. Nor could even the great Lloyd Bird, founder of modern thaumaturgy, produce such effects.

The only defense Donal could think of in this rushed moment was the Jenkins Flash.

But even the Jenkins Flash wouldn't have done more than make the assassin feel a stinging slap, without the spells that established a thaumaboxing ring.

And even that seemed to be beyond Donal at the moment. His mind whirled in spells of deception and conjuration — his specialties — as well as all he had been learning of the Enochian system.

But he had no time. The assassin closed on him—

—and a woman leapt out of the mirror.

The woman was tall, with immense waves silver-blonde hair flying wild behind her, as though she ran through strong winds. Her ethereal beauty emitted a soft, silvery glow, and was only enhanced by her gown of gossamer and moonlight.

She grabbed the assassin before that knife could strike again. She planted her luscious lips on lips cloaked in shadow, clutching the back of the assassin's head as she might a lover's.

Only the briefest of kisses. Then she withdrew her grip and let her hands drift out wide. Her silvery-blonde hair fell to her bare ankles like a cloak.

She smiled a wicked smile at Donal, her sunset eyes and berry lips full of lascivious promises.

The assassin fell to the floor. Coppery smoke drifted up from his lips.

And it was a him. The would-be assassin was short and slight, clad all in black cotton. His features were Asian. Korean, if Donal was correct.

And the knife wasn't single-bladed after all. It was a double-edged dagger, coated in a greenish film. Likely poisoned.

Even the knife had been part of the disguise.

Donal leaned back against the wall and recovered himself. Steadied his heart rate. Eased the tension in his muscles.

When had he started holding his breath? He'd need to watch that.

He had to swallow before he could speak.

"Morna," Donal managed at last, panting a bit as he spoke. "You saved my life."

Morna was a *leannan sidhe*, originally sent to ... "aid" him by the Duke of Shadows, one of the great peers of the Winter Court.

Despite their beginnings, this latest incident wasn't the only reason Donal knew he could trust her.

"Ah," Morna said longingly, in a voice sweet as crystal chimes, "how I've yearned to hear you speak my name in such breathless tones, master. Perhaps you will *reward* me for my service? I have a few suggestions..."

Donal didn't need to hear her suggestions. Her very nature was sexual. *Leannan sidhe* were said to provide great inspiration to their lovers, even as they led those lovers to seemingly inevitable destruction.

"How did ... where did..."

"I was at the Courts, as you had bid me, master." Did she have to savor that title so? "Her grace noticed that your life was in danger, and permitted me to use her pathway, that I might come to your aid."

"Her grace" could only have referred to the Duchess of Mirrors, the Summer Court's counterpart to the Duke of Shadows.

The idea that a fae duchess was watching Donal with this sort of regularity was more than a little troubling, but not the most pressing point at the moment.

"Is he dead?" Donal asked, nodding at the assassin.

"No," Morna said with a disappointed sigh. "I would happily have ended his life for threatening you, master. But I knew you would not wish it."

"Will he be out long?"

Morna cocked an eyebrow. Put one wrist on her hip.

"He will not stir before the dawn, master. Unless you wish it otherwise."

Donal reached out and clasped her free hand in both of his. Looked into her eyes so she could see his sincerity.

"*Thank you*, Morna. You have done me a great service tonight and I will not forget it."

Morna shivered with pleasure, and Donal held his gaze on her adoring face so he might not be distracted by other sights. Moonlight and gossamer were not the most concealing materials.

Then Donal remembered where they were.

"No one can find you in here," Donal said, raising one hand to forestall her objections. "This is a public restroom, and your presence here would imply things we weren't doing."

"We *could* do those things," she said, and her voice shivered pleasure down his spine.

"Morna," he warned, but even that seemed to thrill her. Nevertheless, she removed that little bit of extra from her voice.

"Yes, master."

"I mean to say that I must ask you to meet me back at my hotel room." Donal summoned Fionn from the silver faun pendant about his neck.

Fionn appeared in a flash of emerald light, and took in the scene with a glance before turning to Donal.

"Fionn, take Morna to the hotel. Morna, tell Fionn all about what happened here."

Donal frowned. "In fact, brief Fionn on what you learned at the Courts, too."

"May I not have the pleasure of reporting to you directly, master?" Her voice wasn't quite a whine, but it was close.

"You may," Donal said, "but this way Fionn gets time to consider your report before I hear it. I'll need his take, as well as yours and my own."

From Morna's smile, she was satisfied with that answer. She turned to Fionn. "Lead on, great *cú sidhe*."

Fionn left straight out through the wall, while Morna herself melted into the shadows.

Donal drew a deep breath, and stepped out the restroom to summon the management and the police.

DONAL THOUGHT HE HAD SEEN POLICE IN ACTION BEFORE. HE'D EVEN seen San Francisco Port Authority apprehend murderer Imenand bin Zuka.

But Donal had never seen anything like this.

It seemed that no more than a minute could have passed between the *maître d'* linking the Washington DC police department and two dozen officers entering the restaurant.

They'd already surrounded the building.

No fewer than three of the investigating officers were Journey-men, and that only included those inside the restaurant.

More startling was that every officer entering *La Petite Coupure* looked and sounded like a member of the court of Louis XIV, until the *maître d'* provided them with tiny clips that exempted them from the illusions.

Everyone was interviewed. Everyone. From the lowliest busboy to the senator from Idaho, to the ambassadors themselves. Each was taken, in turn, into the employee break room, chosen, presumably, because none of the restaurant's illusions penetrated there.

The break room looked positively mundane, compared to the main dining room. Schedules and employment law information on the walls. Simple tables and chairs of cheap, unmatched wood. The odor of fried food seemed to seep from the walls.

Of course, the ambassadors were offered the opportunity to assert diplomatic immunity and refuse the police interview. But the implication lay heavily upon the air that refusal might be taken as a statement of its own.

The senator might have been offered the opportunity to decline the interview as well. Donal wasn't sure.

The compromise appeared to be that everyone above a certain level of prominence was allowed to wait for their attorneys to arrive, with the others being interviewed in the interim.

Donal and Rowan both declined representation. True, Mr. Mancuso would have lectured Donal for that — at length — but Donal had nothing to hide. Further, he had no wish to find and retain counsel at this point. Not when he was due to leave the planet in the morning.

Donal himself was interviewed three different times. Twice from the general police perspective, and once from the strictly thau-maturgic perspective.

It was during that last interview that Donal realized something. During the attack he had shifted awareness with such speed and skill that he had assessed any and all magics about the assassin without even realizing he'd done it. No deep analysis, but still.

He'd come a long way from the newly minted Journeyman who needed time and predictable breathing patterns to look for or examine spells.

When asked how he subdued the assassin, Donal held back the presence of Morna. Investigating magicians would be able to determine the presence of fae magic, though, so Donal took flagrant advantage of his position.

"I *am* an ambassador for the Fae Courts," he said. "That comes with certain ... advantages. Anything more than that, I'm afraid, is considered classified information."

Donal did concede that the assassin would regain consciousness with the dawn, if not awakened before then by thaumaturgic means.

Other than that detail, Donal withheld only the official business discussed among himself, Rowan, Ms. Matsuo and Mr. Dos Santos.

He even made certain the local police knew about the last time someone had sent an assassin after him, back in San Francisco. Also just after Donal returned from a flight to Venus...

By the time enough of the interviews were completed that Donal and Rowan were given permission to leave it was approaching midnight.

The police offered to run Donal and Rowan back to their hotel, but Rowan asked if they could take a runner cab instead. The police weren't happy about it, but apparently accustomed to dealing with ambassadors. They put up little struggle before settling for agreeing to settle for providing an escort.

Might have helped that both Rowan and Donal agreed to allow the police to take them to the spaceport in the morning.

Donal knew without asking why Rowan didn't want to ride back in a police car that night. Police would be friendly and helpful, but would listen intently to every word spoken.

Cabbies were less likely to care.

This particular runner had four great, orange, lizard-like legs, a matching covered top, and an interior done in ornately carved, weathered woods that felt more comfortable than Donal would have expected. Especially as no thaumaturgy was involved in that comfort.

The driver was a heavy-set man who looked as though he'd spent too many years boxing. Or drinking. Or both. His face was reddened by broken blood vessels, as were his previously broken nose and his swollen ears.

At least his hands were steady on the reins.

He chattered loudly about the weather, but Donal and Rowan weren't listening. They chatted instead in soft voices, speaking Gaelic.

"Brazil still wants the introduction," Rowan said. *"Their envoy will meet us at the spaceport in the morning."*

"Japan stands by withdrawing its request?"

"Absolutely." Rowan shook her head. *"And both will be going home to cold, angry beds tonight."*

Donal chose to leave that topic alone.

"Did you say where the introduction will happen?"

She shrugged. *"I'm pretty sure Luna was implicit, but I didn't specify."*

"Good," Donal said. *"I'm going to Venus in the morning. It's already been arranged by the UNAS."*

"Oh?"

"I met with President Gutierrez this afternoon. Pretty much the same discussion. You don't have to go, if you don't want to, but I hope you will."

"Of course I'll come," Rowan said dismissively, then frowned. *"All the Celtic heritage in this country, and they're asking favors from the fae."*

Suddenly the answer was so obvious that Donal laughed. He even had to reassure the cabbie, in English, that it was an inside joke and by no means an insult, before he turned back to Rowan's puzzled expression.

"I represent the fae," he said, returning to Gaelic, *"but I myself am human. These are people so accustomed to thinking in terms of loopholes and details that they believe that makes a difference here. That they're asking a favor from me, a human, so they'll escape the potential consequences of a fae debt."*

"Do you think?"

"What else could it be?"

"Well," Rowan said with a sigh, *"I think we made the situation as*

clear as we could have tonight, and I'm sure you did as well this afternoon. The rest is on them."

Donal shrugged helplessly. *"Wish I could have refused."*

Rowan patted Donal's forearm. *"If you had, their majesties might have had you disemboweled and burned alive."*

"Both?" Donal asked, surprised enough to slip into English.

"They're very thorough."

It was nearly midnight by the time Anna finished a series of discussions with some very angry people.

The Lunar ambassadors were led by Cynthia Jordan, a dramatically skinny middle-aged woman who traced her lineage through the United North American States and back to Nigeria. Jordan had this habit of stroking her lips while listening, then staring at the ceiling as she spoke. As though she were an oracle, divining her words from the swirls of red and yellow paint decorating the ceiling of her office.

Jordan was good. She hid her anger well enough that Anna believed even Jordan's own staff might not have known just how furious their leader was at the latest *Fomhóraigh* rebuff.

Anna had done her best to find a clause that seemed too complicated and confining for the *Fomhóraigh*, and written a five-page rejection of the clause, with another ten pages of suggested amendments, which included subtle modifications to three other clauses.

Jordan had been good enough to catch at least most of the implications on a single reading.

And fury had blazed in her dark eyes as she calmly raised objections to both the fact of the changes, and that the objections had not appeared in the previous three rounds of negotiations.

Anna, of course, had merely smiled and provided a lengthy explanation that contained not so much as a single word of real information.

Oh, Anna had not lied, of course. Nothing so *bourgeois*. She had simply offered a complex obfuscation that concealed the barest hints of truth within a good twenty minutes of oration.

Father would have been proud.

In fact, Father should have been there. Given Father's involvement in the Lunar Independence Movement, he should have been present for negotiations with the *Fomhóraigh* representative.

Even if the local government wished to empower Jordan as their representative, the chance to counter one member of a great family with another should not have been missed. Especially when both were from the same great family.

No one understood the weapons of diplomacy so well as the great families of Luna.

Well. Perhaps a few of the masters of those interplanetary corporations. Surely rising to that level was comparable, and required similar skill sets.

Immaterial, at the moment.

That Anna's father was not present was interesting. It meant he had to have been involved in something pressing. Something the Lunar delegation had chosen not to share with the *Fomhóraigh*.

Well, if the *Fomhóraigh* were seriously considering the alliance, that show of mistrust might have hurt the Lunar cause. Instead, it might have indicated that Luna was realizing they were wasting their time.

Anna would have to remember that.

Anna had then met with the Martian delegation in the conference room of their hotel. Not what Anna would have considered a nice place. Their chairs swiveled, and she felt them too generic to provide true comfort for anyone. Ash gray ceramics for a table, and taupe ceramics for walls, ceiling, and floor.

Only the presence of a pair of ferns were any nod to character at all.

The Martians had been even angrier. Their lead ambassador was tall and scarred Orlando Sanchez, with his dark Honduran skin tinted deep red through years inside Martian Barriers. Sanchez had not hesitated to curse out his frustrations in Spanish before reverting to English to angrily voice his complaints.

Even a child would have been able to tell that Sanchez was under tremendous pressure to seal the alliance.

Sanchez, to his credit, did not simply kowtow to the issues Anna raised. He pushed back at each point, and insisted on long counterarguments punctuated by fervent gestures and occasional bits of Spanish.

In fact, he even tried to play off his tirade to his advantage. Stopping to calm himself, renew his smiles, and attempting to put Anna at her ease before raising immediate modifications to some of the many changes requested by Anna.

It was skillfully done. Anna had no doubt that many negotiators Sanchez had dealt with prior might have been fooled into believing that his fury had been entirely planned, and not a weakness to exploit.

Anna allowed Sanchez to believe she was taken in by his ploy. After all, the point was moot. The negotiations were a smokescreen. The *Fomhóraigh* were never going to agree to an alliance.

One thing Anna had managed to determine, through her hours of otherwise pointless discussions — the Du Mak had not yet come close to any kind of alliance with Luna or Mars.

Oh, both sets of ambassadors had pretended otherwise. They had hinted and implied now and again, attempting to lead Anna to believe that an alliance with *them* would be an alliance with the Du Mak, without ever coming out and saying so.

But Anna needed only listen to their words to hear the truth behind them. Those negotiations were failing as well.

Not a surprise, really. The Du Mak were represented by her friend Edik Barshai, as well as Rasputin Pajari. Pajari would not agree to any deal that would not benefit his own family at least as much as the Du Mak. And Edik, dear Edik, would try to foil Pajari as much as help the Du Mak.

Privately, Anna wondered whether Edik and Pajari would ever agree on anything themselves, much less on behalf of the Du Mak.

In all, it had been an exhausting day. Dealing first with the *Fomhóraigh*, and then two sets of angry delegates.

Anna wanted nothing more than to return to the luxurious hotel room provided by Luna to the *Fomhóraigh* ambassador and stretch out in a hot bath. She did some of her best thinking while soaking in soothing hot water, and she desperately wanted to figure out what cards the *Fomhóraigh* clutched tightly to their chests.

How could they possibly counter warships?

But there was the other matter to attend to.

And so Anna strolled through the spacious blue-white stone hallways of Kennedy Spaceport, on her way to one specific landing bay. She lamented not having had time to change. Yes, her dress was elegant, and matched her eyes, but she'd been wearing it for too many hours for comfort.

Besides, when she could she preferred to change her outfit for the evening, in the manner of all members of Lunar great families, both the men and the women.

But alas, at times, it could not be helped.

Having grown up on the Lukyanov estate, with its superior conditions, Kennedy Spaceport always seemed to Anna like the city equivalent of a budget hotel.

In terms of cheap furnishings, the air in Kennedy smelled not of clean air, but faintly of licorice. And the water tasted less like that of a clear mountain spring, and more as though its imperfections were covered with liberal squeezings of lemon.

Even the black night sky above — visible through periodic windows in the blue-white walls — yet carried hints of its pale green day color, where stars could be seen.

Anna understood those little imperfections as the legacy of the first terraforming barrier ever assembled. A brilliant, if imperfect, blending of thaumaturgy and alchemy that allowed humans to live on Earth's moon without the aid of *Fomhóraigh* magic.

Not that anyone had known *Fomhóraigh* magic was an option. Not until only a few months ago...

Finally she reached docking bay Two-Hundred Eighty-Six-Bee. The bay where her favorite helioship waited.

The docking bay itself was on the small side. Scarcely more than thirty-five meters across, it was of a size more suited to an airship than most helioships.

Otherwise, it looked much as many other bays at Kennedy Spaceport. All blue-white stone, lit at night with the reddish-yellow light of cheaply bound fire elementals.

But the bay itself mattered little. It was the ship, and its captain, Anna sought.

The *Third Son* was small, for a helioship. A class they designated "runabout," intended for a small crew and few passengers. Day trips, by design, rather than the kind of extended voyages most helioships could make in comfort and style.

Still. Even had she not been friends with the owner, the *Third Son* would have been her favorite helioship. If only for its form.

The *Third Son* was shaped like a brilliant crimson firebird out of Russian folklore. Beautiful, from beak to the tip of its tail. And though it may not have had cabins, Anna knew from experience that the eight large, padded seats of real Terran cow leather in the main cabin reclined for perfect comfort.

And the ship was owned by a man she had come to regard as a true friend, Captain Edik Bashai.

She approached the passenger hatch, but it opened before she could knock.

Edik looked as tired as Anna felt. His normally excellent posture sagged a bit, but at least he had a smile for her.

Good, because the aroma of borscht coming out of the *Third Son* implied that Anna had interrupted a late meal.

"Good to see you, *mladshaya sestra*," Edik said, gesturing with one hand for her to come in.

"And you, as always, dear Edik." She smiled and squeezed his shoulder in passing. A more familiar touch than she might normally have allowed herself, but she already knew it was just the two of them, plus Dola, wherever he was.

Edik only ever called her "little sister" when no one else could overhear. It was sweet of him, though entirely inappropriate, of course. If he ever said it when others were around, she would have to stop the practice.

She was a Lukyanova, after all. Certain formalities had to be observed, in public.

Oh, but the soft leather of those plush, main cabin seats felt good as she sat. If Anna could have closed her eyes right then, she could easily have fallen asleep before she finished even a single breath.

Golden carpet for the center aisle, between the two rows of seats, each with its own meter-wide viewing porthole, trimmed in fiery red, and small shelf for drinks and snacks. The positioning of the seats and portholes reminded Anna that the *Third Son* served primarily to give flying tours of the sights of Luna.

Though that might no longer be true. Edik might need to redecorate.

For now, the carpet matched most of the interior, and the single decoration was one Anna thoroughly approved of.

Down the length of the cabin's ceiling, a mural of the mythical firebird's tailfeather, done in the same blazing crimson as the outer hull of the ship.

Anna smiled at the tailfeather as she sat. She almost — *almost* — allowed herself a sound of pleasure as she settled down. But that would have been too much. She did at least allow herself to ignore the five straps of the safety harness.

Edik sat across from her, on the forward edge of his chair, while Dola sauntered in from the bridge.

To have a familiar alone would have been enough reason to study thaumaturgy, in Anna's view. A bosom companion, always available, such as this great, shaggy gray cat.

"Your day must have been as rough as mine," Edik said, voice full of humor. "It's been nearly a minute since you got here, and you haven't told me the reason for this visit."

"Must I have a reason?" she asked, arching an eyebrow and matching his humor.

"Never," Edik said with a slight shake of his head. "You are always welcome here." He leaned forward slightly. "But you *do* have a reason, don't you."

He didn't even bother making it sound like a question.

"I do," Anna said with a sigh. "I find I am in need of accommodations for a flight to Venus. And I suspect it is a flight you'll be taking soon."

Edik was apparently too tired to even attempt to hide his shock.

"How did you know that?"

"I didn't," Anna admitted with the barest shrug. "But as the Du Mak have made no agreement with either Luna or Mars, it struck me as likely that Pajari is trying to find a way to bring Venus into the mix."

Edik started to speak, but Dola said something Anna couldn't understand, in a harsh language that reminded her somewhat of Gaelic.

"I ... can neither confirm nor deny that," Edik said with a caution that caused Anna a pang inside. Why must they be on different sides in this?

"Of course not," Anna said. "Nor would I expect you to. My friend Edik asked a question, and I answered."

"I'm sorry," Edik said quickly. "I—"

"You are new at this," Anna said, raising a hand to forestall more apologies. "And no apology is necessary. But whether you are going to Venus for pleasure or for business, if you are leaving soon, it would be my pleasure to fly with you, rather than seek other arrangements."

"You're always welcome to fly with me, *mladshaya sestra*."

Something inside Anna eased. "Thank you, Edik."

"We'll be leaving at ten hundred tomorrow."

"That would be perfect."

Edik tugged briefly at his charming, nearly roguish Van Dyke.

"Have you heard from Carl?" he asked.

Carl Jones. Master duelist, unlicensed magician, formerly some kind of agent for the Terran Navy, and a good friend to both Anna and Edik.

"Would that I had," Anna said through a sigh that had no agenda. "I know only that whatever he's about is dangerous."

"I know a little more than that," Edik said. "I know he went to Earth, and from there I suspect he headed to Mars."

"What makes you think so?"

Edik shrugged. "Nothing I could point to. Just ... something in his behavior. The way he watched the news reports."

"Well," Anna said, rising to her feet before she fell asleep, "if anyone can survive the madness of Mars right now, it's Carl. I hope he succeeds in whatever he's doing."

"As do I," Edik said, standing as well.

They said their goodbyes, and Anna headed off for her hotel. The hour was late, but she would have her bath all the same. It would ease her worries, as well as her muscles.

And with this business on Venus coming up, Anna suspected she'd need that.

DC POLICE INSISTED ON GUARDING DONAL'S AND ROWAN'S ROOMS THAT night, but at least that put them *outside* of Donal's room, as well as his wards.

Speaking of Rowan's room, apparently she hadn't been staying at the Washington Arms. Nevertheless, the smiling, efficient woman at the front desk made sure Rowan got a suite just down the hall from Donal. As smoothly and quickly as though Rowan had had a reservation all along.

Eager to please the Fae ambassadors, it seemed. It also seemed, to Donal's amusement, that as soon as the escorting officers realized Rowan and Donal weren't a couple, they became a little more obvious in the way they checked Rowan out.

Nothing too offensive, at least. Just taking less effort to hide their glances. Donal was certain Rowan noticed, but she gave no indication. Probably just used to it.

At last, though, Donal was back in his suite once more. He

reclined on a dark blue sofa, with his stocking feet up on cherry coffee table. He held a tumbler of orange juice, and lamented the firmness of the couch.

Right now he would have loved to just sink down into someplace comfortable, and sleep.

Not yet, though. And for that reason, that the couches were firm was probably a good thing.

Morna, of course, draped herself across the matching couch opposite Donal as though hers were entirely soft, comfortable and inviting. Her expression said that she'd be more than happy to share with Donal.

Fionn had already told Donal twice that there was no use in asking Morna to stop with her offers and come-ons. It was her nature. Forcing her to fight her nature would weaken, and eventually destroy her.

Speaking of the *cú sidhe*, Fionn paced the chocolate brown carpeting beside the coffee table.

"I should have been there," Fionn said.

"It's not like you to repeat yourself three times," Donal said, frowning.

"I wish to ensure you understand." Fionn stopped pacing and put a paw on the couch beside Donal, floppy ears forward with worry. "You allow others to exclude me from conversations in your continued attempts to set others at their ease. Politics is deadly serious, master. I *must* be your second set of eyes and ears. Had there been no mirror nearby when the assassin struck, you might well be dead."

"Why *do* you allow others to exclude him?" Morna asked. "He is your familiar. He should be considered part of you."

Donal sighed, his cheeks burning with a touch of embarrassment. He might have said something about how few magicians work as ambassadors, and more along those lines.

But here and now, it was better to be frank.

"Nicholas Mason rarely seems to have his familiar present, even during important meetings."

Fionn growled for a moment, then let that growl subside before speaking.

"Hierophant Nicholas Mason involves himself in many, simultaneous activities. His familiar, Clixic, is nearly always off on some task or other."

Fionn dropped his ears back against his head for a moment, then brought them back up.

"Must I also add," he said, "that Hierophant Nicholas Mason has been a master wizard since before you started high school? Or that he is a master swordsman as well? Or that his command of strategy and tactics—"

"All right," Donal said, sitting forward and staring straight into Fionn's blazing emerald eyes. "I get it. I'm no Nicholas Mason."

"Yet," Morna said, raising an index finger as she made her point. "Do not underestimate yourself, master. If nothing else, remember this — his grace sent me to aid you, yes, but he also believed I could best you. That I am not your mistress but your slave should tell you that you are no one to be trifled with."

Donal's stomach twisted a bit at her word choice. He'd never wanted a slave. Hated the idea of it. He would have freed her, except that this would have gone against her nature.

She would have withered and died in painful misery.

In that sense, Morna served as a constant reminder of the alien nature of the fae.

"I do not wish my words to be taken as derogation," Fionn said softly. "You are cleverer and more powerful than you allow yourself to believe, especially for a wizard of your age and experience. However—"

"I have blind spots," Donal said, shaking his head and not even bothering to correct Fionn's choice of terms from "wizard" to "magician."

"Just so," Fionn said, approvingly.

"All right," Donal said. "Consider your point taken. On to the events of this evening."

Donal sipped his juice. Fresh squeezed, and with just the right amount of pulp. Odd that a little thing like orange juice could help ease his mood. Settle his stomach.

"This assassin carried a poisoned dagger," Fionn said.

"Just like Smithson did in San Francisco, after my last trip to Venus."

Donal remembered those events clearly enough.

Some group called the Consortium had sent an assassin named Jeremy Smithson, first to try to intimidate Donal into making an attempt on Mr. Mancuso's life during that flight to Venus.

When Donal not only made no such attempt, but saved Mr. Mancuso's life and his very mind in the process, Smithson returned to try to kill Donal.

Might have succeeded, if not for the intervention of Hierophants Nicholas Mason and Jane MacDougall.

"Might even have been the same type of dagger," Donal said. "I never got a good look at Smithson's. He tried to keep my focus on his rapier."

"Nevertheless," Fionn said, "the correlation cannot be discarded at this time."

"Thaumaturgically," Donal said, "this was entirely different. Smithson had carried items enchanted to help him kill quickly and effectively. This assassin's only magic was the shadowy disguise."

"Tell me more about this Consortium," Morna said, and those her pose remained lascivious, the focus in her eyes was sharp.

"Sounds sinister, doesn't it?" Donal said with a frown. "I don't know much. They tried to hire Li Hua away from 4M, as well as keep her off that Venus flight. They sounded just like a group of businessmen in competition with 4M."

"They tried to kill you," she said slowly, "and you never thought to find out more about them?"

Fionn turned and said something to her in what sounded like that language that familiars spoke among themselves. Which seemed unfair, as Morna was not a familiar.

To Donal, their words sounded like a form of Gaelic he didn't speak. But he knew that to Esme, familiars talking among themselves sounded closer to Aztec or Mayan.

Donal sighed, as he let them finish.

"Well," Donal said, "let's see. Not five minutes after Smithson was stopped by Hierophants Mason and MacDougall, those two offered to have a job waiting for me when I get my doctorate."

Those two storied Hierophants wanted to put together a special task force to investigate interplanetary magical crime. And they wanted Donal to be part of it.

"Then, of course," Donal continued, "I started graduate school, which can take a fair amount of attention, let me tell you."

"Master," Morna started, but Donal kept talking.

"During a break I got sent on a mission out to Ganymede to help the Du Mak people. And then, oh, yes, I got tapped to act as ambassador for not one, but *both* Fae Courts, which has kept me pretty busy, as you know. Then there's the small matter of a coming war between the Courts and the *Fomhóraigh*, which I'm still trying to figure out how to avert."

He shook his head, running out of steam. "I still think the key to that is finding Fintan mac Bóchra. Wherever he is now."

"Finished?" Fionn asked.

"I'm sorry, master," Morna said, sounding miserable.

"No," Donal said through a sigh. "I'm sorry. I'm tired and I think the stress is getting to me. You didn't deserve to have me snap at you. The short answer is that, no, I haven't tried to find out anything more about this Consortium."

Donal shrugged. "I figured they'd forgotten about me by now."

"Perhaps they have," Fionn said, "and perhaps they have not. But you have a resource in this matter that you did not understand when Smithson tried to take your life."

"Mr. Mancuso," Donal said, sitting forward.

"He would ask you to call him Donatello," Fionn said, "but yes. Perhaps you should contact him in the morning before you leave."

"Definitely. Remind me, if I need it."

"I shall. But we must also consider that this assassin may be unrelated."

"Master," Morna said, voice brimming with excitement as she sat forward. "May I have the task of investigating this assassin?"

"I'm not sure I should interfere with the police investigation," Donal said slowly.

"I assure you," Fionn said, "that the Courts will assert the right to investigate any attempt to take the life of their ambassador."

"He's right," Morna said. "Their majesties will likely send an inquisitor with the dawn. But they will not object to you conducting your own investigation. If anything, it will build esteem for you at the Courts."

Fionn titled his head in that way that Donal knew was his equivalent to an encouraging nod.

"All right, Morna," Donal said. "Please do investigate this matter for me."

Her smile looked positively feral. "I swear you will be pleased with my results, master."

"Speaking of your results, what did you learn at the Courts?"

"The Courts are abuzz with activity," she said with sigh and the barest hint of a frown. "Their majesties work with the peers to settle or dismiss disputes among the lower nobility."

"So they're unifying," Donal said. "Does that mean what I think it means?"

Morna nodded.

Fionn was more explicit.

"Such has always been the first step, when the Courts prepare for war."

Morna supplied further details, but Donal left those to Fionn for the time being. Too much was happening today for him to properly assess the minutia of it all.

When she finished, Morna stood and curtsied to Donal, so deep a movement that she practically prostrated herself.

"My report is complete, master. How may I best serve you now?"

"I thank you, Morna. You continue to impress me at every turn.

Your report was as thorough and complete as I have come to expect from you." Donal frowned, thinking about the hour. "Please rest and refresh yourself as you please within the strictures we have previously discussed" — meaning she would take no liberties with Donal — "then begin your investigation of the assassin when you are ready."

Morna smiled, looking both pleased and flattered.

"Your esteem is more refreshing than a week of sleep and fine food, master. I shall begin at once."

She melted away into the shadows.

Fionn looked Donal up and down. "You should rest as well, master. Tomorrow will seem long."

"Right as usual, Fionn," Donal said, reaching out and ruffling that spot between Fionn's ears. Nothing sounded better to Donal than sleep.

He pulled his feet up under himself on the couch. His back straightened reflexively, and he lay his hands on his thighs, palms up.

Sleep would be delightful, but evening meditation came first.

3

THE FOLLOWING MORNING, EDIK SAT WHERE HE WAS HAPPIEST IN THE universe — in the captain's chair of his ship, gazing out the forward viewport at the distant stars. Enjoying the lingering scent of his lunch of homemade borscht.

The *Third Son* was a small ship, and had a correspondingly small bridge. Only one seat for the crew, ever since Edik had re-routed the communications and scanners from a separate station to come instead through his own pilot/command station.

Edik was no master magician, by any stretch. But when he'd studied for his Associate's in Thaumaturgy, he'd taken as many classes devoted to conjuration and the magic of space travel as he could. Enough that he and Dola, with the aid of his elementals, could handle not just running his ship, but nearly all its maintenance.

Here in his captain's chair, he was truly home.

Smooth, level, white ceramic surface under his hands, unblemished by any unnecessary mechanical controls. All the true controls of the ship were phantasmal.

At the far port side of the station floated the snarl of blue strands that formed the communications array, with a red slap-pad below it, for answering any urgent, incoming links.

Two three-dimensional displays in the air above that ceramic station surface — one just to port and one just to starboard — showed the space around the *Third Son* in excellent detail, out to a good range for a ship its size. Two golden handgrips waited below each of those displays, in case Edik needed to seize control of the scanners and search for something specific.

Finally, the pilot controls themselves. Three, in gold, for pitch, roll, and yaw, and a single red handle for speed, including all-stop and reverse.

There were larger, more expensive helioships on the market. There were helioships with more features, larger crew or cargo capacity, and designs more cutting-edge in ways Edik might not even be able to imagine.

But to him, this ship was perfect.

With Dola sitting on the deck beside him, Edik felt that he could do anything.

And these days, it almost seemed he could.

As the captain of a small helioship running little more than tours of Luna's features, he'd never garnered much respect.

But now, he was an *ambassador*.

Even Port Authority treated him like a *king*.

Oh, but Edik would be only too happy to hold onto that particular advantage for the rest of his life.

You need to fly out in the morning, Captain Barshai? But of course. When would be convenient? No, no, there'll be no question of customs or cargo checks. Just let us log your official destination and expected time frame, and we'll handle the forms. Luna would appreciate, however, if you would be willing to provide us with a passenger manifest...

Oh, but that was a sweet conversation. If Anna hadn't been right there beside him when he took the link, Edik might have even declined the passenger manifest as "ambassadorial privilege."

But she gave him the raised eyebrow. And from Anna, that expression felt as though she were gauging everything Edik had ever done in his life, and that the balance of whether or not he was a good person depended entirely on what he did *right now*.

Anyone else giving Edik that kind of look would have gotten a laugh in the face, at best. Anna, though, somehow always made Edik want to be a better person.

Perhaps because — despite being hampered by the privileged, selfish upbringing of one of the two most prominent families on Luna — Anna honestly seemed to care about other people.

Usually a very good thing. But sometimes, it was just ... inconvenient.

So under the influence of Anna's raised eyebrow, Edik had turned in a passenger manifest. And he'd included Dola, just to spite Luna's "humans only" tendencies about such things.

Luna officially still disregarded familiars, even though they were now interested in tracking the movements of the fae, Du Mak and Fo... Fav... Fu-vor-ee ... *Fomhóraigh*.

Edik still had trouble with that mouthful. He firmly believed that the written form of the Gaelic languages had been designed to make fun of a perfectly functional alphabet.

Then again...

Perhaps the ancient Celts would have made their languages more sensible if they'd had the Cyrillic alphabet available on their islands, instead of what the Romans thrust upon them.

As it was, the spelling the old Celts went with might even have been a form of revenge against their would-be conquerors.

If people like Donal Cuthbert and Nicholas Mason were typical examples, they might be obstinate enough...

"Edik," Anna said, drawing him from his musings.

She sat behind him to the starboard, at what was once the scanners and communications station. Edik had re-routed the controls, but he had left the seat and its counter.

Edik made a vague, interrogative noise, but kept his attention on the scanner displays, to make sure none of the local traffic behaved strangely.

Last thing he needed was to get followed and attacked, as had happened the last time he left Luna on a mission like this one.

Traffic looked normal today. Private vessels and liners headed into or out of the ports of Luna. The few awkward, cigar-like gunboats Luna kept on regular patrol.

In the distance, the cruisers and gunboats of the Terran Navy, designed to look like the old steel ships that sailed the seas of Earth only a few decades before Edik was born.

The Navy vessels stopped and boarded all inbound and outbound traffic, snarling normal transit to a near halt.

But the *Third Son* had been designated an ambassadorial ship, so—

"Edik," Anna said, adding just a touch of impatience to her voice.

Dola cleared his throat, and gave Edik an expectant glance.

"Sorry," he said, chagrined, and turned to give Anna a smile.

She wasn't smiling, but she didn't look cross either. Her face held a look of infinite patience that didn't quite match the question hiding in her eyes.

Even now, she made Edik feel underdressed. Even with her hair down and dangling past her shoulders. Wearing nothing more than a simple red blouse, with cream slacks and short, tan boots.

Of course, the clothes were airsilk and the boots were ... some kind of leather that looked softer than anything Edik owned.

Then again, how would she have looked in good spacer gear...

Oh, who was he kidding? She'd probably look better in his clothes than he did.

"I do enjoy the taste of good borscht from time to time," she said. "It isn't what I was raised with, of course, but still. I have enjoyed yours, have I not? Your grandmother's recipe, I believe?"

"That's right," Edik said.

"Here it comes," Dola said, pitching his words just for Edik's ears.

"*Must* we smell borscht everywhere we go on this ship? The galley. The main cabin. The bridge. Even the head carries a touch of that particular aroma."

Anna blinked. "Admittedly, in the head, the aroma could be far worse, but the point remains."

"I like it," Edik said with a one-shoulder shrug. "It's comforting."

"And I would never attempt to dissuade you from eating your

favorite meal. Nor would I refuse it on those occasions you are good enough to serve it to me. But, Edik." She raised that eyebrow again. "Everywhere? All the time?"

"She does raise a point," Dola said carefully, still allowing only Edik to hear his words.

"Very well," Edik said, turning back to check the scanners. No unusual activity so far.

Varia was the sylph, or air elemental, dedicated to handling air quality aboard the *Third Son*, but Edik called forth his ship's lead sylph instead.

"Nixia," he said.

She appeared almost at once. A tiny, beautiful woman composed almost entirely of swirls of air the color of fresh, ripe lemons, save with orange eyes. Only a dozen centimeters tall today, which was shorter than usual but not too odd.

She dressed today in a yellow mimicry of Edik's preferred outfit, down to an imitation of his saber. That was unusual for her. She favored dresses, when she wore anything. But at least she didn't imitate his hairstyle, or beard. Her own long hair floated behind her, constantly moving.

"Yes, Edik?" she said, her voice as breathy as that of all air elementals.

"How long until Xincapph will be able to take over flying?"

Xincapph was the *Third Son's* sole lacuna, the elemental handling both travel and scanners within his native environment of space.

No spirits were more alien than lacunas. And yet, Edik seemed to have established a positive, working relationship with his that went beyond the typical interplay of bindings and commands.

But then, Edik treated all the spirits of his life as people, and tried to relate to them at least as well as he did with other people.

Usually better.

"Perhaps five minutes, Edik," Nixia said with a smile, "if we maintain our present speed. At that time, Xincapph will be ready to carry the *Third Son* to Venus along the route you plotted."

"Perfect," Edik said with a smile. But the smile faltered. "One more thing. Could you please have Varia remove the smell of borscht from the *Third Son's* cabins?"

"Are you sure, Edik?" Nixia asked with a frown. "You've always specified—"

"I know," Edik said, pointing with a glance toward Anna. "But for this voyage, remove it."

"From all the cabins?"

"Please."

"Is there a scent you would prefer?"

"Leave nothing but clean air for this voyage."

"Of course, Edik. Will that be all?"

"For now. Thank you, Nixia."

The sylph nodded and dissolved.

"Edik," Anna said softly, "I feel as though I've asked you to do something a great deal more important than you're letting on—"

"It's nothing," Edik lied.

"...if you're certain," she said, sounding as uncertain as he'd ever heard her.

"Really. Don't think any more about it."

"All right then. Thank you."

Edik shot her a quick smile, then turned his attention back to the scanners. He had the feeling this trip was going to be very long indeed.

At the southern tip of Washington DC, all three of its ports faced each other across the Potomac River.

On the west bank sat the river port, which Donal suspected saw no commercial traffic at all anymore. He couldn't see why anyone would bother with water travel, except for personal entertainment.

On the north bank, the airport, with a steady stream of airships flying in and out all hours of the day and night, most of which were designed to look like birds. The airships came and went along the same five approaches, passing through clouds the color of disappointment.

Finally, on the east bank, the spaceport, where Donal and Rowan were arriving right now in the back of a blue-and-white, Washington DC Metropolitan Police runner. The bench seat beneath them was padded, at least, which was good because the interior was otherwise entirely off-white ceramics, alchemically treated for toughness.

Four other police runners served as escort — one in front, one behind, and one to each side.

Donal tried to keep his mind on the spaceport he approached. Wasn't easy, the way his day had gone so far already.

Donal had been awakened by the arrival of a *sidhe* knight, standing over his bed.

The knight, who had not identified himself beyond his role as inquisitor, had skin like the sky at midnight, and hair the colors of storm clouds that hung to his waist in one long, tight braid. He stood tall, and lean, and inhumanly beautiful in antique formal clothes that might have fit in at *La Petite Coupure*. He wore a broadsword at his hip with more comfort than many professional champions wore rapiers.

The knight's cerulean eyes seemed to analyze everything they saw, missing nothing. His voice sounded soft and neutral, and yet as he asked Donal all about the assassin the night before — he asked about Smithson back in San Francisco as well — the knight gave the impression of a predator poised and ready to strike.

Donal's later whirlwind conversation with incisive Mr. Mancuso had felt peaceful and relaxing, by comparison.

Mr. Mancuso had claimed not to know anything about the Consortium, but Donal recognized the tone of the denial. Mr. Mancuso knew or suspected something, but wouldn't tell Donal what until he had confirmation.

Such dizzying ways to start his day. Donal was only too glad to sink deeply into his morning meditations and regain his clarity and balance.

If only he could have had longer.

Left to his own devices, Donal would have meditated for an hour or so last night before bed, and another hour this morning, between awakening and breakfast.

But with all these demands on his attention, it seemed Donal's meditation times were getting shorter and shorter these days.

Nothing Donal could do about that, though, riding in the back of a police runner on his way to the spaceport. Nothing more he could do about the about the investigation, either, from where he sat.

So Donal focused his mind on his arrival at the spaceport.

The spaceport was designed as a tribute to the early days of the old United States. All weathered brick façades for the buildings, and a red brick or cobblestones for the walking surfaces.

Hardly the poured stone of the nicer streets Donal had seen, but he had no doubt that earth elementals had worked just as hard to get the look and feel right.

Much lighter traffic here, but then, it was a minor spaceport. Very little shipping came to DC from space. Some commercial transit, but most commercial helioships coming to this coast from Luna or Mars would come in through Toronto. Their DC bound passengers would then take an airship down.

A little extra time, but minimizing direct space traffic in and out of the UNAS capitol was said to be important for security reasons.

So most of the transit that did come in and out of the spaceport was private or military, with the odd political or ambassadorial ship making up the remainder.

To be honest, Donal was glad to have the logistics of Washington DC travel to distract himself this morning on the ride to that spaceport. And not just because of *sidhe* knights and worries about bargains and assassins.

The runner he rode in smelled like stale bread and old socks. And the two patrolmen in the front had chattered the whole way about how Donal had no need to worry, that they would find the perpetrator and stop him and any others who might be involved, and on and on and on.

They meant well. Donal knew that. But he strongly suspected that the assassin himself was a dead end. Likely knew only who his target was, where, and when to strike.

Which meant that Donal had been under observation at least since sometime after his arrival in DC yesterday.

He couldn't help but think about those efforts to scry his hotel room. Not to mention Bran's warning of incoming danger.

Had Bran been trying to warn Donal about a possible assassin? Or was the danger Bran warned of something else? Something yet to come?

What could Bran have learned on his way to Ganymede that would affect Donal all the way back here on Earth? And why send Res with a wards message? Why the old code? Why not have Res deliver a spoken message?

Donal was certain that thoughts such as these had made him a poor traveling companion this morning. But Rowan, sitting beside Donal, appeared perfectly at ease. Even chatting a bit with the policemen, between their assertions and reassurances, and a little more with Fionn, who sat on the floor between her and Donal.

Donal wondered briefly where Rowan had gotten her change of clothes. She carried no baggage, and yet she sat beside him wearing not the gown she'd worn the night before, but the same suit she'd worn the day they met, in the New Leningrad Spaceport on Mars — smoke gray and cut to emphasize what it concealed.

The clothing was real enough. Donal could tell that without even reaching for his tuning fork. He'd have to ask her sometime.

The runners bypassed the public drop-off point, and continued through a red brick tunnel to the landing bays out back.

Along the way through the tunnel, Donal spotted illusory displays scattered here and there about gates, flights, and other tourist information. Every one of them designed to look like paper on wood, with their information handwritten in black, looping letters.

The runners emerged from the tunnel onto cobblestones beneath a dingy sky. The cobblestones were grayish through the common areas in back, but color-coded around their landing bays and corresponding paths into the main building of the port.

Donal didn't need to ask which bay they headed for. Right now only a dozen of the landing bays were in use. Some with older style mythical creatures for their designs. A roc, a dire wolf, even one that looked like a hut on chicken legs.

Others were done in more modern styles. Not the bird trend so popular with airships, but sleek designs. An arrowhead. A swirling curve. One that might have been a manta ray.

On its lonesome, way off to one side, a design that Donal took to be a rocket ship out of some old science fiction novel — a steel gray tube with huge red fins, and a large transparent bubble over the bridge.

None of those ships could have been Donal's destination. Not when there was a boring white flat-bottomed shuttle dead ahead, designed to look like ... oh, some kind of old sea vessel. Donal didn't know the types well enough to differentiate.

It was flat and wide at the back, and tapered toward the bow. It had a single, boxy protrusion above a flat deck. On the side, in black, block letters, the designation *Galileo*.

Odd to name a shuttle after an artist, but no one had asked Donal's opinion.

Four Terran Marines — in their tan uniforms and carrying crossbows in their hands and black clubs on their belts that were presumably military-grade Pacifiers — stood waiting by the ... gangplank?

Yes, Donal thought that was the right word for the broad stretch of white wood leading from the cobblestones to the deck of the *Galileo*.

A fifth person stood in the center of their assemblage, wearing the pale blue uniform of the Terran Navy. This was a man with the chin and cheekbones to have at least some Germanic ancestry. He was pale, as many Caucasian spacers were, but he looked fit enough, and his dark hair had the same close-cropped cut as his companions.

The naval man was as young as the marines too. Likely no one in the receiving party was older than Donal or Rowan.

Donal's runner stopped. The escort runners continued moving, circling the runner and shuttle.

Donal's door opened.

The air smelled surprisingly clean. Apparently the spring stench of the Potomac wasn't allowed near the spaceport. A vast improvement over the odors of that runner.

The marines took up positions around the runner, their weapons held high and their eyes scanning for threats.

At least Donal couldn't complain that the attempt on his person wasn't taken seriously.

His mouth frowned at doing so, but he got out of the runner preceded only by Fionn. His mother would have thrown a fit at not letting a lady exit the vehicle before him, but both Rowan and Fionn had insisted.

It seemed likely that anyone trying to kill Donal would know of his ... more polite tendencies. Thus, by preceding Rowan, they hoped to surprise any last-moment attempts.

"Up the gangplank quickly, if you please, Mr. Ambassador," the naval officer said. And Donal knew the man was an officer now. He could see his ensign's bar. "The sooner you're aboard, the safer you'll be."

Two of the marines flanked Donal and hurried him up the gangplank, with Fionn leading the way.

Donal crested the gangplank, crossed two meters of exposed deck space, and continued on into the main cabin of the shuttle. Rowan followed, only a step behind him.

The cabin was a simple affair. Two seats up front for a pilot and copilot. A row of padded, gray ceramic seats against each of the port and starboard bulkheads for accommodations.

Donal sat and strapped himself into the five-point safety harness, while Rowan did the same beside him.

Donal's luggage was brought up by the marines a moment later. They carried it to the rear of the shuttle, where they secured it among other cargo before all four marines strapped themselves to their nearby seats.

"Fionn," Donal said, "please go thank the officers for their escort."

"No time, sir," the ensign said, while the hatch closed behind the last marine. "We need to lift off now."

"Now?" Donal asked.

"*Wait*," Rowan said. "We're supposed to be meeting an envoy from Brazil."

"Yes," Donal said, quickly. "This envoy is supposed to be coming along. It was arranged last night."

"I have no orders about any envoy from Brazil, sir," the ensign said, shaking his head. "My orders are to get you two safely out of port and aboard the *Pegasus* at best speed, and I intend to do just that."

The ensign nodded at the pilot to lift off.

"Stop," Donal said, but the pilot only cringed, and grimaced an apology.

"Go," the ensign said to the pilot, then turned back to Donal.

"I'm sorry, Ambassadors," the ensign said, strapping himself in as the shuttle lifted off and zoomed into the sky, heavily buffeted by turbulence. "You'll have to take it up with the captain when we dock."

Rowan started to speak, but at a glance from Donal she nodded for him to take the lead.

"Thank you for doing your duty and getting us aboard this shuttle safely, Ensign..."

"Taverner, sir."

"Ensign Taverner. And for seeing us aboard the ... *Pegasus* is it?"

"Aye, sir."

"Captained by..."

"Captain Klimek, sir. Captain Iwona Klimek."

"Well, the Fae Courts of Winter and Summer both acknowledge your efforts on behalf of their ambassadors. However. Your Captain Klimek had better show more flexibility in terms of her orders, or she risks provoking humanity's first *interrealm* incident."

Donal kept his voice calm and steady through his little oration. He was pretty sure Mr. Mancuso — Donatello — would have approved.

And Donatello would definitely have approved of the way Ensign Taverner visibly paled at Donal's words.

———

BETWEEN HIS TIME TRAVELING AS AN INTERPLANETARY COURIER, HIS time riding around with Mr. Mancuso, and now his time serving as an ambassador, Donal had flown aboard a large number of helioships.

Small ones, big ones, private yachts, tiny runabouts, huge passenger liners...

Of them all, Donal was convinced that military vessels were the worst, in terms of passenger comfort.

They were always cold, for one thing. As though military service required temperatures below anyone's casual comfort level.

Perhaps this was an attempt to cut corners on the alchemical reagents that made their long-term spells and bindings practical?

That was a possibility. Donal noted to look into the correlations between temperature and the thaumaturgy and alchemy of space travel, when he had time.

Either way, the *Pegasus* also stank of metal and some kind of oil. That had been true in the docking bay, and it was true now. Donal wasn't even sure what kind of oil he was smelling. Certainly nothing that had to do with cooking.

Ridiculous, that perpetual smell of metal. It wasn't as though the *Pegasus* were actually made from steel, despite its pretensions. No, it was made from space-grade ceramics — along with some carterite, of course — the same as every other helioship.

Donal did have to admit that the odor fit the theme, though, because decks and bulkheads both had their ceramics enchanted to seem as steel. Even down to the point that the boots of his security escort had clanged off the deck with every step, as they escorted Donal and Rowan to the briefing room, to await Captain Klimek.

Was it an appeal to the Law of Similarity? Did it make military vessels hardier than others?

Another point for Donal to research. In his abundant spare time.

The briefing room was small, with a single door. No more than a handful of meters across in both directions, with a round, simple ceramic table in the center — the brown of unpolished, cheap loafers — and surrounded by black ceramic chairs that Donal thought might be useful for teaching meditation.

He doubted anyone could get comfortable on the flat, hard, straight-backed things. Certainly no one could fall asleep in one, and anyone unfortunate enough to have to sit on one for any length of time would be only too happy to distract their thoughts from their physical discomfort.

And this room, too, smelled of oil and metal.

A gray, ceramic pitcher of cold water sat on the table, along with four matching cups. Donal had poured a cup each for himself and Rowan before sitting, but neither of them had touched their drinks yet, while they waited.

Rowan, of course, looked perfectly at ease in her chair, though Donal couldn't believe she was.

Fionn sat on the deck between them, looking up at Donal. Studying him.

After a few minutes, Fionn's thoughts came to Donal's mind.

You have yet to grow accustomed to so little time alone.

Donal frowned. *What do you mean?*

You traveled alone as a courier. Spent much time alone in hotels, restaurants, aboard ships...

You were with me, Donal thought to his familiar.

Fionn didn't bother pointing out that he didn't count. Fionn had once been a completely independent spirit before answering Donal's call for a familiar. But in taking the role of familiar, in this world, he became a part of Donal, and would remain so until Donal's death.

You socialize in school, of course, Fionn continued, *but still take a great deal of time to yourself. Or to the two of us, if you prefer.*

But my ambassador work...

Indeed. Fionn flicked his ears the way he did when he felt a point was nearly understood, but needed more clarification all the same.

Now you are disturbed at all hours, often without warning. Dealing with that, along with the many directions that demand your attention, has begun to affect your moods. You must take steps to prevent that.

Donal sighed, and gave Fionn a small smile. *Think I could work office hours into my contract, if I renew?*

I believe it would be worth the effort. But in the interim, you must remember to keep your focus in the present. Last night's assassin, the coming war, those are not matters for you to handle here and now. Meditate. Rowan MacPherson will understand.

Does she meditate?

After a fashion, but not the way you mean it.

Before Donal could ask what that meant, the door opened, and in came someone who had to be Captain Klimek. And not just because of the captain's bars on her uniform.

She was short, only perhaps a meter and a half tall, but she had the square, solid build of a woman who could probably dismantle this table with her bare hands.

Though only likely in her forties, Captain Klimek's black hair was already shot through with gray streaks, and her pale skin had to begun wrinkling in patterns that indicated a lot of stress, anger and frowning.

She was frowning now, and spoke quickly, in clipped tones, as she took her seat.

"I understand you have some pressing need to speak with me that cannot wait until we're underway?"

"Captain Klimek, I presume," Donal said, letting his words out slowly. Just one of the little tricks Mr. Mancuso had taught him for controlling a conversation. When someone rushed, slow them down.

"Yes," Captain Klimek said, voice full of irritation, "I'm Captain Klimek." She pointed at Rowan. "You're Rowan MacPherson." She pointed at Donal. "You're Donal Cuthbert. I'm a captain in the Terran Navy and in command of this ship and this mission. And you're ambassadors for the Fae Courts of Earth."

"The Fae Courts," Rowan corrected, her tone and pace as casual and calm as Captain Klimek was clipped and rushed. "Earth has no claim to them beyond alliance, and the Courts will not have their domains limited through inference or implication."

"Whatever." Captain Klimek looked unimpressed. "Are we done with the introductions then? I have a schedule to keep."

"Your schedule is not our problem," Donal said, fighting the urge to steeple his fingers the way Mr. Mancuso would have, and settling instead for folding his hands on the cool ceramics of the table.

"Look here," Captain Klimek said, raising one index finger in anger, "The *Pegasus* is no one's taxi service. I'm ferrying you two along as a *favor*—"

"Not to us," Rowan said.

That stopped whatever tirade Captain Klimek had started.

"I'm sorry?"

"You might be doing *someone* a favor," Rowan said. "However, you are not doing *us* a favor, nor are you providing a favor for the Fae Courts."

Captain Klimek closed her eyes and flared her nostrils in a long, slow breath. Donal spoke before she could.

"That difference may seem unimportant to you, but I assure you it's crucial."

"I hate dealing with politicians," Captain Klimek grumbled, possibly unaware that her words carried in the small room. Louder, she said, "Fine. But you aren't my mission and I have a timetable. So what the hell do you want?"

Rowan nodded to Donal.

"There is to be a third passenger. An envoy from Brazil."

"Ridiculous," Captain Klimek said. "You don't get to give your friends a lift—"

"*Captain Klimek,*" Donal said, snapping the words out.

Fire blazed in the captain's eyes, but Donal matched her glare.

"We have said you are not doing us a favor, and I am not asking you for one now. Nor am I in the habit of taking joyrides on military vessels. Nor have I ever invited a 'friend' on ambassadorial business."

Donal smiled, and knew that nothing like happiness came through that smile. "Now I suggest you remember that when you speak to us, you are representing the United Terran Government and addressing ambassadors of an allied power. If you are not qualified to do that, then I suggest you call for someone who is."

Donal placed his hands flat on the table and leaned forward.

"Either way, I assure you that if this vessel leaves Earth without our problem being resolved to our satisfaction, it will mean the end of your career, and possible charges for treason. Depending on how *your superiors* decide to play it."

Captain Klimek frowned, thinking, while Donal leaned back.

"If transporting us was billed to you as a 'favor,' Captain, it is not. By agreeing to take us to Venus, you *have* placed yourself in a complex political position, and thus, potential jeopardy."

"I'm beginning to understand that."

"I assure you that we have no wish to cause you trouble, nor put you off your timetable. But this ship *will not* leave Earth until we have linked the Brazilian envoy who waits for us even now in the Washington DC Spaceport, and shuttled that envoy aboard."

"Trust me, Captain," Rowan said, "you do not wish to test us in this matter. Do not believe that because we are aboard your ship, we have no means of communicating directly with the Courts. We do."

Captain Klimek ground her teeth, but growled, "Fine. Of course. Anything for our allies."

She stood. "Come on. Let's get this over with."

DONAL ALMOST LAUGHED WHEN HE FINALLY SAW HIS "CABIN."

To say that the *Pegasus* wasn't designed for ferrying about VIPs was putting it mildly. They'd put Donal in an unused officer's cabin, and he pitied any officer who got stuck with it.

The cabin had no porthole. No view of space outside at all, because it was toward the center of the vessel. Close to the transport bubble, yes, as many of the cabins set aside for officers were, but without that little bit of relief, the small space would get confining on long voyages.

Fortunately, three days didn't count as long.

But *small* was putting it mildly.

The cabin was no more than three meters long, if that. And across, hardly a meter and a half.

For a bed, it had a hard cot that could be popped out of the bulkhead with a double-tap. Much like the efficiency desk that could pop out of the other side (at the right height, if Donal didn't mind sitting on the cot while he worked. Not that he had another option, in this cabin).

At least officers' cabins had their own showers and toilets. Those popped out of the short wall opposite the door. Both were not available at the same time.

Tiny. Absolutely tiny.

For a light, there was a single square in the center of the ceiling, whose minuscule fire elemental would take orders from any occupant of the room.

Clearly the *Pegasus* was an older ship. Newer ships had alchemically enhanced enchantments to provide lighting in the cabins. Donal remembered reading an article about it last semester.

And, of course, this cabin — like the rest of the ship, so far as Donal could tell — smelled like metal and oil.

Donal was going to have to ask someone about what kind of oil that was. Greasy, and vaguely metallic in its own right.

"Well," Fionn said, glancing around. He had to stand in front of Donal, because there wasn't enough room to stand beside him. "It's not exactly the top suite on the *Horizon Cusp*, but better accommodations than you were given for some lunar flights, when you worked as a courier."

"It's perfect," Donal said with a smile, shaking his head.

"Perfect?" Fionn cocked his head to the side, letting his tongue loll just a little. Curiosity and amusement.

"Are you kidding?" Donal asked. "Listen to that."

He held up one hand. There were no sounds but Donal's breathing, and his heartbeat.

Fionn chuckled. "Tired of the yelling?"

"Exhausted," Donal said, sinking straight down to sit cross-legged on the cold faux-metal floor.

And exhausted was a good word for how he felt. All the arguing and bureaucracy of the day were getting to him.

He'd been aboard this ship for more than three long, loud hours. And they were only now finally leaving Earth.

First, there had been the matter of getting back to the port.

Apparently, the *Pegasus* had already accepted clearance to depart, and even though they never left the atmosphere, turning right around and coming back to the port was considered ... unusual, for a military vessel.

There were procedures to follow, codes to cite, people to talk to and quite likely asses to either chew out or kiss, as appropriate.

Donal hadn't seen that part, but his time with Mr. Mancuso had made him expect it to work that way. Mr. Mancuso always said that bureaucracies kept things from getting done only to the extent that people allowed them to.

Donal had needed that one explained twice. It just hadn't made any sense. At least, not when Donal had thought of bureaucracies as systems in place to establish *how* things were done.

No, Mr. Mancuso had explained. They were gates that had to be passed through or battered down. That bureaucracies existed to keep people from trying to do too much, too quickly.

Actually, the explanation went on from there, and Donal didn't even want to revisit it in his head. Not when the day felt so long already.

The key element was that Mr. Mancuso seemed to be right, and that the *Pegasus* had to pay a toll in time and effort for accepting its cue to depart, and then reneging on the deal.

Once back to port — well, in the sky above the port, as the *Pegasus* didn't land itself, but sent down a shuttle again — then there was the matter of finding the envoy.

And oh, how Captain Klimek had been less than thrilled to learn that neither Donal nor Rowan knew the envoy's name.

Very colorful vocabulary, the captain.

Once Donal had weathered that particular storm and forced the links to open and get port security looking, the envoy hadn't been too hard to find. Apparently, in a city like DC, all diplomatic personnel were expected to log their entries and exits from ports.

Donal did wonder then if that was supposed to apply to himself and Rowan as well, since as far as he knew neither of them had ever done so.

Rather than ask, Donal decided that it had to be an internal matter of the UTG, and not his concern.

At last, though, the envoy was tracked down, led out to the shuttle, and finally brought aboard the *Pegasus*. At which point, Captain Klimek immediately abandoned Rowan, Donal and the envoy in a small ready room with some minor officer whose duty it was to show them to the officers' mess, where they'd take their meals, the cabins where they'd sleep, and the meeting room set aside for their use.

Not to mention instructions to stay out of everyone's way, and to not go wandering on the ship.

Under normal circumstances, that last order would have been the most difficult for Donal to follow. Back when he'd been a courier, he'd developed the habit of wandering everywhere he could, aboard ships. Seeing what their was to see, as well as getting a little exercise.

But not this trip. Not after meeting the envoy from Brazil.

No, now Donal hoped to spend the majority of his time in his cabin, meditating.

At least, as much as he could get away with.

It wasn't that the envoy was unpleasant. No, if anything, the problem was just the opposite.

The Brazilian envoy's name was Alessandra Bueno, and she had the kind of look and style Donal would have expected from a talk show hostess, rather than a politician. She was only a few years older than Donal, and every centimeter as tall, with a slender build, dark eyes, and exceptionally white teeth. She wore her lustrous black hair long, but not long enough to get in her way.

Her outfit was a dark blue skirt suit would have looked more at home at an ambassadorial reception than aboard a ship like the *Pegasus*.

Then again, maybe she was a better judge of that than he was. Donal certainly had no doubt that even her clothing was a tool of her trade.

Conversation, however, was clearly her primary tool.

Ms. Bueno was the kind of lively conversationalist that Donal considered hazardous. The sort who could put anyone at ease by saying just the right thing, and then keep a conversation flowing so smoothly that, if Donal wasn't careful, he might let something slip that he shouldn't.

Mr. Mancuso had warned him against diplomats like Ms. Bueno. Called them the most dangerous creatures this side of accountants.

Donal wondered if Esme had to deal with diplomats like Ms. Bueno. It had been too long since he'd spoken with Esme. He'd tried linking her from the hotel that morning, after he spoke with Mr. Mancuso. He couldn't reach her though.

But maybe Donal was overthinking the situation. Maybe Ms. Bueno was actually just a friendly person.

He looked at Fionn, where the meter-tall emerald *cú sidhe* sat before him.

Fionn had that patient look in his eyes right now. But then, Donal often sat and reviewed his last few hours before beginning a meditation. And often when he did, he had at least one question for Fionn.

"Fionn," Donal said finally, "do you think Ms. Bueno—"

"Was trying to put you at ease to the point that she could finagle additional benefits for Brazil? Absolutely," Fionn said, his voice as matter-of-fact as it ever got. "It is my opinion that she was given this assignment partially as an excuse to see if they could send someone who could get close to you. It is also my opinion that the means by which the meeting came about … threw off her normal approach."

"What do you mean?"

"Only that Alessandra Bueno strikes me as a confident, competent woman, who is accustomed to reading men easily, and drawing them out in conversation."

"And I didn't give her anything to work with?"

"More than that," Fionn said, twitching his floppy ears as though holding back a laugh. "I think she'd already had in mind how she was going to approach you in the spaceport. Likely she had studied whatever information was available, and had selected just the right gambit to allow her to set and control the tone of your conversation."

Fionn actually allowed himself a wag of his tail as he continued. Under the circumstances, another sure sign of contained hilarity.

"Then you appeared to forget about her entirely. Then the military escort — the *abrupt* military escort. On arrival, of course, she was introduced to Rowan MacPherson first, and Rowan MacPherson ... interfered."

"Oh?" Donal wasn't sure if he should have been flattered, amused or offended.

Fionn sounded amused.

"Oh, most certainly. She has explained to you, I believe, her idiomatic mastery of body language?"

Donal nodded.

"Well, she sent Alessandra Bueno such a complicated set of signals, the poor woman would have been excused for believing you were married, preferred the company of men, or had no interest in sex of any kind. Perhaps even all three."

Donal blinked in confusion.

"Why? Ms. Bueno didn't seem to be hitting on me."

"No, but undoubtedly the file her government provided identified you as heterosexual, single, and in a relationship of uncertain status. By confusing so basic an issue, Rowan MacPherson threw into question the quality of all the information Alessandra Bueno had obtained. This caused her to move from a targeted approach to a more general approach. Which, of course, was easier for you to resist."

Donal considered that through a breath.

"How did I not see any of this?"

Fionn's tongue lolled out for a moment. "You have long had a blind spot where Rowan MacPherson stands. Ever since you met in the New Leningrad Spaceport."

"Well," Donal said, feeling both tired and grumpy and letting it show in his voice. "She did come across as trying to make me choose sides in a war."

"Which you have done since then," Fionn said. "Twice. Both decisions involved Rowan MacPherson in some way. So, in that sense—"

"By the end of that flight back from Mars I'd thought she was responsible for killing Hassan al Rashid and trying to kill Mr. Mancuso."

"Who would tell you to call him..."

"Donatello." Donal shook his head. "Hard habit to break."

"But worth the effort, I think you'll find." Fionn glanced over Donal, nodded to himself, and continued. "At no time, however, did you question your conclusions about Rowan MacPherson. Not until circumstances — and direct conversation — forced you to do so."

"All right," Donal said with a sigh. "If I admit you're right about this can we move on?"

A disgruntled wave passed down Fionn's shaggy fur. "If we must. But seeing how often you deal with Rowan MacPherson, you might wish to again revisit and reassess your conclusions about her."

"Are you trying to set me up with her or something?"

"It is not my place to matchmake for you. Especially as I think you did quite well for yourself with Esmeralda Villaseñor, although I admit to being no more certain than you are about the status of that relationship."

"Wish I'd gotten her on the link."

"And yet..."

"I didn't," Donal said with another sigh. "But I'm here now, and Esme will have to wait. Do you think Ms. Bueno will cause me trouble?"

"I think Alessandra Bueno has enough on her plate right now."

"What do you know that I don't?"

"On this topic? She has been talking with Rowan MacPherson. I suspect Alessandra Bueno will come away from that conversation confused along more than one line. Alessandra Bueno is quite skilled, but she is ill-equipped for the likes of Rowan MacPherson."

Donal said nothing through a long, slow breath.

"Think anyone would mind if I spent most of this voyage in meditation?"

"If you wish to do so, I shall be more than happy to ferry messages and make excuses."

Donal shook his head, chuckling. Fionn would have done those things anyway. Pointing it out was just another way of encouraging Donal to meditate more.

And his familiar had a point.

Donal straightened his back. Rolled his shoulders to loosen them. Rolled his neck next. Shook out his hands, then lay them, palms facing up, on his thighs.

He drew one deep breath, from the base of his diaphragm all the way until his lungs were full to bursting.

He released that breath the same way, from the bottom to the top.

He did that again. And then a third time.

By the time he finished the third repetition, his body felt more relaxed and loose already.

Time to begin.

His breaths came and went now, slow and deep and steady.

His thoughts began to drift away with each exhalation. His concerns about Ms. Bueno, about Rowan, about Esme, about Captain Klimek, about what he was to do on Venus…

All of them, just fading into the background as Donal eased his mind down into the proper channels.

Donal continued to follow his breaths for a time. It was the easiest way to focus attention, and the first method taught to anyone studying modern thaumaturgy.

But after only a few breaths, Donal left that focus behind with his thoughts.

He slipped his attention from his breaths to his heartbeat and then to the self behind them both. Behind his thoughts. Behind even his awareness of his own awareness.

He drifted then, into the purity of deepest silence.

No fixation for him to ruminate on and puzzle through. No magical conundrum to solve. Not this time.

This was true silence. True emptiness. The most centering, refreshing form he'd encountered yet. A depth of meditation he hadn't realized was possible even a year ago.

Donal's final thought as he sank deeper and deeper was to wonder what he didn't believe possible today, that would become part of his life a year from now.

THREE DAYS. THIS TRIP FROM LUNA TO VENUS WAS ONLY SUPPOSED TO take three days. From lift-off to landing, just about seventy-hours even.

So why did Anna feel as though this voyage were taking weeks?

It wasn't as though Edik was restricting her movements aboard the ship. He'd even made his hammock available to her, when he wasn't using it.

Anna could not imagine herself sleeping in a *hammock* anywhere at all, but certainly not on the lower deck of the *Third Son*, near Edik's storage and laundry.

Crates and dirty clothing? Not her idea of a conducive sleep environment.

Still, she appreciated the gesture.

Anna was allowed on the bridge anytime she wished. Even when Edik was asleep, and their transit was handled entirely by the elementals under his command.

From what Anna understood of space travel, few captains would allow their elementals such control. They would insist on having the bridge "manned" at all times. But not Edik.

One of the things she liked about him was the respectful way he handled his spirits. Not just his familiar, but every spirit she ever saw him interact with.

The man was only an Initiate — *only, as though she were even that well-versed in thaumaturgy* — and yet Anna felt he handled his spirits better than some Magisters she could name.

Still. Though he called her *mladshaya sestra*, spoke when she wanted conversation, and gave her free run of his beloved *Third Son,* Anna felt that things were wrong between them.

A tension lay thick in the air. Thicker than the smell of borscht had ever been aboard the *Third Son.*

Anna had tried three times over the first day or so. Three times she'd told him he could restore the scent, if he wished. Three times she'd reassured him that it did not bother her.

Each time he dismissed her concerns, quickly and decisively, and turned away to do something else.

He hadn't even made borscht once by the end of the second day of their flight. Normally he ate it every night, as predictable as a dispute between great families.

But on this voyage, so far, only sandwiches. Moonfish, or lunar ham, on those sticky slabs of what passed for bread to most of the lunar populace. Spiced with decent mustard, at least, which made up for the wilted excuse for lettuce.

Anna hadn't realized Edik still ate so badly. She would have to see about getting him a higher quality of food, when they returned to Luna.

She offered no complaints about the meals, of course. Wouldn't have, even if everything were normal between them. He was her host. Complaints about the fare would have been rude, even if those sandwiches did not sit well in her stomach.

She wished she'd stayed as silent about the smell of borscht. Clearly, something about that aroma was important to Edik. Even if he wouldn't admit it.

But she had an idea.

It was the third day of their voyage, and lunchtime was approaching. Edik sat at his pilot's seat, wearing one of his more dashing spacer outfits. Silver stripe down the side of his many-pocketed black trousers, which were, as always, tucked into those tall, shiny black boots of his.

The long-sleeved shirt he wore today — also covered in more pockets than anyone could possibly need — was an off-white, not quite a cream color, that worked well with the reds in his complexion, and the darker blonde highlights in his hair and beard.

Whatever else could be said of the man, he knew how to dress for the image he liked to project.

He was busy chatting with Dola about something, in that strange not-quite-Russian language they shared. A conversation that had started when Anna had returned to the main cabin to read, but left the door to the bridge standing open, as it often did, when Roger North was not aboard.

Someday Anna wished to bring peace to the odd, tense alliance between those two men. Perhaps even get them to develop more of a friendship.

Of course, it might be easier to bring about peace between the Fae Courts and the *Fomhóraigh*...

One problem at a time.

Neither man nor cat seemed to notice when Anna had set her book down and stole away into the galley.

It was the only ship's galley Anna had ever been in, so she had nothing to compare it to. It certainly did not even belong to the same category as the magnificent kitchens she knew back home on Luna.

The counters were plain white ceramic, and surprisingly clean. Four circles on the left-hand side for the stove units, with heat supplied by salamanders, according to a sliding lever set by the cook. One slider per circle.

Directly underneath the stove circles sat the oven cabinet, with part of its ceramic door a pane of glass.

More controls for the oven cabinet. A number of touch-buttons for specific dishes such as steak, roast, turkey, chicken, popcorn, and re-heat. Below the buttons a sliding lever with the proper centigrade degrees laid out, for those more traditional cooks.

That lever could even be flicked up for baking, or down for broiling.

Cabinets above and below the counter, that same plain, white ceramic. The only exception were the two pale blue cabinets above and below the counter to the far right. Preservation units.

Of course, calling anything "far left" or "far right" in this galley felt like an exaggeration.

The galley was so narrow that Anna could stand in the center and touch all three walls. The fourth "wall" was nothing more than a pale brown door she'd had to slide closed to keep her work secret until she finished.

Although speaking of secret...

"Nixia," Anna whispered, unsure she would receive a response.

"Yes?" came the breathy reply, as the air elemental coalesced into form in the air before Anna.

Nixia stood a half-meter tall this time, and the swirls of air that made up her humanish form and wild, flowing hair had the color and sheen of lemons that had ripened late into the season. As did the elegant ball gown she seemed to wear, though Anna suspected the dress, too, was a part of Nixia.

Amusement and curiosity danced together in those tiny orange eyes.

"Can I ask you to do me a favor?" Anna asked, her voice sounding unsure even to herself.

"A favor?" Nixia echoed.

"Yes," Anna said. "I want to do something for Edik. I feel terrible that I asked him to remove the aroma of borscht from his ship. I wish to make some for him. But I don't want him to smell it until I can bring him a bowl on the bridge."

Nixia tilted her head, smiling. "He has asked me to keep the smell of borscht off his ship. Nothing would be easier, or more in alignment with his expressed wishes. Of course I will do this."

"Thank you," Anna said, letting out a nervous breath and turning to the cabinets.

She almost jumped out of her skin when Nixia spoke again. Anna had expected the little sylph to swirl away as she so often did.

"Would you like to use the recipe Edik uses?" Nixia asked. "I know it, of course."

Anna smiled.

Many skills had been taught to Anna during her formative years in the Lukyanov household, both through schooling and private tutors.

Cooking, however, was notably and deliberately absent from the list. In fact, if Father had ever discovered Anna cooking in their kitchen, he would have punished her severely.

Cooking was peasant work. Not for the likes of a Lukyanova.

However. Now that Anna was attempting it, cooking was not so very unlike alchemy.

And once Anna had discovered alchemy, in school, she had begun a secret study of it at once. It called to her in a way Father never understood. Would never allow himself to understand.

Alchemy, too, was beneath a Lukyanova.

Of course, Father had punished Anna each time he had discovered her practicing and studying her chosen craft. But no punishment would dissuade her. Alchemy was not only an interest for Anna, it was a gift. She understood the way various blends and concoctions came together as though she'd been born to the craft.

Her need to pursue alchemy had been the reason she'd run away from home in the first place, which had led her to Edik and Carl and Roger, as well as Oolaut, and the Rhian people.

Oolaut, who turned out to be Nalacha. And the Rhian people, in truth the *Fomhóraigh*.

And now look at her. Cooking. Father would be *scandalized*. A thought that made Anna smile as she scrupulously followed Nixia's directions.

Fortunately, Edik had the ingredients all ready, in the preserver. Enough to feed an army, which had been intimidating until Nixia made clear that she would tell Anna how much of each Edik usually used, and when he added them.

Nixia had just assured her that the smell was right for ladling into one of Edik's brown ceramic bowls when the door opened.

"Why is this..."

Anna turned to see Edik, standing in the doorway and blinking in confusion. Dola padded up behind him, ears forward in feline curiosity.

"...door ... closed?" Edik finished.

Anna gave him a hopeful smile and offered him a bowl of borscht. Nixia had already vanished.

Dola remarked something, but Anna couldn't understand it. Whatever it was made Edik shake his head in wonder, his face caught somewhere between a smile and a slack jaw.

"You ... made borscht?" Edik said.

"I tried," Anna said. "Nixia helped, so it should be edible, but I'm not exactly a top chef."

Edik, still wearing that stunned expression, accepted the bowl from her.

Anna felt ridiculous. Her cheeks were flushed red and her heart was in her throat. She was very nearly on the verge of perspiration.

Over a bowl of borscht.

Edik held the bowl under his nose, and the smile that spread across his face made Anna's heart sing.

"Grab a bowl, *mladshaya sestra*," he said in the most relaxed tones Anna had heard from him in days, "and let's eat our lunch on the bridge."

Anna rushed to fill a bowl for herself.

WITHIN AN INFINITY OF SILENCE, A SINGLE PULSE. THE GENTLEST reminder of separation. That within the oneness of all things, there remains a level of duality. Of plurality.

A world waiting for Donal, full of people who were not him, in very basic ways.

The pulse of awareness came from Fionn, of course. Donal would have known that, even were he to have overlooked the feel of his familiar.

Here, within his quarters, within his wards, and deep within himself, no one else could have reached him. Not like this.

Donal's mind slowly surfaced from the deepest phases of meditation that he could yet achieve.

There were deeper levels still. On some level, he was aware of that. And the contradictory nature of that idea intrigued him.

Layers within oneness. As of stripping away dead skin to reveal perfectly healthy tissue beneath?

A flawed analogy, but the one that occurred to Donal as his mind eased slowly out of the depths of his meditation.

Odd, that the image, the analogy, was so physical this time. He would need to ponder that later, and wonder what it said about his view of reality that his mind had supplied the image.

For now, though, he allowed himself to slowly become aware of his thoughts again. They raced around as they always did. A never-ending whirl of speculations, memories, worries and more.

He could still remember being in high school and first learning to meditate. How he believed that he really would learn to *stop* his thoughts, instead of simply realizing that the thoughts were not him, and moving beyond them.

Of course, until one had gained enough mastery of meditation for that sentence to sound like more than noise, there was no point in even trying to explain it to anyone. Least of all to a high school student eager to learn his first spells.

Slowly, ever so slowly, Donal became aware once more of the content of his own thoughts.

This was the third day of his voyage. Likely no more than hours before the *Pegasus* was due to shuttle him down to the surface of Venus, while going about whatever mission brought it out here.

Assuming that Captain Klimek had been honest about not being in the taxi business. Donal wondered about that, in spare moments.

If this was the third day, perhaps they were already arriving?

He'd know soon enough.

For now, what mattered was regaining the feel of his heartbeat, slow and steady. Regaining the feel of his muscles. Letting his shoulders and hips roll. Reminding himself that his body was part of him, on this level.

Of course, it was part of him on all levels, at this phase of existence. This moment in time and space and awareness. This...

No. Donal could not go back into that right now.

Donal felt his lungs expand and contract, the muscles of his chest and diaphragm moving along with them. The flare of his nostrils as air came in and out. The passage of that air through his throat.

The feel of his eyelids, fluttering open, allowing his eyes to adjust to the currently dim light of his cabin.

In some ways, this cabin had been everything he could have asked for, in terms of this voyage.

No distractions. No books. No shadow plays. Just a bare room. Perfect for catching up on his meditation, and getting his mind right before arriving on Venus.

Three days now since Donal had seen anyone other than Fionn. Well, apart from brief glimpses of Yeoman Kerrigan, the poor young man who had the job of bringing Donal his meals.

Yeoman Kerrigan was absent now, of course. In the room, only Donal and Fionn. Sitting on the fake metal floor, smelling fake metal and oils, while regarding each other.

Wait. That wasn't quite right. There was a third person in the room.

Donal's neck cracked as he turned his head to see Morna, leaning against one wall and smiling at him.

She wasn't dressed the way he was used to. So often, Morna preferred to wear as little as possible. Gauzy, filmy things that revealed as much as they covered, or more, flowing around her skin in a suggestive way as she moved.

Not today though.

Today, Morna adorned tight clothing, black, and concealing everything that lay within, save the basic outlines of the shapely body it covered.

Neck to wrist to toe, all midnight black cloth that might have been spun from the darkness inside an unopened crypt.

Even her long, silvery hair was concealed within a netting of the same material. Only her face and hands were revealed, and Donal knew that the latter was only because she was not wearing the gloves tucked into her belt.

At her side, she wore a rapier, within a scabbard of what looked to be the same black material. Even the handle wouldn't have glinted under direct sunlight.

"Welcome back, master," she said, letting her smile stretch. "I must say, I don't think much of these accommodations. Although, if you ever wish to play the monk and the tempting demon, this would be a perfect setting. Well, perfect if we altered the scent from something so military to something more … cloistered."

She fluttered her lashes. "I can promise you I make an excellent tempting demon."

"I just bet you do," Donal said, rising to his feet in a motion that was smoother than he expected. He rolled his shoulders and neck again, and was pleased not to hear any more cracks.

"Wait," he said, before Morna could speak. "Do you know what kind of oil is part of that smell?"

"Of course," she said, looking puzzled. "Humans used to use it to grease machines. Back when they trusted to machines."

"Oh," Donal said, the idea coming together in his head. Had to be part of a larger application of the Law of Similarity.

Then again, for all Donal knew there and then, it might have had to do with continuing the naval tradition or something.

"More important at the moment," Morna said, setting aside her smile for an expression of business, "I have returned with my first report for you."

"Excellent," Donal said.

"A moment, if I may," Fionn said, waiting for Donal's nod to continue. "Morna's timing is excellent. I was due to rouse you in five minutes time, but not for lunch in your cabin. Your presence is requested in the officers' mess, to join Rowan MacPherson and Alessandra Bueno for the final meal aboard the *Pegasus*, before you land in approximately three hours."

"All right," Donal said with a small sigh. "After Morna's report, tell them I'll be along presently."

"May I then?" Morna asked, glancing from Donal to Fionn to Donal again, and continuing only when Donal gave her the go-ahead.

"The DC police are, in my opinion, well-meaning and competent, but insufficient to the task as set them. They have hit a dead end with the assassin, and strike me as unlikely to ever see a way past it."

Morna rubbed her hands together, warming to her topic.

"The United Terran Government has sent investigators of their own, who are making more progress. They have already made headway into the possibilities roused by your mention of the Consortium, and are tracing references to this organization through their own information network."

"They told you all this?" Donal asked, surprised.

"Not in the least," Morna said, waving away the possibility. "Now, the Courts' inquisitor has managed to track the individual who hired the assassin, and is currently tracing the thread from that direction."

"Is the inquisitor sharing this information with the UTG?"

"Of course not," Morna said, again, as though such an idea were outside the realm of possibility. "The queens will inform their allies only once the matter has been handled to their satisfaction."

"They will not want outside opinions regarding how the matter should be dealt with," Fionn added. "I believe humans have a saying about forgiveness and permission that might be relevant here."

"Yes," Donal said, frowning. "But the Courts don't care about forgiveness any more than they do about permission."

"Exactly," Morna said, smiling, "so why trouble the human governments with the possibility of an opinion?"

Donal sighed. "Thank you, Morna. I appreciate—"

"Oh, my report is not yet complete, master."

"Excuse me," Donal said, slightly disturbed that those words sent a shiver through her, but finishing his thought anyway. "Please do continue."

"For my own part, I began with your Donatello Mancuso. He has agents of his own, and an impressive network of information." She turned to Fionn. "He would have made a formidable *sidhe*."

Fionn nodded absently. Donal agreed.

"Connecting the information I gained from the human inquisitors, the *sidhe* inquisitor, and the early data from Donatello Mancuso's informants, the clearest link tying them together is a Martian corporation called Aetheric Dynamics."

Aetheric Dynamics. A would-be competitor to Mr. Mancuso's company, 4M.

Donal remembered them best as the company he'd been told was behind the attempt to *blow him up* in the spaceport in New Leningrad.

"Corporate espionage," Li Hua had called it.

"Specifically," Morna continued, "four individuals who seem the most common elements. Now that I have made this report, I wish to trace them, follow them, and learn the truth."

Malice gleamed in her eyes. "May I have permission to ... punish the guilty, master?"

Donal's instinct was to say no. His lips parted to do so, but a quick mental communique from Fionn stopped him.

Once Donal looked at his familiar, Fionn explained, mind-to-mind.

Your instinct is to refer this matter to human law. I both understand and commend this instinct. However, in this instance, I advise against following it. The Courts will take care of this matter, if you do not.

But the UTG investigation— Donal began, but Fionn intruded.

Even if the human investigation finds the culprits before the Courts' inquisitor, they will still send him in to ... finalize the matter.

Donal sighed. *Then what difference does it make what we do?*

If you allow Morna to conclude matters, the Courts will accept her report in your name. You will gain standing at the Courts, and avoid the potential incident that would follow the Courts' overruling human justice.

Donal bit his lip. If his movement was the cause behind Morna's sigh just then, he didn't want to know.

He shook his head. Flared his nostrils in a quick breath.

"Here is my decision," Donal said, turning to Morna. "Investigate. Impress me with your thoroughness. Then come to me with your findings. As you will be acting in my name, I want to know and agree with any ... concluding action before you take it."

"Of course, master," Morna said, with a slight shiver of apparent enjoyment. "May I go now, to continue my inquiries?"

"Please do," Donal said, "and thank you for your work. You're doing quite well."

The smile she gave Donal was filled with evident pleasure, but for the first time Donal thought that not all that pleasure was sexual in nature.

Interesting. Perhaps there was more to her than the seductress side of her identity?

Once she faded into the shadows, Donal turned to Fionn.

"How is she getting all this information?"

"She is a *leannan sidhe*," Fionn said, as though that were enough answer.

When Donal's continued stare proved otherwise, Fionn continued.

"She is, at her heart, a creature of inspiration and idea. All she need do is remain near the investigators for a time, and feel their ideas and the connections they make."

"Impressive."

"And part of the reason that your victory over her was so important," Fionn said. "Had she overcome you, not only would she have been the mistress and you the slave, she would have reported your every notion and connection, plan and intention, to his grace."

Donal needed a moment to process the thought of the Duke of Shadows having that kind of insider knowledge of not only Donal's actions, but his *intentions*.

Not for the first time, Donal wondered if his mother hadn't been right about avoiding all contact with the *sidhe* as a standing policy.

"They play a very deep game," Donal said, finally, "the peers of the Courts."

"You are not the first to say so."

Still. At her heart, a creature of inspiration and idea...

"Would it be good for Morna," Donal asked, "if I allowed her to be present when I do research and perform experiments?"

"Very. There is even a chance she could provide a ... safer level of inspiration for you."

"That doesn't matter," Donal said, turning toward the door to his room, "I mean, I wouldn't refuse her aid, at a safe level. It's just that..."

Donal paused and looked at Fionn. "She's going to be with us for a long time, and I'd like to keep her as happy and healthy as I can without ... well, *without*. So if I forget, please remind me to invite her to my next experiment."

"Of course, master." Fionn fell into step beside Donal as they made their way to the officers' mess. "And I must say, sometimes you make me very proud to be your familiar."

4

ANOTHER THING ABOUT BEING AN AMBASSADOR THAT EDIK COULD *definitely* get used to.

Military escorts.

The last leg of the flight to Venus took the *Third Son* within half a decan of registered zuglodon hunting grounds.

Well, registered in the sense that someone had been smart enough to label a section of the charts appropriately. Wasn't as though anyone was speaking for the zuglodons and trying to preserve areas of space for them.

Not a thought Edik wanted to voice aloud, lest Anna — currently sitting in what he'd come to think of as the bridge "visitor's chair" — decide to take up the cause of the zuglodons.

Oh, it might have been a cause worth taking up. They were just spirits, after all, doing what came naturally to them. And space *was* their natural environment. Beyond that, Edik didn't know much about them.

He suspected they had some kind of kinship with lacunas, but he didn't know what. Perhaps they were different varieties of space elemental?

He did know that spacers talked about zuglodons as though they were the closest thing anyone living had seen to a real dragon. Capable of ripping apart a ship from the wards on in, and feasting on the lacuna inside.

Part of the reason Edik was more than happy to have a quartet of Terran Naval gunboats escort the *Third Son* safely past those zuglodons and on the final approach to Venus.

Venus.

The last time Edik had been to this part of space was five or six months ago, for that big meeting in the Terran Naval no-fly zone that actually turned out to be in Faerie.

But he'd never come close enough to Venus to get a look at the planet itself.

It was beautiful, in its own way. Yellowish white, and it seemed to glow softly. The way the sky back on Luna seemed to, some evenings, after the sun had set, but night had not yet really risen.

"It reminds me of the sun," Anna said softly. "If someone could dim the sun, it might look like this."

Edik didn't know how to answer that, but from the distant tone in Anna's voice, she might not have expected a response.

Edik reflexively checked his scanners, but the only other ships in space around him were those Terran Naval gunboats.

So little traffic was just ... creepy. Gave Edik a shaky feeling in his guts.

True, the only spaceports he'd really been to had been the busy ones on Luna and Earth — mostly Luna — and the nonexistent one on Ganymede.

But that was the point. The one on Ganymede, that hadn't been busy apart from the military blockade going on at the time. And even that involved more ships than Edik was picking up on his scanners.

So even at Ganymede, there had been more space traffic than there was here. Edik knew that Venus discouraged travel, but still.

One incoming, non-military ship? Total?

That just did not seem right.

And it was only the *Third Son* making a landing approach. Even the gunboat escorts were already peeling off. Going back about their business.

Edik was about to reach for the links to make sure there wasn't some alert he'd missed — perhaps a zuglodon sighting — when one strand of the mess glowed a brighter blue.

Edik twisted it, and the head of the person he'd been dealing with for the last few hours formed a spectral manifestation above his communications web.

Officious looking little man. Greasy black hair that Edik kept expecting to drip oil down his narrow face.

Midshipman Erikson.

"This goodbye?" Edik asked, before the midshipman could speak.

"We've gotten you safely to Venus. No thanks are necessary."

Edik swallowed his first response, even before he felt Dola's warning claws on his foot.

Those words had just sounded so ... belittling.

"Well, if there's no need for thanks, then I guess this is goodbye," Edik said, not at all sure what the proper protocol was supposed to be under circumstances like these. "At least, until next time."

The midshipman didn't bother saying anything further. Just cut the link.

"I didn't like him," Anna said, which was more severe a condemnation than Edik expected from her. "He should have shown more respect to the ambassador of a foreign power."

Edik scoffed. "And Earth wonders why the Du Mak show no interest in an alliance. Even without Ganymede, they haven't represented themselves well."

"They should have had a diplomatic officer handling all communications with us," Anna said, frowning. "But they did not. There must be a reason."

"Think something big is going down?"

"Perhaps," Anna said, tapping the fingers of one hand against the palm of the other. "Something that drew the normal escort vessels away. Possibly away from Venus entirely."

"Mars," Edik said.

"Likely. Perhaps they've finally started negotiating."

Edik might have said something then, but another strand of the communications web lit up.

"That must be Port Authority," Edik said, reaching out and twisting the right strand.

It was a woman's head that appeared above the web. At least, Edik assumed that the owner of those dark eyes was female. He'd never seen any men wearing a burqa, even a red one.

"This is Daria Alavi of Venus Port Authority," she said, and her voice sounded older than Edik expected. Somewhere in middle age, maybe. "Am I addressing the Du Mak ambassador, Captain Edik Barshai?"

"You are, Ms. Alavi," Edik said, pleased at the change in tone from that midshipman. "And traveling with me is *Fomhóraigh* ambassador Anna Lukyanova."

Those dark eyes widened. "We were not told to expect the *Fomhóraigh* ambassador."

"That's quite all right," Anna said. "The trip was quite last-minute. I can make my own accommodations while I await the convenience of the Venusian representatives."

"That will not be necessary," Ms. Alavi said. "A room will be waiting for you at the Zanzibar, and transportation there will be provided shortly after you land. Ambassador Captain Barshai, I'm sending your landing route now. For your own safety, please do not vary from it."

A soft pinging noise sounded.

"Landing route received," Edik said. "Anything else I should know about my approach?"

"Negative. Welcome to Gilgamesh."

Both Edik and Anna thanked Ms. Alavi before Edik cut the link and focused on flying. Normally he would have handed off the landing duties to Nixia, but the thrill of landing for the first time on a planet he'd never been to before was just too strong to ignore.

The *Third Son* soared down from space into the skies above

Venus, making the transition from the lacuna of the main drive to the sylphs of the air drive as smoothly as any ship in the skies.

And speaking of skies, the one around the *Third Son* now looked almost pure white.

"Like eggshells," Anna muttered behind him, a touch of awe in her voice. "So many things get called that color, but this ... the little variations here and there..."

Edik didn't have the attention to spare for figuring out the precise color of the sky. It wouldn't be the same once they made it inside the barrier anyway, and he'd see it again when they left.

For now, Edik let his eyes run over the yellow-white landscape of Venus. Of the two main continents, only Istar Terra was said to be settled, and only the "city" of Gilgamesh had a port of any kind.

In fact, according to what Edik had been able to learn about Venus before the flight, Gilgamesh was the largest settlement on the planet, which was just about the only excuse for calling it a *city* at all.

No more than a thousand people, according to the general information guide. Almost all of them from the region of Earth known these days as New Mesopotamia.

It was true that, apart from the bright yellow column of the Gilgamesh's Barrier, the terrain Edik could see looked uninhabited.

Beautiful, though, in its way. Mountains and canyons, craters...

...forests?

"Are those forests?" Edik asked.

"I believe so," Dola said slowly, in English, "though I am not sure what kind of trees."

"A new local blend," Anna said, still sounding distracted. "Derivatives from three different varieties of tree from southern Asia, on Earth. Primarily a strain of acacia mixed with Greek strawberry, though last I'd heard there had been some disagreement about the third."

Edik started to ask, then answered his own question. "Alchemy. Of course."

"It was covered in Brewer's Digest ... perhaps two years ago. When the first reports were released prior to the arrival of settlers."

Then Edik had to keep his attention on his flying. The skies might not have been crowded, but the route assigned to him was unusual.

Instead of flying straight in, he had to follow a number of curves and dips in the air that didn't seem to make any sense at all.

"Nixia?" Edik said, while following a wide spiral to starboard before curving back toward the port.

"Yes, Edik?" Nixia said, swirling into form small and near his right ear. She knew better than to block his view at a time like this.

"Can you check with the other sylphs and find out why this route is so strange?"

"No need," she said. "The magic of Venus is unlike the tamed magic of Earth. It whorls and eddies in delightful ways that could potentially knock an unready ship out of the sky. The route you've been given will easily avoid those hazards, at this time."

Edik chuckled. "They have their own reef."

"And they didn't really warn us," Dola said, disapproving in both his tone and the way his fur stood up. "An ambassadorial ship."

"Take their privacy pretty seriously, I guess."

"Why don't they just land ships by remote thaumaturgy," Anna asked, "as many ports do?"

"Takes a lot of investment," Dola said. "Not just hiring the magicians, but also registering their port with the Commission for Space Safety, so they get the right links to incoming ships. Without those links, it's impossible to guarantee a smooth, safe landing."

Anna must have looked puzzled, because Dola continued.

"Edik hates dealing with the red tape of bureaucracy, so he has me do most of that kind of research."

Well, whatever whorls and eddies might have been going through the skies seemed to be dulled by the Barrier, because the moment the *Third Son* passed through it, the rest of the flight in was straight and true.

"Not much of a landing field," Edik said.

Thirty circles in all, each with a glow that would probably be brighter after sunset. No poured stone underneath them though. Bare, yellowish dirt.

Only one other ship in port at the moment. A largish helioship —
roughly three times the size of the *Third Son* — in the shape of a
double-headed eagle.

"Pajari beat us here then," Anna said.

"Guess he didn't wait until morning to leave after all," Edik said
dryly.

Well, at least Pajari didn't have the most comfortable place to
wait. The buildings of the port didn't look any more impressive than
the landing field.

No single large structure at all. Wait. Scratch that. There was a
single building that looked to be maybe twice the size of the *Third
Son*, made from flimsy-looking pale wood. Likely wood from those
forests.

A few other small buildings were made from the same wood, but
not many. Most of the structures around the port were those alchemical things. Sold as blocks of solid, grayish stone. Once positioned
and triggered they'd pop up into conical or cylindrical buildings. Pre-
furnished, with reasonably large windows.

Those pop-ups were only intended to last five or ten years. Edik
hoped the locals weren't planning on pushing that too hard. He didn't
know what happened when they ... expired.

He brought the *Third Son* down in a perfect landing.

Local time looked to be early afternoon. Sun still bright and high
in the blue sky inside the Barrier...

"Blue sky," Edik said, turning in his chair to face Anna. "But the
dirt isn't brown. I thought they tried to replicate Earth inside
Barriers."

"Dirt is often too much trouble," Anna said. "The newer Barriers
try to work more with whatever is there natively."

"Let's leave the luggage for now," Edik said, thinking mostly of
Anna's. He wasn't sure he intended to sleep anywhere off his ship
anyway. "Might as well go play ambassador right away."

Anna said nothing, but her eyes danced with either amusement
or excitement.

VENUS. ANNA WAS ACTUALLY ABOUT TO SET FOOT ON VENUS.

Excitement shivered up her spine, and danced in her belly.

She felt silly. Girlish. Almost ridiculous, to be so excited over this.

She may have been born on Luna, but she'd been to Mars more than a dozen times, and Earth, closer to a hundred.

She'd been to deeper space than most would expect, in that Terran no-fly zone.

She'd even been to *Faerie*.

And yet here she was, nervous as a child and on the verge of giggling over getting to step outside the hatch of the *Third Son* and tread on the dirt of Venus. Dirt only trod by perhaps a thousand or two before her. Not like the hundreds of thousands or millions on Mars or Luna, or the billions of predecessors on Earth.

Venus still felt new. Special. Unexplored.

Which was, again, ridiculous. Humans had settled here ... was it two years ago? Something close to that. She wasn't quite sure.

But Anna did not force down her excitement. She kept it from her face, but not her thoughts. She knew better. She'd been taught directly by Father, and through example by Natalia Romanova.

Face your excitement when it comes. Experience it. Only then may you truly set it aside and focus on what matters.

"Ready?" Edik asked, with a grin that said Anna wasn't masking her excitement as well as she believed. But then, Edik had gotten to know her pretty well this past year.

Anna checked herself quickly.

Her pale orange dress was perfect. High collared, long-sleeved and ankle-length. Tight enough to be flattering, but not so tight as to distract someone in conversation. Her hair was still up in the complicated mass of curls and braids that would keep it out of her way, yet catch the eye when she needed it to.

Oh, yes, her hair, her outfit, even the short, pale brown leather shoes she wore, these were the first line of weaponry in diplomacy. Creating the correct first impression.

Edik would not have truly understood that even if she tried to explain it. It would go against the way he liked to view his world.

And yet, Edik understood enough to use his clothing to project the kind of image he favored.

Or did he? Perhaps he'd merely built his look based on the shadow plays he'd favored watching in his youth.

Perhaps Anna would ask him one day.

At the moment, he wore a red stripe on the outside of another of his pairs of black pants with many pockets. The shirt he wore was long-sleeved and white, and seemed to have almost as many pockets as the pants.

All those pockets. Anna would have loved even a single pocket, somewhere in this dress. Instead, she carried a bag that matched her shoes.

Ah, well. At least, the bag allowed her to carry more alchemical reagents than she could have tucked into ... pockets...

Of course. Edik did his own alchemy aboard the *Third Son*. In all likelihood, his pockets were as stuffed with reagents as her purse.

Odd that she'd never made the connection before. But then, Father hadn't exactly encouraged her to think about spacers and their clothing...

Edik cleared his throat. Fingered his Van Dyke.

"Ready," Anna confirmed, and Edik spoke the words that would open the hatch. *Open sesame*, in Russian, which she found too adorable to mention.

Edik allowed her to exit first, for which she felt immensely grateful.

The dirt beneath her boot was thin, yellowish, and even drier than the hot air of the afternoon. Good thing she'd checked weather conditions before packing, or she might have worn something too heavy for this environment.

But Anna's dress wasn't just made from airsilks, it was made from *Gustav* airsilks. Finest quality on Luna, and rivaling the best made on Earth, and certainly finer than anything made on Mars.

The gentle, dusty breeze clung not at all to her clothing, and did nothing to overheat her. One of the benefits of wearing a Gustav ensemble.

The air of that breeze. It smelled faintly of citrus and something fresh and green. Not grass. Clover, perhaps?

Interesting that the air had any such scent at all, if they were using modern Barrier techniques. Perhaps the alchemy of Venus might prove as interesting as the magic.

Edik joined her a step later, Dola beside him. Both their necks craned to take in as much of their surroundings as they could, while Anna focused on the detail that mattered most.

The approaching runner, crossing the landing field.

That the runner came from Pajari, Anna did not doubt. On Luna, Pajari was well-known for favoring runners large enough to cause traffic problems. Runners with not just one bench seat in the back, nor two facing benches, but four total, forming a rectangle so all the passengers could face each other, with a table in the center for his chessboard, drinks, food or whatever struck his fancy.

This particular runner required eight legs, and its lizard-like skin was a dark ocean blue. Two doors up front for the driver, and four in the back.

The runner halted a respectable distance away, to avoid covering Anna and Edik with dust.

A man in black got out of the driver's compartment.

He looked to be Romanian, to Anna's eye. He had that kind of black hair, worn swept back over pale skin. He looked fit enough to stand as a champion, and he wore a cavalry saber at his side.

His suit was traditional. The cut and style of a manservant, confirming that he'd been sent by Pajari. As he approached, his shoes kicked up a small cloud of yellow dirt, which stuck to his shoes, and the legs of the man's pants.

Just a little reminder to Anna why Pajari would never ascend higher than his current position in the hierarchy of the great families of Luna.

Pajari had no mind for the little details.

No Lukyanov or Romanov servant would return from an assignment like this with dirt on his pant legs.

"Greetings," the man said, when he was still a good half-dozen meters away. "My master, Rasputin Pajari, sends his regards to Anna Lukyanova, and hopes that she will do him the great favor of joining him for dinner this evening."

Edik cleared his throat.

"Forgive me," the manservant said, not sounding or looking the least bit embarrassed or contrite. "In truth, I had come to issue *you* this invitation, Captain Barshai. And to include your familiar in the invitation, of course."

Of course? That was odd. Issuing a dinner invitation to a familiar. Edik seemed to smile, though, as this were some personal joke shared between himself and Pajari.

Interesting.

"But since Anna was standing right here..." Edik said, one eyebrow high in judgment on the poor man.

"She is a Lukyanova. I have standing orders to address any member of the Romanov or Lukyanov families first, and then to carry out any other orders, including the offering of invitations."

"So Rasputin didn't send you here to invite me to dinner?" Anna asked, showing the poor man a gentler raised eyebrow.

"No, Ms. Lukyanova. I extended the invitation because I know my master would wish me to do so. I did not expect to see you here when I arrived."

"When will dinner be?" Edik asked, his hands on his belt now.

"Early, in keeping with the local fashion. Five o'clock. Approximately three hours from now, if you wish to refresh yourselves first."

"And where?"

"In my master's suite at the Zanzibar." The manservant frowned, as though irritated with himself for getting something out of order. "My master has arranged the adjoining suite for your use, Captain Barshai. He bids me assure you that it is private, even from himself."

Anna had to smile at that one. Pajari had many flaws, but the man had a sense of humor.

"I think I'd prefer to stay on—"

"Don't," Anna said, her voice soft and sharp all at once. When he looked at her, surprised, she said quietly, "You're here as an ambassador. The Venusian government will take it as an insult if you trust only the accommodations of the ship you arrived on."

Edik grimaced and sighed, but nodded.

"All right then," he said, then muttered something Anna didn't understand, but Dola was overcome with a sudden urge to sneeze, which Anna suspected was covering laughter.

"All right..." Edik started, louder and in English, but his words trailed off and he sighed again. "Look. What's your name?"

The manservant drew himself to attention and clicked his heels together, kicking up a little more dust in the process.

"Funar, sir."

"All right, Funar. Lead on."

"Your bags, sir?"

"We'll send someone from the Zanzibar for them," Anna said, dismissing the question with a wave. She had no intention of trusting Pajari's people with her luggage.

"I'll wait here then," Dola said, possibly to coordinate the luggage. Possibly to keep Edik from objecting. Perhaps even both.

Funar held the runner door for both Anna and Edik, before returning to the driver's compartment to take the reins.

The interior of the runner was as Anna expected — overdone in its comfort. Cut glass bottles of liquor on the central table, along with a selection of charcuterie.

She ignored the offerings, though Edik tested a small piece of honeydew melon wrapped in ... likely a slice of turkey breast. He seemed pleased with the results.

The runner began its trip to the Zanzibar, but Anna's hopes for the accommodations weren't very high. Not when all she could see from where she sat were dirt roads, uncertain-looking wooden buildings, and prefabricated alchemiblock structures.

Not very encouraging.

WHEN EDIK GOT HIS FIRST LOOK AT THE ZANZIBAR, HE GASPED AND wished the Dola were beside him, to share the moment.

Gilgamesh had seemed only a token attempt at a settlement, with no real effort put into anything.

Edik could understand why, now.

All of their effort — and probably all of their money — had gone here. Into creating this masterpiece.

The dirt road transitioned into a gleaming marble street, surrounded on both sides by vast, beautiful gardens. And so many fountains, it was a wonder that the air still seemed so dry that static made Edik's clothes cling to themselves.

At the end of this road, a tremendous four-story palace of gold and marble, shining in the sun in defiance of all the dust in the air.

"Aladdin," Anna said, sitting beside Edik in the back of Pajari's runner cab. She looked just as struck by the sight ahead of them as he was, which made it all the more astonishing.

"Who?" Edik asked.

"From the tales of the Arabian Nights," she said quietly. "Well, the expanded editions, at least. He wishes for a palace, and this ... this is what I always imagined it looked like."

Edik didn't quite follow what Anna was talking about. Arabian knights and wishes. He just knew that he had never in his life seen anything so ... opulent. Yes, that was the word. In fact, Edik suspected that the word existed only for places like this ... hotel?

This was a hotel?

Edik was accustomed to hotels being places with huge signs, pronouncing themselves to the world. But the Zanzibar had no sign. He was used to stables for horses and lots for private runners. But the Zanzibar had neither of these, unless they were concealed around back.

This looked like the finest estate of whatever equivalent Venus had to the great families of Luna.

He desperately wanted to make sure this was the right place, but couldn't bring himself to ask.

Anna, beside Edik, looked impressed, though less surprised that all this effort and expense had been gone to for a hotel.

Still, he couldn't help one muttered question to Anna.

"We definitely don't have to pay for this out of our own pockets, right? I mean..."

His words trailed off when she patted his arm reassuringly.

The runner pulled up in front of ornate teak double doors trimmed with polished bronze. Flanking the double doors were two statues of bearded men with swords at their sides, but that description didn't quite do them justice.

The men depicted had plates of armor, but they also wore long ... robes? Edik didn't feel right thinking of them as dresses. He didn't know the term for them, though. Whatever cloth wrappings they were, they extended up to wrap around the men's heads — leaving faces visible — and were topped off by round hats — probably helmets — each with a single spike on the top.

Maybe these were the Arabian knights Anna mentioned?

Funar opened the runner door to let them out — Anna first, of course — and the front doors to the Zanzibar opened as Anna and Edik approached.

The air wasn't quite so hot or dry here, closer to those double doors. Likely due to all the fountains.

Edik was glad to have Anna to follow right now. On his own, no way he could have looked like anything other than a small time pilot and captain out of his element.

But Anna, she always looked confident. And her confidence and poise helped Edik draw himself up tall and proud. To stride boldly forward with confidence he didn't feel as they passed those teak double doors and entered the Zanzibar.

Welcoming cool air, scented with lilies and something else. Some kind of exotic spice that Edik couldn't quite place.

The interior was so overwhelming that Edik just stopped walking, two steps inside.

A domed ceiling rose high above him. All marble, to look at it, but instead of echoing the way marble would have, it somehow swallowed those echoes, rather than spreading them.

Stone tiles for the walls and flooring in ornate designs and supplemented with occasional artwork that all looked so classy Edik half expected to have some doorman escort him back outside, certain there'd been some mistake.

The reception desk and concierge were off to his right, polished woods that had to have been transported here from Earth. All of this, every tile and every centimeter of marble. All of it had to have been brought up from Earth. The expense in just the transportation alone was staggering to consider.

And the opulence continued. Scattered across the lobby, sufficiently apart for the illusion of privacy, were sitting areas highlighted by plush, broad couches and more coffee tables and end tables than anyone could possibly need.

It all seemed so ... wasteful.

All those couches, but no one sat on them. There should have been families on vacation, or businessmen holding important meetings. Or maybe a — what was the word? — a sultan?

Yes. That was the word. There should have been some sultan and his ... wazer, vizer, something like that. Holding court.

"Edik," Anna said, refraining from letting the amusement in her eyes infect her voice, "the reception desk is this way."

Chagrined and flushing a bit, Edik caught up to her as she stepped up to the young man behind the counter whose nametag read "Ahmed."

"Welcome to the Zanzibar, Ms. Lukyanova," Ahmed said, which made Edik frown. Could she possibly have been here before?

If the greeting threw Anna, she gave no sign.

"Thank you, Ahmed. I'm ready to check in."

Edik drew a deep breath slowly, and let it out.

Odd. But even in Faerie, Edik hadn't felt quite as out of his depth as he felt here.

And he hadn't even seen his room yet.

LUNCH HADN'T BEEN NEARLY THE TRIAL DONAL HAD EXPECTED. IT seemed that either three days of Donal's hiding in his cabin — or perhaps some skillful work from Rowan — had convinced Ms. Bueno to ease back on the conversational throttle.

Instead she'd been friendly and sociable, talking about her native Brazil, and asking about the places Donal and Rowan had been, the things they'd seen.

The conversation ran easily among the three of them, with no one demanding or denying the spotlight. And no business allowed.

Donal did, however, watch what he said. Just in case.

By the time lunch was finished, Donal almost felt guilty for having spent the vast majority of the trip in his cabin. Though neither Rowan nor Ms. Bueno — Alessandra. She'd insisted he call her Alessandra — seemed to blame him for spending the trip in meditation.

One of the advantages of being a magician, he supposed. People seemed to take it for granted that he spent a lot of time meditating and experimenting — even more than he actually did.

Who knew? Perhaps spending the trip in his cabin even added a little to the mystique that Magister Ronaldo Machado had once insisted Donal work on developing.

All right, some of his professors encouraged it as well, but it had been Magister Machado who first really drove the point home to Donal, during a flight aboard the *Horizon Cusp*.

In any event, after lunch, Rowan and Alessandra both said they needed to change before landing. Donal didn't understand why. They were both wearing perfectly good suits — Alessandra's a smoky gray and Rowan's a lovely teal.

Donal himself had no intention of changing. He was wearing a pale blue, long-sleeved airsilk shirt, with good black airsilk slacks and fine black leather loafers that matched his belt. A combination that was practically the modern equivalent of wizard's robes.

He did run a comb through his hair. He'd been paying more

attention to his hair since Morna became a fixture in his life. She was forever asking to brush it for him, though brushing wasn't really the right word. When Morna ran her fingers through his hair, it was not only a marvelous sensation, he came out of it looking as though he'd paid a stylist a lot of money.

The results had made him at least want to be better about keeping his hair combed.

Yeoman Kerrigan made sure Donal's bags were handled, and finally he was brought down to the docking bay, where a shuttle would take him, Rowan, and Alessandra down to the planet's surface.

The docking bay was much smaller than that of the last Terran Naval ship Donal had been aboard, but then, that ship had been a cruiser. This was just a gunboat.

The docking bay was large enough to house two shuttles, the *Galileo* and the *Copernicus*. Identical in their white, flat-bottomed, boring pretense of being seafaring vessels. It was a wonder they weren't the same gray as everything else on the ship.

For that matter, it was a wonder that Terran Naval crewmen didn't go mad on these ships.

Then again, maybe they did and the navy just covered it up. Given the attitude of Captain Klimek...

Fionn cleared his throat, shaking Donal out of his reverie. Rowan and Alessandra were arriving. Rowan had changed her teal suit for a skirt suit of Kelly green that practically screamed *If the hair and complexion weren't a clue, I'm Irish!*

Alessandra, on the other hand, wore a skirt suit of dark cream that went well with her skin tones.

Both skirts ended at the knee, and Donal couldn't help but wonder if that was coincidence, planning, or just the current state of fashion.

Donal was in the middle of offering a greeting when Ensign Taverner poked his head out of the *Galileo* and said, "Forgive me, ambassadors, but we have a tight schedule. So if you could please come aboard and find your seats, we'll be off."

Once they were seated and strapped in, facing each other across the "passenger" section of the shuttle — which felt like a glorified cargo section to Donal — Alessandra was the first to speak.

"What is the plan once we land?"

"I say we check into our rooms first," Rowan said. "The facilities aboard the *Pegasus* were functional enough, but I'm looking forward to once again enjoying the positively sybaritic showers of the Zanzibar."

Donal agreed. Perhaps the Zanzibar had a good masseuse as well. He could certainly do with a massage.

The shuttle lifted off and flew out of the landing bay. Donal could only just see the forward view port from the corner of his eye, as he looked across at his two traveling companions.

Well, two of three. Fionn sat on the faux metal floor at Donal's feet.

"That is your hotel?" Alessandra asked. "The Zanzibar?"

"It's the only place worth staying, around Gilgamesh," Rowan said. "You'll definitely want a room there."

"Did you link ahead?" Donal asked Rowan.

The crease between Rowan's eyebrows told him she hadn't, even before she said, "When you mentioned that you had our travel arranged, I assumed the rest."

"I should have thought of that," Donal said. "The only arrangements were to meet the Du Mak ambassador."

"Ambassador? Singular?" Rowan asked.

"Far as I know, our meeting is just with Rasputin Pajari." Donal shrugged. "Probably for the best. If Edik isn't along, he won't feel the need to tell Anna Lukyanova, which leaves the *Fomhóraigh* out of the loop."

"When will the meeting be?" Alessandra asked.

"In the morning," Donal said. "And there'll be someone else along. This was all arranged by the—"

"UNAS?" Alessandra asked with a sly smile. "That sounds like their president. He'll probably be angry to find out Brazil managed to tag along."

"Think the UNAS will object?" Rowan asked, tilting her head just enough to drape her long hair down her shoulder.

"Doesn't matter if they do," Donal said through a sigh. "The introduction is a favor. It'll happen."

Alessandra's eyes widened, and she paled. "A favor? Did you say this introduction is a *favor*? From the Fae Courts? To Brazil? Does Andre Dos Santos realize this?"

"We were quite clear," Donal said, feeling pleased that at least *someone* from Brazil seemed to understand the hazards involved in dealing with the fae.

"*Mãe de Deus,*" she muttered, crossing herself. "*Ele vai* ... he'll be fired for this."

"Won't help," Donal said. "Better make the most of the introduction."

"You're telling..." Alessandra frowned. "He made the deal with you?"

"Both of us," Rowan said. "But we were representing the Courts, and Dos Santos was representing Brazil."

"As I said," Donal said. "Quite clear."

"What about the UNAS?" Alessandra asked. "Is this introduction a favor for them?"

"That's privileged information, I'm afraid," Donal said. "Sorry."

"You know," Fionn said, pitching his words so that only Donal understood them, "I do believe you're beginning to understand your role."

Alessandra could not have understood Fionn's words, but on hearing him speak, she seemed to remember he was present.

Her lips parted and she stared wide-eyed at Fionn, as though realizing for the first time that he wasn't just a familiar, but a fae hound. A *cú sidhe.*

When Alessandra looked back at Donal, the look in her eyes was haunted. As though she were trying to replay every conversation, every word she'd spoken to Rowan and Donal over the last few days, desperately trying to make sure she hadn't dug herself any deeper than the hole she'd started in.

The inversion of her normal role no doubt terrified her.

"You're fine," Rowan said softly. "We represent the Fae, but we don't set conversational traps the way *sidhe* nobles might."

"Very kind of you to say so," Alessandra said, but her tone had changed. Far more formal than she'd been before. "I find myself reassured that I have not incurred any further debts for myself or on behalf of my government."

"You haven't," Rowan said, but her words didn't matter. Donal could tell. Alessandra — or maybe he should go back to calling her Ms. Bueno — looked as though she'd never again let her guard down enough to be friendly. Not around Donal or Rowan.

Sadly, Donal couldn't help agreeing with the decision.

The rest of the flight to the surface passed in silence.

DONAL, ROWAN AND MS. BUENO WERE BARELY OFF THE BOTTOM OF THE shuttle's ramp and stepping onto the dry, yellowish dirt inside the landing circle when their luggage was deposited beside them and the ramp began to close.

"What's their hurry?" Ms. Bueno asked, irritation as plain on her face as in her voice.

"It's their captain," Rowan said. "It seems that since she knows she's leaving a bad impression, she might as well go all the way."

Donal, meanwhile, glanced around the nearly empty landing area of the Gilgamesh spaceport. The mid-afternoon sun was hot, and the air was far too dry to merit its scent. Anything that smelled so much like lemon and clover should have been refreshing.

The spaceport looked much the same as the last time Donal had seen it. Cheap, simple wooden buildings — mostly small though there was one main building of decent size — and a scattering of those alchemiblock structures that Donal had really expected to be replaced by more permanent construction since his last visit.

That they weren't was more likely a statement than an oversight. A message to visitors that they shouldn't get comfortable. That they were more than welcome to leave the moment their business was concluded.

Appropriately enough for such a place, only two of the space-port's landing rings were in use, and Donal likely knew by whom.

Off to Donal's left, a mid-sized helioship in the shape of a double-headed eagle. Donal had seen such a ship before, and the last time it had been carrying Rasputin Pajari. Chances were good that this was his ship.

Off to his right, he saw the much smaller firebird shape of the *Third Son*. Edik Barshai's ship. Just the sight of it made Donal smile. He and Edik had flown all the way out to Ganymede and back on that ship. The trip that led them to meet the Du Mak in the first place, which led to Edik becoming their ambassador.

"Looks as though both Du Mak ambassadors will be at the meeting," Donal said, pointing out the *Third Son*.

"Dola is there," Fionn said, in English.

"Excellent," Donal said. "Tell him we're here, and we'll be getting rooms at the Zanzibar, in case Edik wants to talk before the meeting tomorrow."

Fionn nodded and trotted off.

Ms. Bueno looked as though she wanted to ask a question, but changed her mind and shook her head. Instead she slung one small suitcase over her shoulder and picked up her other, larger suitcase in both hands.

Donal glanced at his own bags. A suitcase, garment bag, and what his mother always called a valise. His instinct was to heft his own luggage, maybe even help Ms. Bueno with hers. But he could just imagine the response from the Courts if word got out that he was doing what they would call "servant work" while acting in their name.

"I'm going to send someone for my bags," Donal said, before Ms. Bueno could start off. "Since we're all going to the Zanzibar—"

"The sentiment is appreciated," Ms. Bueno said, "but such actions are unnecessary. The United Terran Government will have a repre-sentative at this spaceport..." She frowned, looking over the ... unimpressive structure of the largest wooden building, and the even less imposing cones and cylinders of the short-term alchemical buildings. "I hope. And if not, there has to be one nearby. What time is the meeting?"

"Ten," Donal said, trying not to feel discouraged by her caution. It was smart and sensible, and not at all personal. No matter how it felt to him.

"See you then."

She didn't look back.

"We're not in this business to make friends, Donal," Rowan said softly, but Donal could hear the unhappiness in her own voice. And she'd been dealing with fae a lot longer than Donal had.

"Rowan," Donal said, and he waited until she looked at him before speaking again. "I consider you a friend."

She looked away then, and unless Donal was mistaken, he'd seen tears well up in her eyes before she did. He looked away as well, to give her privacy, and noticed a runner approaching, kicking up pale yellow dust.

Odd, this runner. Most of the vehicles that got designated "runners" looked as though they'd been fashioned from the bodies of giant lizards.

No reason that was the shape they had to have, so far as Donal knew. After all, it wasn't as though there were any such giant lizards out in the wild. Not since the days of the dinosaurs in the distant past.

Still, this was the first runner Donal could remember seeing that looked more avian than saurian in its design.

The runner had a closed top, but looked long enough to accommodate not only a driver's section up front, but seating for at least four in the back. Six legs that looked as though they'd come from two-ton chickens supported the vehicle, suggesting it could carry a great deal of weight.

But the hide. It was all covered in downy, sky-blue feathers. The abbreviated tail in back, as for a duck, must have been where the trunk was kept. Donal couldn't even see any latches or grooves on the sides, for doors. There must have been some way inside, though, because Donal could see *somebody* at the reins.

Ms. Bueno glanced at the runner, then back at Donal and Rowan, but kept walking. Perhaps she knew who was in the runner, or perhaps she assumed that Donal and Rowan had managed to send for one without telling her or giving her the opportunity to send for her own.

The runner stopped a few scant meters in front of Donal and Rowan, just far enough to avoid covering them with dust as it halted.

A door in the back popped open, and out clambered a heavy man just past middle age. His complexion was dark as mahogany, and both his short beard and the tight curls on his head showed more gray than black. The suit he wore, though, had lost some of its fine, navy blue coloring to the yellow-white dust of Venus.

A simple spell had ensured that none of that dust would cling to Donal's clothes or bags. And Donal doubted that any dirt would have *dared* try to cling to Rowan or her clothing.

The man smiled brightly, though he moved as though he'd hurt his back badly in his youth, and it had never quite healed correctly.

"Welcome," he said in a strong voice as he approached. "My name is Ezekiel Collins, and I'm the UNAS ambassador. Hope you don't mind, but I've taken the liberty of informing Venus that you'd be arriving, and arranging suites for each of you at the Zanzibar."

He shook hands with Rowan, and then Donal. And Mr. Collins was the kind of man who gave a handshake with both hands, though he didn't try to make it a challenge. More as though the gesture was intended to be as welcoming as his smile.

Nevertheless, Donal confirmed Mr. Collins' credentials. Mr. Collins presented a small, silver representation of the UNAS seal. Donal tapped it with his tuning fork and listened for any disharmonious overtones in the sound.

Pure and clean. He was exactly who he said he was. Donal slipped his tuning fork back up his shirtsleeve.

Donal and Rowan, of course, were not expected to present anything. From what Rowan had told Donal, early in the alliance, the

UTG had asked a *sidhe* knight about proving an ambassador's credentials.

That knight's smile had chilled the room ten degrees, and all he said was, "If anyone attempts to impersonate one of our ambassadors, we'll handle it."

No one had ever asked again.

"Pleasure to meet you, Mr. Collins," Rowan started, but Mr. Collins held up both hands and turned his head away as though he could not bear to witness what she'd just done.

"Please," he said, "*please*. For this afternoon, let me be Ezekiel. Obviously you had to be certain that I am who I say I am, but now that that's established let us be informal today. No reason to get formal before the meeting in the morning, unless we decide we simply *must* discuss business later."

Donal couldn't help but smile at that. "That would be my pleasure, Ezekiel. And I do hope you'll call me Donal."

"And please do call me Rowan," Rowan added, while a young man in a rumpled brown suit got out of the runner.

His tanned skin was already sweaty enough to suggest he'd been working hard for most of the day.

"This is Jenkins," Ezekiel said. "He'll get your..."

Ezekiel frowned. Shook his finger at Donal and Rowan. "Now, now, which of you is trying to pretend you don't have any luggage?"

"I've been serving the interests of the Courts for quite some time now," Rowan said with a small smile. "Any answer more than that would require a formal conversation."

"Well," Ezekiel said with an even broader smile, "we can't have that, now can we? So let's just leave that topic on your shuttle. Wherever it is."

Ezekiel gave a tight shake of his head while Jenkins grabbed all three of Donal's bags at once and made his way to the trunk.

"Don't take their quick exit personally," Ezekiel said, pointing vaguely upward with his chin. "They treat me the same way, as though ferrying me about is a hassle, and not part of their job. Now then!" He clapped his hands together and rubbed them rapidly. "Shall we go?"

Donal had been concerned that the cabin of the runner would be as stiff and unwelcoming as the spaceport, but he needn't have worried.

Soft leather and thick padding for the facing bench seats. After days of functional-but-not-comfortable Terran Naval furniture, Donal couldn't help sighing in pleasure as he sat.

There wasn't any more of Gilgamesh to see than the last time Donal had been here. Small buildings, most of them of the alchemi-block short-term variety.

Only one or two other runners on the dusty dirt roads that served as streets in Gilgamesh, and those were of the two-legged, saurian variety. Otherwise, the locals appeared to prefer horses for their transit.

Ezekiel was just starting to say something about Gilgamesh when Donal felt the first wild wave.

A flowing pulse of raw, untamed magic. Tiny and swift. So swift it might almost have gotten away, had part of Donal not been ready for it. Hoping for it.

He immediately did what he had not gotten to do — might not have been skilled enough to do — the last time he was on Venus.

Donal closed his eyes and shifted his attention as fast and deep as he could, forgoing any sense of what was physically going on around himself for the sake of experiencing the remains of that wave.

It was undeniably powerful. Magic. But ... it felt unlike anything Donal had studied. Had really experienced before.

This was not the elemental magic he had studied. The powers of earth and air, fire and water. Not even that of the fifth element — spirit or space, depending on who described it.

He had no direct comparison in any of the magics he'd studied. Not the power of the moon or sun, not that which seemed to flow down from the heavens or up from the underworlds.

It was like nothing Donal had ever tapped into, among the human magics of Earth.

But it was nothing like the magics of the fae either, which varied from light and airy to dark and terrifying, and yet always contained a through line he could only think of as *fae*.

Fae magic felt ... elusive. Ephemeral. Transient. Even an effect that had been in place for thousands of years — and Donal had noticed at least three such effects while in Faerie a few months back — felt to him as though it might collapse at any moment. Or maybe shift into something entirely different.

No matter how many times he'd tried to describe fae magic in his personal notes, he had yet to get any closer than that.

The powers of the Du Mak and the *Fomhóraigh*, those Donal did not know as well. Had not spent nearly as much time around them as he'd spent around the fae and their magics. And yet, both the Du Mak and the *Fomhóraigh*, though as different from fae magic as oregano and cumin were from rosemary, somehow felt related. As though, somewhere at their base lay a magical kinship of a type that Donal might be able to parse, if only given enough time...

But this wild pulse of magic here on Venus. It felt like something different yet.

Citrus was the first descriptor that occurred to him. As though the lemon taste of the air was not a consequence of alchemy, but an indication that the thaumaturgic elements of Gilgamesh's Barrier had not been able to take into account the variations of the local power available.

But there was more to it than that. It was as though ... that wild pulse had some of the *tanginess* that Donal associated with citrus. That border between sweet and sour.

All of that was metaphor, flitting through Donal's mind in an instant. A means of trying to interpret the unknown through the known, to understand the connections it produced in his mind.

Donal was trying to reach for more data while simultaneously puzzling at the ways in which the concepts of sweet and sour might track into useful analytical information when the pulse vanished.

And with it, that taste. That momentary experience.

If only Fionn were here. He could have helped Donal hold this moment. Recreate it. Study it. But Fionn was off talking with Dola, and Donal had not established a memory circle.

The opportunity was gone.

Donal could only hope he would have another before he left Venus.

5

EVER SINCE ACCEPTING HIS POST AS AMBASSADOR, WHENEVER DONAL checked into new accommodations — whether a hotel room or a ship's berth — he considered them from two perspectives.

The first, of course, was his personal response to the quality of the accommodations. From any wards already in place, to the amount of space, the furnishings, and all the little details.

Donal worried occasionally that he might become spoiled, and fail to appreciate fine appointments. Or, worse, become offended if the offering was below the standard that had been set in his mind.

Neither would be productive for a magician.

The second perspective was to determine the *reason* behind the selection of accommodations. He worked in politics now, and — as Mr. Mancuso had driven home to him — every aspect of the way his hosts treated him was information he could not afford to overlook.

The Washington Arms had been a fine hotel, but it would never have been mistaken for D.C.'s ritziest. Not by a long stretch. Which, Donal had deduced, was one of the reasons he had been boarded there. President Gutierrez had wanted to show respect for Donal's position, without being obsequious.

A good move, and had the salutary secondary effect of keeping Donal conveniently close to the D.C. centers of power.

No doubt Gutierrez, and other presidents before him, had made a habit of boarding ambassadors at the Washington Arms. And the Washington Arms, correspondingly, had been well-versed in dealing with diplomats.

Their front desk had certainly been quick to find a room for Rowan, despite having no warning that she would need one.

On the other hand, berthing Donal in a low-level officer's cabin aboard the *Pegasus* was an awkward move on Gutierrez's part.

First, although Donal had not been personally offended by the tiny cabin, he could have chosen to interpret it as a sign of disrespect. Offering it to him was a decision that certainly risked becoming offensive.

Which meant Gutierrez must've had a compelling reason for it.

Unless.

It was *possible* that the choice of berths was Captain Klimek's, and that more suitable lodgings had been bypassed in favor of petty revenge for her earlier disagreement with Donal and Rowan over holding the voyage for Ms. Bueno.

Donal didn't consider that likely. The captain had seemed to understand the peril of her position. More likely a mere gunboat like the *Pegasus* simply had no more appropriate lodgings available.

Adding these details to the fact that no political liaison had been assigned for the journey, and the ... political ineptitude of Captain Klimek, Donal was able to draw two solid conclusions about his accommodations aboard the *Pegasus*.

First, that a gunboat was the best Gutierrez could do, for a military vessel. Which meant that the pickings were slim, which meant that the Terran Navy was dedicating a lot of resources elsewhere. Likely Mars.

Second, that Donal, Rowan and Ms. Bueno had been berthed aboard the gunboat — rather than berthed aboard a more comfortable helioship and *escorted* by the gunboat — meant that Gutierrez was likely restricting information about the presence of ambassadors as much as possible.

Certainly Captain Klimek had not been pleased to have them aboard, and kept insisting that "ferrying" them about was interfering with her mission. Not to mention the restrictions on their movements...

Internal matters to the UTG. Troubling, though, especially since Donal would probably be expected to mention his speculations in his next report to the queens.

Donal had no doubt that political juggernauts like the queens would wrest depths of understanding from these details that he himself might never begin to suspect.

More important, though, at the moment, was that Donal was getting his first look at his suite in the Zanzibar.

His room — no, his *suite* — was on the fourth floor, in the northwest corner. The door that admitted him was teak, and guarded by simple, yet strong wards that Donal had already been told he could supplement however he chose, so long as he did not interfere with those already in place.

The suite had four large rooms, and Donal took them in slowly as he wandered, all his senses alert.

The entryway led straight into the lounge. Plushly carpeted in shades of yellow that seemed to echo the surface of Venus. Textured walls in muted swirls of color that managed to be interesting, when considered, but easy to ignore.

Four armless divans faced each other in the center, surrounding three small, cubical coffee tables.

Currently a coffee and tea service was set there. Polished silver pots kept steaming not through bound elementals, but alchemical extension of thaumaturgical techniques.

Interesting. Donal made a mental note to see if he spotted any bound elementals on Venus, and to discuss the subject with Fionn when he returned.

In fact, he noted that the moderate temperature of the room was maintained without elementals either...

...something woven into the wards. Had to be. Well, perhaps not *had to be*, but that would certainly have been the most efficient way to handle maintaining a constant temperature, without the use of elementals.

He would determine the answer later, when he had time to sift through the wards personally. Or at least to have Fionn do so, if time pressed on Donal.

For now, though, alongside the silver pots sat four fine China cups bearing flowery patterns (similarly enchanted and treated to maintain a requested level of temperature).

Next to the coffee and tea service, a small plate of baklava. Donal smiled at that, already considering his first taste of the honeyed pastry. He hadn't enjoyed any baklava since he'd last been to the Jade Monkey in San Francisco.

Too long.

On the wall past the divans, far to his right, a door that likely led to the bedroom. To his left, a double door that led...

Where *did* that lead? He'd find out soon enough.

Next to those double doors, a pale, finely carved desk with an armless and backless padded seat. The desk's single, central drawer was likely empty.

At least, most hotel room desk drawers were empty, in Donal's experience. No reason to expect this one to be different.

A red slap-pad sat on the far left edge of the desk. The link to the front desk, which could, from there, be routed elsewhere in the hotel, or to anyplace beyond that the hotel could reach and the customer could pay for.

Presuming the customer was willing to let the Zanzibar listen in. Because there was no way to know if they weren't. Not with a slap-pad setup.

To Donal's right, a mustard-colored divan with arms and no back sat beneath a window, which Donal found a touch odd because it was next to the glass double-door leading out onto the impressively large balcony.

Enough room and wicker furnishings to host a party for twenty, out on that balcony.

Why bother with a viewing couch that looked out over the balcony, when the door to said balcony was a scant meter away?

But then Donal felt the tug of magic from window before the mustard-colored divan.

Ah. A scrying spell. Whoever sat on the divan and asked, could get a visual tour of Venus.

Donal snorted a chuckle and wondered what areas the scrying window would simply fail to show. Because he had no doubt that, if he looked into the literature about the suite and hotel — actual, paper materials in this case, resting on a table inside the front door, beside a vase of violet roses — the Zanzibar would claim a "complete" view of Venus, or similar.

Not that Donal could blame them for keeping secrets. Everyone did.

Moving through the double-door beside the desk, Donal found the dining room. Opposite the double-door, a long wall full of windows that looked out over orchards and a courtyard full of fountains.

Between Donal and those windows, a mahogany dining table with seating for sixteen. Backless mahogany chairs surrounded it. The edges of both table and chairs looked to have been carved, though Donal couldn't tell the design from where he stood.

The lounge had been one thing, but this was ridiculous.

Seating for sixteen?

Venus discouraged visitors. Just who, exactly, did the Zanzibar expect to *need* seating for sixteen in the dining room of a suite? Surely their restaurant would have...

Donal stopped himself there. Not point in plunging down that rabbit hole. No doubt the Zanzibar had its reasons.

The air smelled fresh and clean, and Donal noted that he could not even smell the coffee from the lounge. Which meant that...

Yes. There it was. A small privacy spell on the frame of the double-door, confining the aromas and conversations of the lounge and the dining room to the room of their origination.

In the far left corner of the dining room, a small door that had to have led into the hallway...

No. That wouldn't have made sense. It had to be...

Of course. The suite had no kitchen. Food for the dining room would be delivered through that door, and the remnants removed the same way.

A moment's study confirmed for Donal that this door would open for anyone bearing a kitchen tag.

Donal frowned at that for a moment. Seemed a potentially serious security breach. He shook his head. He would exclude this room from his protection wards, but include even sharper detection wards here. Just in case.

On the wall beside the door, another red slap-pad. Presumably linking directly to the kitchen, or room service, or similar. Interesting.

One other door here in the dining room, leading to a small — relatively speaking — yet comfortable bathroom. Counting the one Donal had spotted in the lounge next to the closet, that made two so far, and Donal had not even reached the bedroom.

Donal went back through the lounge, then through the single door near the scrying window into the next room of the suite's four.

That next room was smaller than the lounge. Only about the size of the dining room. "Only." Donal chuckled to himself as he evaluated what lay before him.

The room was scentless. Perhaps spring air, if Donal wanted to give a name to the little information his nose could bring him.

A round, teak table sat in the middle of the room, surrounded by four backless, armless chairs positioned equidistant from each other.

In the center of the table, a small snarl of blue strands of light. Links. Direct links, without going through the front desk.

Huh.

The table sat in the middle of the room. Windows on the far side, and the right-hand side, but they were designed in the Martian style. Not from glass nor transparent ceramics, but portions of wall that could be made transparent or given varying levels of opacity with the proper command word.

The only other features of the room were a door on the far side, and whorls of color along the walls, in the manner of the lounge.

Was this a private meeting room? That would explain the link setup...

A quick glance at the spells woven into the walls suggested that it was. Privacy spells seemed paramount.

Might also be a good place for Donal to cast his own spells, while he was here.

For now, though, there was the one remaining door...

The bedroom.

Donal had read that in the days of the sultans, they'd kept multiple wives and concubines. That would certainly have explained the bed, which looked large enough to sleep a dozen.

Or more. Perhaps all sixteen diners were expected to be able to retire to the bedroom for an orgy.

Donal shook his head. No point in wasting a joke like that without Fionn around to disapprove.

Instead of the usual earth magic work to make the bed as comfortable as possible, it seemed that the comfort spells were tied to human physiology. They would work to relax and soothe muscles gently, but directly.

The designers seemed to at least acknowledge that the bed was oversized. In addition to the two large nightstands, a shelf ran the length of the headboard, with a red slap-pad in the middle. Like the nightstands, the bedframe and headboard shelf were a smooth hardwood of some stripe, stained a faint orange color that worked with the pattern of the textured walls.

The air carried the faint scent of oranges.

Windows to the right. Three doors to the left. One led to a walk-in closet, where all the diners could have hung their entire wardrobes.

Another held a bathroom too grand for the word. Sweeping vistas of white marble, veined with gold and silver and onyx. A bathtub large enough for half the diners to share, while the other half — assuming they were friendly — could reasonably pack into the shower.

Silver racks certainly bore enough huge, fluffy white towels to accommodate the crowd.

A three-meter-long counter beneath a mirror that had to have measured six meters square. For the bathers to watch themselves?

That there were only two sinks with polished silver fixtures almost felt strange, considering the crowd the Zanzibar appeared to expect to share a bathroom.

That there was only one toilet and one bidet felt stranger still.

And where did they get their water?

Donal knew well the telltale signs of elemental magic, yet none were present here. Which meant that the Zanzibar had to be using at least some old-fashioned piping systems to move water through the building.

A combination of spells and alchemy handled temperature, certainly. But not purification, much less production. Both had to have been handled elsewhere...

Fionn trotted in then, looking around as he joined Donal on a plush yellow rug near the sink.

"The luggage will be brought into the dining room in a few minutes," Fionn said. "I told the handler to leave it there. Dola would not disclose Edik's business on Venus, beyond your morning meeting, which makes me suspect that the Du Mak wish to negotiate with Venus. A suspicion I feel is confirmed by the arrival on Venus of Anna Lukyanova who, no doubt, will be doing the same on behalf of the *Fomhóraigh*."

"No real surprise there," Donal said. "Everyone wants to consider all their options. I suppose we'd better arrange a similar meeting with the Venusian representatives. See about that first thing tomorrow, will you?"

"Of course, master," Fionn said, "One last detail. Ezekiel Collins left a message for you at the front desk, regarding dinner, which is to be in three hours, in the main restaurant of the Zanzibar."

"Thank you, Fionn." Donal shook his head and looked over at his familiar. "Overwhelming luxury, with no reason to leave the hotel.

Think the point is to keep us so focused here that we never look beyond what the Venusians want us to see?"

"Perhaps. Have you examined the wards yet?"

"And another thing," Donal said with a frown. "Where do you suppose they're getting their water?"

"That's a no, then," Fionn said, and his ears gave a flick of disapproval. "May I suggest we get started?"

Donal frowned, still considering the water question.

"Unless you'd prefer to trust our safety and privacy to the hotel's wards?"

Donal shook himself. "You're right. The water question can wait." He slipped his tuning fork out of his sleeve. "Might as well get started."

THE "CHAIR" HAD NO SUPPORTS IN ANY DIRECTION EXCEPT DOWN, BUT Edik sat on it anyway. He leaned back against the ornate desk which sat against one wall. His eyes cast suspicious gazes about the tremendous sitting area.

His shoulders and back were tense. His legs were poised, ready to spring at the first sign of trouble. His right hand itched for the grip of his saber.

This wasn't a freaking hotel room. This was ... he wasn't sure *what* this was. More square footage in this room alone, than available to him on the whole of the *Third Son*.

Three couches? One of them off under a window, for some reason? A coffee and tea service with some kind of honeyed pastry?

All right. Maybe that part made sense as a greeting for an ambassador.

Still. The rest of it? And that balcony?

Had to be a mistake. No way all this was for him. And if it was for Edik, then it had to be a trick. Maybe intended to lull him past his natural wariness.

Surely at least the dining room — on the other side of the wall behind the desk — was a common area of some sort. All those chairs? Who needed so many chairs? If it were a common area, though, that would explain the dining room's extra door that could only lead out into the hall.

Then there was the ridiculous size of the bed in that bedroom. And the way-overdone bathroom.

Hell, the bureau was in the walk-in closet? What the hell was that about? Who needed to leave their bedroom to grab a pair of socks?

The great families of Luna didn't go this far in their ostentation.

The great families...

Was this Pajari's doing? Some kind of trick?

Edik thought about that, as well as why any one sane person might need three bathrooms, while he waited for his familiar.

Dola *finally* came trotting back into the ... front room. This was way too big for Edik to think of it as a living room.

"So?" Edik asked. "Are there any elementals?"

"None," Dola said, then paused and bathed a fluffy gray, slightly transparent paw. "I know the magic here is not so tame as that of Earth, but—"

"I don't like it," Edik said.

Dola blinked cerulean eyes at him. "Which part?"

"Any of it," Edik said, springing to his feet and pacing the thick carpeting for want of something better to do. "This is way too much space for one person. And that bed. And that bathroom. And that dining room. And where are the elementals? And—"

"Breathe, Edik," Dola said, but the big cat's calm only irritated Edik further. "One thing at a time."

"All right. The elementals. What's the deal there?"

"The magic of Venus is largely wild. Perhaps using that magic to bind elementals has proven ... too unreliable for a place like the Zanzibar. Perhaps we should ask Journeyman Donal Cuthbert—"

"And what's he doing here anyway?"

"According to Fionn, he and Rowan MacPherson are here to provide representatives from the United North American States and from Brazil with an introduction—"

"You told me that part already. What else are they doing here?"

Dola gave Edik a sardonic glare and set about washing his face. Something he only did when he wanted to stall for time, or when...

...when Edik was being rude.

Edik stopped pacing and drew a deep breath. Let it out slowly. He crouched down before his familiar and best friend.

"I've been interrupting you, haven't I?"

"You have," Dola said, continuing to wash.

"I'm sorry, Dola," Edik said, voice so full of sincerity and worry that Dola stopped bathing immediately. Edik continued, "It's just ... I'm so far out of my depth here I could have drowned ten times over. Even the magic is wrong here. How am I supposed to understand anyplace that doesn't have elementals?"

"Elementals exist here, as they do everywhere," Dola said, patiently. "What you must understand is that Luna has been intimately involved in Earth magic for so long that they have developed an intrinsic connection. What works on Earth works just as well on Luna."

Dola must've felt Edik's urge to interrupt well up, because he flattened his ears for a moment. Edik plopped down to sit on the thick, yellow carpeting, and nodded for Dola to continue.

"After the early difficulties with the Barrier on Luna, the Mars settlers didn't want to risk the same, or worse, issues. So while their Barriers weave in the native magics of Mars, they also established a firm foundation of Earth magic as well."

"They didn't do that here?" Edik asked.

"It is too soon for me to say for certain, but I believe they did not. Thus, they have had to take a different approach to their local magic, while no doubt their own researchers are busy adapting to the new clime."

"Great," Edik said, through a sigh. "What about Donal and Fionn? What are they really doing here?"

"More than arranging an introduction between us on behalf of the Du Mak and certain nations of Earth. That much is certain. Beyond that, ask. Perhaps he will tell you."

"And all..." Edik waved one hand about. "...this?"

"There are six master suites in the Zanzibar. Rasputin Pajari has one, Anna Lukyanova has another, Journeyman Donal Cuthbert has a third, Rowan MacPherson has the fourth, and we have the fifth."

Edik frowned. "So who's in the sixth?"

"I have not been in a position to find out. I could only be certain about Journeyman Donal Cuthbert and Rowan MacPherson because Fionn informed me of their presence, and because I witnessed Journeyman Donal Cuthbert's luggage being delivered. Perhaps the sixth master suite is empty."

"Given the way my life goes, do you really think it's empty?"

Dola tilted his head, curiously. "Who do you think resides there?"

"Baba Yaga, of course."

"By which you mean Natalia Romanova? I've seen no evidence of her presence. Certainly there was no Romanov helioship at the port."

Edik scoffed, certain Natalia Romanova would find a way. Dola considered the implicit question while twitching his tail.

"We simply do not possess enough information to know for certain. We cannot disregard the possibility that the sixth suite is either empty, or taken by someone unknown to us."

Edik puffed out a breath. Put his fists on his hips and glared around at the front room of the suite. Frowned.

"Where's my duffel bag?"

"I had the porter put it in the bedroom closet."

"So, what, a ten-minute walk?"

Dola twitched his tail with enough agitation that Edik had to stop and look at his familiar.

"You are being treated the same as every other major ambassador," Dola said. "True, the accommodations are beyond anything we could have expected or planned for, but they were not built just for you. You are not being singled out for special treatment."

Dola stood and trotted closer to Edik as he continued.

"In fact, as they provided similar accommodations to other ambassadors, to give you anything lesser would be an insult to the Du Mak people, whom you represent."

Edik slumped with a sigh. Hung his head. "Right. Right."

"The selection of these suites is a message, Edik," Dola said. "The Du Mak are being given the same degree of respect as the Fae Courts and the *Fomhóraigh*."

"Wait," Edik said with a frown. He made himself sit on one of those supportless couches near the coffee and tea service, but stayed facing Dola, who turned with him. "What about the rep from the UNAS? Didn't Pajari say we were meeting with them in the morning as a smokescreen?"

"It is possible that representative resides in the sixth master suite," Dola said, "but I consider it unlikely."

Edik tugged on his Van Dyke as he considered that.

"So you think a diplomat from the one of the most prominent nations on Earth is being afforded less respect than we are?"

"It follows," Dola said. "And it makes sense. Only representatives of the United Terran Government itself could attempt to lay claim to the same level of importance as the Du Mak and the others."

"Or," Edik said, his back straightening as he pieced details together, "Venus has nothing to gain from the UNAS."

Dola twitched his whiskers as he considered that.

"You think the representatives from the *Fomhóraigh* and the Fae Courts are here to negotiate with Venus?"

"Earth is bound by alliance with the Fae Courts. So Anna couldn't be here negotiating with one of their nations on behalf of the *Fomhóraigh*. They wouldn't have standing to strike a deal. She must be here to negotiate with Venus."

Edik shook his head. "I'd be a fool to assume Donal's not here for the same reason. Especially since Rowan MacPherson's along."

Dola nodded agreement while Edik flopped back across the couch, only to have to grasp the sides with his hands to keep from falling off when his shoulder and head missed the cushion.

He centered himself. Sighed at the fancy, textured ceiling, and wished he were looking at the firebird tailfeather painted down the center of the main cabin of the *Third Son*.

"You can do this, Edik."

"I'm not trained for this, Dola." He shook his head. He felt as though every gram of marble in this whole ridiculous hotel had come crashing down on him, burying him alive. "I—"

"Edik," Dola said, propping himself on the cushions with his forepaws, so he could look straight down into Edik's eyes, "you're just flying through uncharted space. How do you do that?"

"Rely on my scanners for all the data I can gather," Edik said, his words coming automatically, "chart the best route I can, and hope I don't get eaten by a zuglodon."

Dola snorted. "I believe the third part is 'and don't fly faster than my scanners feed me information.'"

"Fine," Edik said, agreeing, even though his heart wasn't in it.

He had the distinct feeling that, before all this was over, he'd be eaten by a zuglodon.

———

Anna barely gave her suite more than a quick once-over assessment before she got to work. The appointments were gaudy, if sufficient. The finer details being closer to the standard she preferred — from the pleasant hint of floral scent she could detect in the air, to a temperature so moderate that many would not think to notice it at all.

On the other hand, Anna had to admit, at least to herself, that the thoroughly *decadent* bathtub was calling to her. Add in the varied options for soaps and bath salts and herbal blends and it was all Anna could do to stop herself from stripping down and getting right in the tub.

While she loved Edik like a brother, and thought the world of his *Third Son*, after three days on that little runabout of a helioship, her skin was begging her for a proper soak.

But that would wait.

Work came first.

She rejected the more private system of links in the suite's conference room — its presence a touch she approved of in a suite of such sybaritic design — in favor of the simple slap-pad on the desk in the parlor.

The features of the desk clerk who'd checked her in formed in the air above the pad as he answered her link.

"Front desk, this is Ahmed. How may I assist you, Ms. Lukyanova?"

"I need to speak to a representative of the local government in my official capacity as ambassador for the *Fomhóraigh*. Please connect me with the appropriate office."

"Right away," he said. "Shall he link you in the meeting room? It's a more secure connection."

"That would be fine."

Ahmed suspended the link.

Anna poured herself a cup of anise tea, and carried it into the meeting room. She frowned against the chairs and their casters. Whoever decided that chairs in a meeting room needed rotation? Much less the ability to roll about the room?

Pointless distractions. And positively *skudnyy*, beside the ostentation of the rest of the suite's design.

As though the hotel wanted such a room available, but wished any businesspeople taking advantage of the facility to feel as though they were in any other office. Or perhaps a chain hotel's business center.

To dissuade them from doing business on Venus?

Perhaps. Even so. Odd.

However, whatever her opinion of the chairs, it would not do to be seen standing when the Venusian diplomat linked her. So she tolerated their pedestrian fit and kept her chair from rolling or turning while she waited.

Her first sip of the tea carried the natural sweetness of the licorice taste she'd hoped for, along with an undercurrent of bitterness she found most appropriate for political efforts. And the cup provided that taste at the perfect heat. Not quite enough to scald, but hot enough to truly bring out all the character of the tea. The subtleties in its herbal undercurrents.

How well trained was the Zanzibar staff? she wondered. Would news of her call spread only locally? Or would the other guests learn of it? If so, how long would the dissemination take?

Pajari would bribe the information out of someone, no doubt. Just as he would scoff, and assume that the use of the slap-pad had been a careless mistake on her part.

How the Pajari family had risen so high as third among Luna's great families despite being led by a chauvinist, Anna did not understand.

A strand of the pale blue link web glowed before she'd finished half her cup of tea.

She allowed herself another sip, forcing the diplomat on the other end to wait.

The *Fomhóraigh* had no interest in an alliance with Venus. Nalacha had made their stance on the issue of alliances quite clear.

However. Appearances must be maintained, while she went about her real work her on Venus.

The conversation was a simple matter. The Venusian representative — a stern faced man named Jaleel Nazari, whose beard looked sharp enough to cut — was not so well-trained as he should've been, for his post.

Within his first two sentences, Anna had already determined that he'd been informed of her arrival, and that his superiors wanted him to maintain friendly relations while not committing themselves to anything.

He'd been only too glad to set their meeting for four o'clock tomorrow afternoon. Quite obviously after at least one other meeting.

Still, he'd been polite without risking obsequiousness. Talkative, without offering too much information.

Not as bad as some diplomats she could name.

After she concluded the conversation, and her tea, Anna went through the provided guides to the Zanzibar and Gilgamesh, deducing what she could about what the locals wanted travelers to know, and what they didn't.

As she expected. The literature made the Zanzibar seem like the only thing worth seeing on the whole planet. Only the barest of token nods to a twice-monthly bazaar in town, where no doubt the pickings would be slim. At least, to the eyes of those travelers who could afford to come here in the first place.

But was that because the settlers so valued their privacy? Or because they'd discovered something they were trying hard to hide from everyone else?

And where did her task from Nalacha fit into all this?

More things for Anna to consider while she freshened up for dinner.

She outfitted herself in another Gustav airsilk dress. This one a dark, subtle orange with burnt red undertones. The combination would go well with the walls and carpeting of the Zanzibar, as well as setting off certain highlights in her hair, which she again wore up in a complex, businesslike arrangement.

The gown had simple lines through the bodice and ruffles starting halfway down the skirt. It also had the benefit of covering her from collarbone to calf, and her arms just down past the elbow.

Normally, a certain amount of décolletage would be appropriate at a dinner like this one, where members of different great families would dine together. It was tradition.

In fact, had they been on Luna, she would have chosen a dress that would have recalled the days of the Tsars. An imperial court gown. Off the shoulder, with an intricate pattern, and long sleeves that would hang like cloaks around her bare arms

However, this was not Luna. And that the conversation might descend into business was enough excuse to buck tradition.

Most important, Anna had no intention of offering up her bare skin to Pajari's lecherous gaze.

She had been invited to arrive at five o'clock. A member of a lesser great family than Pajari's would be expected to knock either exactly on time, or early by a minute or so.

Anna did not knock until twenty minutes past the hour.

The door to Pajari's suite was answered promptly by that

Romanian manservant who'd met Edik and her at the port. Funar, as she recalled.

The manservant greeted her with only a gesture to enter, accompanied by a general statement to the room, "*Fomhóraigh* ambassador Anna, of the Lukyanov family."

That was ... proper, but only under the most formal of circumstances. Pajari was many things, but he was rarely formal. Anna would need to be wary.

Her darting eyes spotted no unexpected guests, at least. She noted that his suite was laid out the same way hers was, but that was no surprise.

Pajari himself lounged on a divan in the center of the room, facing the door. His ruddy face wide with a broad smile. A dark beer in one hand, and a sweet of some kind in the other.

Despite the formality of her introduction, Pajari had not dressed for a formal dinner. No Tsarist court outfit for him either, nor even an airsilk tuxedo.

Instead, perhaps anticipating Anna's choice, he'd dressed in a well-cut dark airsilk suit with a tie a dark enough shade of gold to almost make her believe his dark eyes hid flecks of gold as well.

Had the introduction been intended as a joke, then? With Rasputin Pajari, she couldn't be certain.

Sitting opposite Pajari, and looking just as uncomfortable as Anna expected, was poor Edik. He was still in the same spacer outfit as earlier, and he looked ready to spring up and leave at the first opportunity. On the square coffee table before him, his beer sat untouched beside the vast array of meats, cheeses and sweets that Pajari had been helping himself to.

Edik looked at Anna as though sighting a rescue ship after six months marooned in space.

Dola, of course, sat at Edik's feet. In fact, one of Dola's paws rested on Edik's left boot. A reassurance for his master?

"Oh!" Pajari said, eyes wide with mock surprise as he looked over at Anna. "Given the hour, I'd assumed Natalia Romanova had chosen to grace my table tonight."

"Your devotion to your ambassadorial duties is commendable, Raputin. But it has distracted you too far from lunar matters. The Lukyanovs have supplanted the Romanovs as Luna's first family."

"Have they?" he replied, his broad smile and knowing eyes practically teemed with suggestion.

Pajari knew well what Anna's father had accomplished with the Lunar independence movement while Natalia Romanova's attention was on Mars.

Apparently his jest had sought to get a rise out of Anna.

She could only hope her tone had been as bland as she intended. Oh, but the man was irritating.

"Well," he continued, "it is nevertheless wonderful to see you, Anna. You've grown into a woman of such *exquisite* beauty."

Anna quickly turned to Edik, while Pajari's eyes tried to see through her dress.

"It is good to see you, Edik, as always," Anna said with a smile. Then she gestured to the array of snacks and said to Pajari, "Is this to be our dinner then?"

"Certainly not," Pajari said, coming to his feet.

As he stood, Anna noticed that Pajari wore his sashka at his belt tonight. A response to the fact that Edik went nowhere without his saber?

Or was Pajari expecting trouble?

"Come," he said, rubbing his hands together. "Let us eat."

EDIK TRIED NOT TO DRAW ATTENTION TO HIMSELF AS HE FOLLOWED Pajari and Anna from the front room into the suite's dining room.

The great families of Luna. He'd spent most of his life staying as far out of their way as he could. Now he was dining with two of them. One a friend, and one an "ally" of sorts.

That didn't mean he understood them.

At least Pajari's suite had the same style dining room as Edik's had. Same seating for sixteen, with backless, armless chairs, made from the same ornately carved dark wood as the table.

Way too big for a group this size, but maybe having some space between the diners was a good thing, in this case.

The place settings had been arranged by someone who echoed that notion — one at each end, and two in the middle. Finely polished real silver for the silverware. Plates delicate enough that Edik hoped they weren't served steak. He'd worry about cutting right through the ceramics. Crystal glasses for both water and a dark red wine, both etched with matching double-headed eagle designs.

Pajari took one end of the table, and Anna the other, leaving Edik in the middle. He would've been all alone in the middle, except that Pajari had set a place for Dola, complete with a small assortment of fish and bird meats.

Dola took his place and made a show of sniffing his fare.

"Marvelous selection, if I may say so," he said, in words that all could hear and understand, "and quite well prepared. Though I hope you'll forgive me if I do not partake."

"Of course, of course," Pajari said with a booming laugh. "I know you are a thing of spirit, not flesh. But I would see no guest at my table unprovided for."

With those last words, Pajari gave Anna a significant look that Edik didn't understand at all. She accepted his words with no change in expression, though a bare nod of her head. As though Pajari had actually done something she agreed with.

Something had just passed between them, and Edik had no idea what it was. Just one more item in the long, *long* list of things Edik didn't know and probably should. At least as long as he was playing ambassador...

He stopped himself there. Forced himself to breathe. Remembered what Dola had been saying about flying through uncharted space.

This dinner, this was just more uncharted space. So what could Edik figure out about it?

Start with the arrangements. Pajari and Anna, at opposite ends of the table. Positions of equal strength? Or did the superior rank of Anna's family mean she sat at the head and Pajari at the foot?

Edik liked that idea.

Edik, himself, sat equidistant between them. A balance point between the two? Like the fulcrum of a lever?

Wait. Did that mean that Edik's position held some power he hadn't recognized?

He would need to discuss that with Dola later.

Edik would also need to be careful. Pajari might technically be his ally in their roles as representatives of the Du Mak, but Anna was his *friend*. He mustn't jeopardize that.

The door at one end of the room opened. The door that Edik believed led out into the hall. In came that blonde serving girl, the one he'd first seen at the Pajari estate on Luna.

The poor girl wore no more clothing here than she had on Luna. Same low-cut blouse, same high-cut skirt.

She carried a large silver bowl, containing their first course for the evening: a salad.

As she used silver tongs to distribute salads to Anna, Pajari and Edik — in that order — he wondered why Pajari had brought her all the way here. Surely the Zanzibar wouldn't include dining rooms like this one without having a ready waitstaff as well.

Was Pajari having an affair with the poor young thing?

Edik hoped not. He couldn't believe a woman like her, barely past the age of consent herself, would willingly take a man like Pajari to her bed. So if they were having an affair, Pajari might be pressuring her family. Or worse.

And yet, she'd refused Edik's offer to find her better — or at least better clothed — employment.

Focus, Edik. Why else might Pajari have her here and serving tonight?

Maybe Pajari wouldn't trust the discretion of local servers? That seemed likely. The great families were certainly known to fiercely safeguard their privacy. And Pajari might have sensitive subjects in mind for their conversation.

Of course, given the icy glare Anna gave Pajari when she saw the server's outfit, Pajari might have the girl here just to provoke Anna.

Edik realized then, seeing the blonde girl standing beside Anna, that they were of a height, and similar in build...

That settled at least part of the question then. The server was here to provoke Anna. Which meant Pajari'd accomplished at least one of his goals here tonight.

Edik wondered what the other goals were, but forced his attention back to what he knew, and what he could figure out from there.

Pajari might be using his own servers, but surely the food had been provided by the Zanzibar. If Anna had been right that Edik would've insulted the locals if he'd slept on the *Third Son* — and Edik had no doubt that Anna was right — then the same reasoning suggested that Pajari couldn't insist on having his meals prepared by his own cooks...

Edik took his first bite of salad, and lost his train of thought. Iceberg lettuce crispier than any Edik had ever tasted before. Amazingly fresh diced tomatoes and cucumbers were mixed in, along with crispy squares of some kind of flat bread.

The spices were startlingly familiar to Edik, though their tastes were more robust than those he usually enjoyed. Garlic and mint, onion and ... lemon, all mixed in with olive oil.

Edik loved his homemade borscht with an abiding passion, but even just that salad was enough to get him thinking that Anna had a point about broadening his culinary horizons.

A quickly whispered "Edik" from Dola — pitched so only Edik himself could hear it — made him realize that he'd been so involved in his ruminations — and his salad — that he'd missed the start of the conversation.

"...the value of smuggling," Pajari was saying. "I, myself, feel that if your father's points are correct, and Earth has no further claim of sovereignty over Luna, then of course smuggling past the blockade is not only legal, but expected for those of our standing."

Of course they were starting with the politics of the great families. Why was Edik even here?

Anna, for her part, looked as though she considered smuggling distasteful. Or perhaps the speaker himself.

"Certainly you do not expect me to discuss Lukyanov family policies with you," Anna said, and by her tone Edik was pretty sure that was the end of the topic.

But Pajari had his own take on her tone.

"At least, not in front of an outsider," he said. He turned to Edik and added, "Do forgive me, Edik. But fond as Anna and I both are of you, you are not of the great families. I should never have broached such a subject in the first place. You must both forgive me."

"Must I?" Anna said archly, even as Edik was nodding. She tried to say more, but Pajari spoke over her.

"Besides," he said with a dismissive wave that dislodged a bit of lettuce from his fork, to land on the table beside his plate. "What would you know about Lukyanov family policies these days anyway, dear Anna? You are a Lukyanova in name only, are you not? Certainly you must realize your split with your father is well known."

Anna threw her napkin down on her plate and stood, thunder in her eyes and aspect, but somehow her face itself gave away nothing of her feelings.

Edik wondered how she did that.

"How dare you?" she said, her voice low, yet demanding all the attention in the room.

Same trick Edik had seen Donal Cuthbert do. Was Edik the only one who couldn't do it?

"You forget yourself, Rasputin Pajari," Anna continued, in that scary quiet voice. "You are *not* one who may speak to me in this fashion. I am Anna Lukyanova, and all that that means. I will expect your apology by morning, and if I find it insufficient, I will remind you and yours exactly who and what I am."

In that moment, Edik found himself terribly grateful that he wasn't the target of her anger.

She left with an unhurried, yet swift stride, and Edik would've sworn the door opened for her of its own accord. As it closed behind her, the room felt bigger. As though her presence had taken up more space than it should've.

"Well," Pajari said, drawing Edik's attention back to him. "That went even better than I hoped. Shall we see about the main course?"

Edik shook his head and stood up.

"You and I," Edik said slowly, and he couldn't even pretend that his words carried the kind of almost physical weight that Anna's had, "we have to work together for the sake of the Du Mak people."

Edik shook his head slowly. "But that doesn't mean I have to dine with someone who insults my friends."

Dola was already moving to join Edik as he strode toward the door.

"Edik," Pajari began chidingly.

Edik didn't wait, listen, or look back. He just left.

And as he did, he noticed that he had to open the door himself.

———

DONAL COULDN'T REMEMBER THE LAST TIME HE ENJOYED A CASUAL, social meal. Probably not since before Esme took her post working for the First Magician of the United North American States. Possibly not since before Donal took his post as ambassador.

Yes. That had to have been it. Ever since he took this job, he either ate alone, or accompanied by at least one agenda.

Even Donal's last meal at home with both his parents and Bran — over winter break from school — hadn't exactly been *social*. Not once his mother found out about his ... new title.

Well, if such meals were doomed to be rare, then at least he was enjoying one at an excellent location.

The hotel restaurant at the Zanzibar wasn't like any Donal had ever seen before in a hotel, aboard a ship, or ... well, anywhere at all, once he thought about it. Rather than having a single large dining room with the kitchen off to one side, it had a central kitchen, surrounded by small, private dining rooms.

Donal couldn't imagine how they could hold a major event in

such a place. Hard to have, say, a convention lunch with a keynote speaker, if they couldn't accommodate two hundred diners in a single room.

But then, Gilgamesh didn't seem the sort of place to encourage convention business.

The room where Donal, Fionn, and Rowan joined Ezekiel Collins for dinner looked truer to the tales of the Arabian Nights than the lobby did. That much was certain.

The room itself looked to be smaller than any room in Donal's suite. No more than maybe four meters each direction. Hard to be exact, though, because the lights were kept low and soft, and the ceiling and walls were draped with translucent curtains of rich reds, golds and purples.

The floor was covered in thick Persian rugs. The pale hardwood table in the center was small and round, encouraging the diners to sit close tighter, and eat within touching distance.

The table was low, too. Low enough that there were no chairs to sit on. Cushions, instead, with throw pillows, and all of them in soft colors that went with the décor.

The throw pillows were subtly enchanted to provide back support, for those who needed it. Now that was odd. Given that Donal could not think of a single chair or couch in his suite that had a back, why would the restaurant worry about back support? Were people less likely to spill their food when they had something to lean back against?

Either way, it was actually a neat little bit of spellwork. The magics involved weaving strands of thread from the same source through the insides of each pillow and cushion. Donal could tell readily enough that the majority of those strands were strapped to a stiff, supportive chair somewhere on the premises.

Interesting use of sympathetic magic. Likely a hassle to maintain, but decidedly comfortable to sit upon. Certainly, even Mr. Collins seemed to sit comfortably, despite Donal's suspicions about an old back injury.

All three diners had dressed for a casual meal, though Donal noted that none of them tried to fit the theme. Probably for the best.

Mr. Collins — Ezekiel. Tonight Donal was only supposed to call him Ezekiel — was dressed in a dark brown turtleneck sweater over a pair of slightly darker pants. Both shades went very well with his complexion.

Rowan wore a sleeveless chiffon dress, cream in color, that flattered her well.

Donal ... did his best for casual. Mr. Mancuso — Donatello, Donal had to remember to call him Donatello — had emphasized that even a casual meal was an opportunity, and not to take the word "casual" too seriously.

So Donal was wearing airsilks again. A forest green shirt, and slacks that turned out to match those worn by Ezekiel. Donal's shirt was short sleeved, though, and he left the top button undone, so maybe that counted as casual?

They'd begun the meal with piping hot ginger tea. Tangy and delicious and preparing the way for a delightful salad course featuring farro, apple and roasted persimmon. To drink with the salad, they were served water sweetened with slices of honeydew and cantaloupe.

Already, Ezekiel had begun entertaining them with stories of his time at university, training for a future career in diplomacy.

The most impressive part of the stories, for Donal, was watching Ezekiel split his attention equally between both his listeners. (To Donal's disappointment, he didn't seem to consider Fionn a listener worth including in the conversation.)

Donal had half-expected the poor man to be mesmerized by Rowan in that chiffon gown, but he didn't pay her any special attention.

Ezekiel was telling the tale of how his cohort had managed to swap the mascots of two rival universities, so that each would accuse the other of stealing. A story full of expansive gestures and imitated voices, that ended with a good belly laugh from all of them.

Donal was starting to think that, for one evening at least, he could forget politics and just enjoy himself.

They were just finishing the salad course when a man from the hotel staff came in. Not one of the restaurant's servers, either, but someone from administration.

"Ambassador Cuthbert," the man said. "There's a link for you."

The man was young, about Donal's age. Fit. Uniform looked tailored. Looked to be an expatriate from New Mesopotamia, like every other local Donal had seen so far. No magic about him, or on his person.

And yet, something about the man felt wrong to Donal.

Then he realized the man's nametag read "Ahmed."

Now, it could've been that Ahmed was as common a name in Gilgamesh as John was in England. But given that the desk clerk's name was Ahmed, a second Ahmed working here seemed too unlikely to trust to coincidence.

"Good," Donal said, standing. He turned to Fionn and Rowan. "I do hope it's Leeann. She's been trying to reach me all week."

Fionn flicked his ears in acknowledgment as he stood beside Donal. Rowan gave only a slow blink, but somehow Donal knew that meant she'd understood him completely.

Morna, the *leannan sidhe*, would never try to reach Donal by link.

Unfortunately, Rowan seemed to take Donal's warning as a call to arms. She stood.

"I'll come along then," she said. "If it's her I need to speak to her too, and if not, I'll try to reach her again so we can get this straightened out."

She gave Ezekiel a smile that stopped him from objecting. "We'll be right back."

Donal couldn't be certain, but he thought "Ahmed" looked irritated that Rowan was coming along.

"After you, sir," "Ahmed" said, holding a wispy red curtain aside so that Donal could be first out the door.

"Lead the way if you would," Donal said, doing his best to sound distracted. "I get turned around in this place."

"You know magicians," Rowan said, taking Donal's arm and

looking expectantly at "Ahmed." "They'd get lost in their own labs, without someone to guide them."

"Too true," Donal said, faking an embarrassed smile and leaving "Ahmed" no choice but to lead the way.

He led them into a marble hallway that looked to be surrounded by offices. Likely empty, this time of day, since the offices seeing twenty-four-hour use would be back near the front desk...

Donal was watching for "Ahmed" to do anything suspicious. First as he walked, and then as he opened an office door for Donal, saying, "The secure links are in here."

But the man was good. Too good, it seemed, even for Fionn's wary eyes. By the time Donal realized "Ahmed" had drawn a stiletto, the point was almost to his jugular.

Far too late for Donal to stop it.

But Rowan gave a loud, lovesick sigh. And for the first time that Donal could remember noticing, he felt waves of magic coming from her.

Ephemeral magic. Fae magic.

The stiletto froze, its point only just denting Donal's skin.

"Ahmed" stared, transfixed by Rowan. He smiled a sappy smile. His eyes dilated so wide he might've been staring into the sun. His stiletto hand drooped low and the stiletto itself clattered to the marble.

He started spewing platitudes of love and devotion.

"Another!" Fionn snapped, leaping ahead of Donal and into the office.

A second assassin was in there and on the move.

This one wasn't disguised, and he definitely wasn't local. He looked like a war-scarred Viking, so big he might've had ogre blood. He wore black fatigues, and had a Ka-Bar combat knife in one hand.

Fionn tried to distract the assassin by leaping through his face, but the man didn't give a twitch.

Rowan sighed again, but the waves of her magic seemed to break before reaching that second assassin.

Then Donal realized the man wore his clothes backwards. But

why would that help? If anything, it might repel lesser fae, but fae magic was another matter.

Still. It seemed to be working for him, because Rowan's glamour never touched him.

Donal tried to escape back into the hall, but tripped over the first assassin — currently kneeling before Rowan, his clasped hands high as he pleaded for her attention — and went down hard on the marble flooring.

Rowan tried to get between Donal and the oncoming assassin, but he shouldered her aside. His blue eyes focused on Donal and his strike.

Donal clapped a single hand hard as he hit the assassin with the Jenkins Flash. It was a desperate ploy, unable to do more than give the sudden sensation of a rough slap all over the assassin's body. But it might buy Donal at least a moment to think.

No effect at all. Not even a bare shiver.

The man was warded? Couldn't have been anything he was carrying. Tattooed wards? Was that a thing?

There. Donal spotted a ripple that had to be the man's protection. Not a tattoo at all, but something carried in the assassin's mouth, likely under his tongue.

A talisman. Had to be. An object that could naturally ground magic.

Risky. Wouldn't help against anything Donal could do if he had time to work properly. Then again, it might well be more than enough to shut down what little Donal could manage while struggling for his life.

Donal scrambled out of the way as the assassin grabbed for his leg. Donal got his feet under him. Pulse racing. Eyes darting.

There was nowhere to run. The hall dead-ended not five meters behind him.

The assassin knew that. Smiled. Began closing in...

Quick, approaching footsteps grabbed his attention. "Ahmed," holding his stiletto high and coming on the attack.

No grace or subtlety while under the influence of Rowan's charm.

His larger companion growled and laid "Ahmed" out with a single punch to throat.

A momentary delay. If only Donal could find a way to...

Wait. That talisman. A quick shift of Donal's awareness confirmed that the assassin was using a *lodestone* to anchor and ground any magics sent at him.

A loadstone, Donal could handle.

He drew his tuning fork. Struck it on his knee. It chimed its clear, perfect note.

The assassin smirked as he turned back to Donal. Held up his Ka-Bar, as though to say that his was bigger.

Donal didn't care about the knife. He couldn't afford to. Not now.

The lodestone attracted more than magic. It was a magnet. It attracted metal. It attracted metal and magic.

Donal held up his vibrating tuning fork. More metal and magic.

Correspondence, in this case, leading to causality.

Donal shifted his focus further, through Enochian lines that interpreted all of existence as facets of the five elements through three tiers.

He reached for the power of earth-aspected, earth of earth.

The assassin closed with Donal. Barely a step away now. Lifted his knife.

Donal reached through his tuning fork directly into the lodestone in the assassin's mouth. Connected with all of the earth elements of the lodestone. And through the lodestone he reached into the assassin himself, and all the earth elements that were part of the assassin's body.

Earth aspected earth of earth. The very foundations of anything physical.

Donal tied the magnetic aspect of the lodestone to every muscle in the man's limbs, intending to make his muscles seize and paralyze him.

Donal did his job too well.

The assassin folded in on himself, legs and arms all trying to get to his mouth and the lodestone.

Unfortunately, in the process the man plunged the tip of his Ka-Bar straight up his nose and into his brain.

Nausea swept over Donal as he quick-stepped away from the spreading pool of blood.

He'd just killed a man.

"What on Earth?" Ezekiel's voice, from farther down the hall. Apparently he'd opted not to wait for Donal and Rowan to return.

Some casual dinner this was turning out to be.

ONCE, WHEN DONAL WAS VERY YOUNG, HE'D SEEN THE LAST performance of a traveling circus. It had been a circus without real animals, much to his father's disappointment, but there'd been more than enough magic to keep Donal smiling for days.

He'd loved the colorful, fanciful illusions so much, he'd refused to leave. Kept wanting to stay just a few more minutes.

Finally, they began to strike the tent. And the illusions stopped. Without them, the tent looked sad. Washed out. Lonely.

But he had been a child. The wonder lived on in his mind all the same, even though he'd had a glimpse behind the curtain.

But as Donal sat in the Zanzibar's dining room once more, the décor seemed to him as the tent had, after it was struck.

The bright colors of the draped fabrics and cushions, rugs and throw pillows, they all seemed washed out. Their magic stolen by the attempt on Donal's life.

Yet another assassination attempt. Was this what Bran had been warning of?

There'd no one on the link for Donal, of course. The office that "Ahmed" had led Donal to was a human resources office. No outside links beyond a slap-pad to go through the main hotel network.

Donal had asked Fionn to check, just to make sure.

Ezekiel, as a true diplomat, had checked with Donal and Rowan before alerting the Zanzibar's management, and through them, the authorities.

Donal couldn't help wondering what Ezekiel would've done had Donal refused the authorities. Would he have offered to make the bodies disappear?

Perhaps that depended on how badly the UNAS wanted an alliance with the Du Mak.

Perhaps Donatello was right. Perhaps all of life was merely one long negotiation. Donal might've asked Fionn's opinion, but Fionn was double-checking the area for more assassins.

Rowan pressed a hot cup of ginger tea into Donal's hand, and sat beside him on the cushion.

She rubbed circles on his back with one hand, and asked softly, "How are you doing?"

"I killed a man," Donal said, unsure if he sounded more tired or sad. For that matter, he wasn't sure which he felt, apart from vaguely numb.

Shock, likely. He needed to meditate. But he couldn't do that until he was done with the authorities.

"You defended yourself," Rowan said, and her tone carried such certainty that Donal felt it chime a resonance inside him. "That's all."

"I tried to immobilize him. Instead I killed him."

"Donal," she said, sharply enough that he had to turn to look her in those green, green eyes. "Would you rather be dead?"

Rowan and that way of hers. Her words cut right through to Donal's core.

"No. Of course not. But—"

"You had to stop him." She leaned a little closer. Close enough that Donal wasn't sure if the ginger he smelled was from his tea or her breath. "Was there any other way you could've stopped him?"

Donal shook his head without breaking eye contact.

"All right then," she said, her voice softening again. "I know you need to process this, and I know it'll take some time. But I want you to be clear on something. He was going to kill you. I tried to stop him and failed. Which means that if you didn't—"

"Hey," Donal said. "You aren't blaming yourself, are you?"

Rowan looked away. "All my magic, foiled by some backwards clothing. I'd've said that was impossible, but—"

"Wasn't just that," Donal said. "I'm sure of it. The lodestone helped. And he probably had another—"

"Iron," Fionn said, coming back into the room. "He wore cold iron bracers at his wrists and ankles, and more sewn into his shirt as a cross above his heart. I'm fairly certain the cross was blessed by an Eastern Orthodox priest, as well."

"Iron?" Donal said quickly. "At—"

"Yes," Fionn said. "But no, it didn't amplify your working. You were too precise to connect the iron to the spell."

Donal started to say something, but Fionn put a paw on his knee and said, "You did the best you could with your life on the line. You are to be congratulated for surviving, not blamed for the accidental death of a killer."

"Maybe," Donal said, not yet so sure of that. But he turned to Rowan and continued, "But don't you go blaming yourself for not affecting a man warded specifically against fae magic. Plus, you sent that first assassin after him."

"I knew that was only a delaying tactic," she said, shaking her head. "The Lover's Sigh doesn't exactly inspire effective violence."

"Bought me the time I needed," Donal insisted. "In fact—"

Ezekiel Collins cleared his throat from the doorway.

"Port security is ready for you."

"Port security?" Donal asked. "Not Gilgamesh police?"

"They don't have a police force," Ezekiel said, and a woman continued the sentence for him as she entered.

"We never seem to have trouble, except when off-worlders come to town."

Solid was the first word that came to mind when Donal saw the woman. Not much more than a meter and a quarter tall, she looked as though she could've picked up the big, blonde assassin and thrown him across the room.

Her uniform was a gleaming white, with pale yellow trim and the seal of Gilgamesh above her heart — it looked to Donal like a willow tree — also done in pale yellow. She wore her black hair short, and her dark eyes seemed to take in the whole room within a single glance. She wore a white, military-grade Pacifier hanging from one side of her belt, and a sheathed gladius from the other.

She also had an Initiate's aura of power, but there was something unusual about that aura. It seemed to flicker.

"I'm Sergeant Nawal Rahal," she said, then correctly identified everyone else in the room, including Fionn. "I'll be the one conducting this interview."

"May I test your credentials?" Donal asked, voice more weary than polite. Probably because of her opening statement. As though Donal were to blame for people trying to kill him.

"I beg your pardon." Sergeant Rahal might've sounded more surprised than offended, but it was close.

"The last stranger I met wearing a uniform tried to shove a stiletto through my throat."

"Nevertheless—"

"Sergeant," Donal said, setting down his undrunk tea, "I would very much like to work with local authorities to investigate this matter. However. I will not trust any stranger's word about who they are. Not tonight. Not until I feel safe again, which may be a while. So either you provide me with credentials I can confirm, or I'm going to my room."

"And if I arrest you?"

"I have diplomatic immunity."

The sergeant's eyes seemed to darken along with her tone as she replied, "And if I don't care?"

"Well," a voice said from the hall. A male voice, strong and clear and the kind of beautiful baritone that not one in a thousand can claim. "Then perhaps I will consider you in league with the assassins, and deal with you accordingly."

The temperature seemed to drop five degrees as the inquisitor of the Fae Courts stepped into the room. Skin like midnight sky. His storm cloud hair hanging loose to his waist, save for twin side braids, woven at the back to keep his locks clear of his face.

He'd changed his outfit for a tuxedo the color of fresh blood, a sharp contrast to his shirt the color of innocence, but he still wore that broadsword at his hip.

He interposed himself between Donal and the sergeant.

The sergeant looked stunned. Perhaps caught between deciding if this man had stepped out of a dream or a nightmare. But to her credit, she managed to speak anyway, and not sound like a lost child in the process.

"And just who are you?"

"Perhaps I am your death," he said. "The question remains open."

"Look," Donal said, addressing the sergeant. "We can all work together, but you'll have to—"

"We don't have spelled badges," she said, now sounding embarrassed. She shrugged. "We've never needed them, so why go to the expense?"

"Because now that you need one and don't have it," Donal said, standing, "I have no reason to trust or work with you. Goodnight, whoever you are."

But before Donal could take a step, the sergeant spoke quickly.

"I swear on my power that I am Sergeant Nawal Rahal of Gilgamesh Port Security."

Donal felt the small — if flickering — flare that accompanied the mystic oath. She had to be telling the truth, or she'd cripple her magic.

"What *you* have hardly constitutes power," the inquisitor said.

"And yet," Donal said, "it's a valid oath." He sat down. "All right, sergeant. Let's talk."

Apparently she'd already seen the assassins, because she knew both were dead. That was news to Donal. He'd hoped the smaller one had survived. But the sergeant made clear that his throat had collapsed. He'd choked to death.

Still. Rather that begin at the beginning, the sergeant wanted to start with questions about how the assassins died.

Donal wasn't having it.

"Look," he said. "We were having dinner, when the assassins lured us away and tried to kill us."

"But the way they died—"

"Is not your concern." Donal shook his head, anger driving away some of the numbness. "The magics we used to defend ourselves are classified. These are not details that matter."

"I say they do."

"This man speaks for the Fae Courts," the inquisitor said in a soft, yet threatening voice. "If he says that his methods are privileged information, then they are not yours for the asking."

She started to ask another question, but he spoke over her.

"I might, myself, wonder who begins an investigation at the end, rather than the beginning. Perhaps someone who wishes to pass a warning along to the next assassin?"

"I'm here to protect the people of Gilgamesh," she insisted.

"And perhaps you do not welcome the Fae Courts here?"

"That's for the politicians to decide," she said. "This man" — she pointed at Donal — "whatever else he is, he's a guest of the people of Gilgamesh, and I don't want him getting killed. So I'm going to do everything I can to get to the bottom of this and stop anyone else from trying to kill him while he's here."

She shook her head slowly. "But I don't understand why one assassin would murder his colleague. And I've never even *heard* of magic that could do what was done to that big assassin back there. He stabbed. Himself. Through the nostril. And into the brain."

She shook her head. "That's not how people kill themselves. So someone made him do that. And while I may not have enough magic to figure out *how*, I can at least recognize the signature of the caster."

She pointed at Donal.

"If you're carrying some kind of new weapon," she said, "something that could present a threat to the people of Gilgamesh, I need to know what it is."

She was good. She was applying a lot of pressure, even under threat of the inquisitor. And most people — if they'd had Donal's evening — would probably have given in.

But Thaumaturgy training at the level Donal had achieved made even greater demands on the student. If anything, her pressure only rallied Donal's faculties.

"I'm an ambassador," Donal said. "And entitled to carry whatever resources I need to ensure my personal safety."

She started to object again, but Donal stilled her with a raised hand. "I will, however, assure you that I have no intention of using said resources offensively during my time here in Gilgamesh. And so long as no one else tries to kill me, there'll be no need for me to."

Not that he probably could. Not many assassins would run around with lodestones in their mouths.

Finally, she agreed to begin at the beginning. And when Donal asked, she even allowed that "Ahmed" was, in fact, using a stolen nametag from the front desk clerk. When her team had arrived, they'd found the real Ahmed unconscious and bound in the bushes outside. Likely he'd been leaving for the day when he was accosted.

Donal recounted the tale for both the sergeant and the inquisitor. He skipped over the details of his and Rowan's defensive magics — in the process neglecting to mention that Rowan had done any magic at all — but otherwise he told the tale straight.

Based on the inquisitor's timely nods and glances, he was able to fill in the gaps that Donal left.

The sergeant was less pleased with those gaps, but gritted her teeth and accepted them.

Donal left the inquisitor to deal with her, said his good nights to Ezekiel, and left, flanked by Rowan and Fionn.

As they left the hall and entered the huge, nearly empty lobby, Rowan said, softly, "I'm surprised Morna didn't show up."

"Oh, I don't doubt that she's following a lead of some sort," Donal said, glancing about. A young woman waved from the check-in desk, but otherwise they were alone in the lobby. Or at least, seemed to be. Donal returned her wave with a nod.

"Right now," he said softly to Rowan, "we need to get someplace secure to talk. Let's check out the orchards."

6

Anna rode down to the lobby in a steel cage surrounded by a bubble of air and propelled by undines.

Normally, Anna would have savored the fascination of this mode of transit. She only got to enjoy riding in a bubble when she stayed in hotels, or rode on large helioships. The mansions of the great families preferred the look and feel of stairs.

But just then, Anna was too angry to enjoy even the simple pleasures of riding in a bubble.

When the bubble reached the ground floor, she slammed the cage door open and passed swiftly through the Zanzibar's lobby. Her heels clicked sharply on the marble floor. From the corner of her eye, she thought she saw a man and a woman walking toward the back of the hotel.

There was something familiar about the couple, but Anna had neither the time nor the patience to find out what.

The nerve of that man. The audacity. Not to mention the short-sightedness. That Rasputin Pajari would speak to *Anna Lukyanova* that way was bad enough. But that an ambassador for the Du Mak would speak to a *Fomhóraigh* ambassador that way...

Inexcusable. And coming from Rasputin Pajari, evidence that he had no intention of brokering an alliance between the Du Mak and the *Fomhóraigh*.

The man lacked any semblance of the social virtues, but he was not a complete idiot. He knew exactly what he was doing, and precisely what message he was sending.

And apparently, Nalacha must've expected this. Otherwise he would not have asked Anna to handle that second matter for him, on her first night on Venus, after she finished dinner.

Well, there was no time like the present.

Anna stepped right up to the front desk and was quickly addressed by the young woman behind the counter, whose nametag read Fatima.

"Yes, Ambassador Lukyanova? How may I assist you?"

"I require a horse, saddled and ready in fifteen minutes."

"A horse?"

"I assume the Zanzibar keeps a stable for its guests? Or must I hire a horse from someplace in town?"

"We have a stable," Fatima said, still sounding confused. "It's just ... an unusual request at this hour. Most of the shops will be closed."

"I was practically raised on horseback," Anna said. "I can handle night riding in unfamiliar territory. And I have no interest in shopping at this time."

"Then why—"

"Will you have the horse prepared for me, or must I hire one from town?"

"Your horse will be ready in fifteen minutes," Fatima said. "May I provide you with a guide, at least?"

"You may not," Anna said, her tone firm but not cross. She was too well trained to let her anger at Pajari bleed over onto a desk clerk. Even one asking questions one should not ask of an ambassador. "I will sign a waiver if you wish."

"It's not that," Fatima said. "It's just ... there's really nothing of interest to see at night."

"Perhaps I merely wish the exercise of a night ride," Anna said, with an expression that made clear no further explanation would be forthcoming.

"I didn't want to have to say this," Fatima said, "but there's been an attempt on another ambassador's life tonight."

"Who? What happened?"

"I'm not supposed to say," Fatima said, her eyes glancing over away from the guest areas and to a hallway near the dining rooms.

Now that Anna's attention was that direction, she realized she could hear people moving around down there.

She, herself, had been dining with Edik and Pajari. That had all the *Fomhóraigh* and Du Mak ambassadors in one room. Venusian ambassadors were out of the question. They had no reason to be here tonight.

Perhaps one of the representatives of a Terran nation? Or...

The Fae ambassadors.

"Donal Cuthbert and Rowan MacPherson," Anna said, and from the way Fatima's eyes widened Anna knew she'd guessed correctly.

Those two people Anna had seen going down that one hall. The man had dark hair. The woman's was a fiery red.

Yes. That could've been them.

"What's down that way?" Anna asked, pointing the direction she might've seen Donal Cutbert and Rowan MacPherson walking.

"The orchards and gardens," Fatima said, professional smile back in place. "They're lovely by moonlight, and a much better—"

"The horse," Anna said.

"I'll have to inform port security."

"Then do so." Anna turned and strode toward the bubble. Fifteen minutes would give her enough time to gather a few things, as well as change into something more appropriate for riding.

Not proper riding clothes, of course. No, those would make this little jaunt look less spontaneous.

It had to look spontaneous. In case of witnesses. And she had to go alone.

And if port security tried to object, well, Anna was prepared for that too.

"Edik, there's no need for this," Dola said, as Edik thanked the undines and stepped out of the bubble's cage into the lobby. As he did, water swirled in the bubble tube opposite the one he'd just departed. Someone else going up, no doubt.

"How many people could be staying here?" Edik asked.

Dola stepped in front of him, pawing the marble floor with large, if translucent, shaggy gray paws. He looked up at Edik with cerulean eyes.

"You're overreacting, Edik. If you think something needs to be checked—"

"Dola," Edik said, doing something he rarely did — shifting his speech so that his words could be understood only by his familiar — "Pajari is up to something. Which means that everything here at the Zanzibar is suspect. I need to check on the *Third Son*—"

"The sylphs would've contacted me if there was a problem."

"A problem they understood to be a problem, yes," Edik said, and started walking toward the front desk, crossing the fancy tiles and walking between fancy — and empty — couches. "I want more, though. And I want a link I can trust. I need to talk to someone back home."

Dola had no rejoinder for that as they reached the front desk. Edik paid the front desk woman little attention beyond the fact that her nametag read Fatima.

"How may I help you, Ambassador Captain Barshai?"

"I need a runner right away, please, Fatima."

She frowned and blinked in confusion.

"Edik," Dola prompted, softly, in English.

Edik shook his head, realizing he'd forgotten to switch back to a language the poor woman could understand.

"Excuse me," he said, chagrined. "I require a runner, please, Fatima. At once."

"No, you don't." An authoritative woman's voice, from off to Edik's left. Toward the dining rooms?

Edik turned to see a sight he never enjoyed seeing — an approaching sergeant of the local port security. This one looked as though she'd earned her rank by being tougher and stronger than all other comers.

"There's been an attempt on the lives of two ambassadors tonight," the sergeant said. "And I'm tired of—"

"Who?" Edik said, urgently enough that Dola put a steadying paw on Edik's boot.

The sergeant looked Edik up and down for a moment and said, "You're Ambassador Captain Edik Barshai, and this is Dola. Am I correct?"

"Yes," Edik said, nodding quickly, "now who was attacked? And you said 'attempted.' Was anyone hurt?"

"Well, the two assassins are dead..."

She might've said more, but trailed off when Edik spoke.

"It was Donal Cuthbert." Had to be. Something like that happened, odds were it was happening to Donal. Guy seemed to have been born with a target on his back. "So the other ... Rowan MacPherson?"

"Where were you this evening?"

"At a private dinner upstairs," Edik said, inwardly remembering with a warm feeling that he had no reason to fear the authority of a port security sergeant. "I don't believe I'm at liberty to discuss it. Ambassadorial business."

"Technically," Dola said, pitching his words just for Edik, "I think that's even true."

"You know," the sergeant said with a grimace, "if you all keep fighting this investigation, one of you *will* get killed."

"Is that a threat?"

Edik had no idea who the speaker was of that last question, and he half hoped he never found out.

If *menace* were shaped into a vaguely human form, it would look like that speaker. Skin black as deep space. A bloodred tuxedo, over a shirt so white it seemed to glow.

Cerulean eyes the twins of Dola's, which was even more off-putting to Edik than the impressive broadsword at the ... *man's* side?

No. The faerie's side. Because this guy, he had to be one of those high-end Celtic faeries. The kind Edik had only seen once before, at that ill-fated meeting in Faerie itself.

The sergeant turned and faced the faerie.

"If I threaten you," she said, "you'll know it."

All right. Edik was now impressed enough that he didn't want to cross the sergeant *almost* as much as he didn't want to cross the faerie.

The faerie in red looked Edik over.

"Edik Barshai," he said in a baritone so rich it probably clogged arteries at ten paces. "Captain of the *Third Son*. Initiate in the ways of magic. Ambassador for the Du Mak people."

He turned his attention to Dola, and said something that sounded vaguely like ... Russian? Almost. But not quite...

Dola responded in kind. The faerie nodded. He turned back to the sergeant.

"This man had nothing to do with tonight's assassination attempts, and he represents a power beyond your ken. Let him be about his business."

"But how can I be sure that—"

"*I* am sure. That is all that matters."

"Now look here," the sergeant started, but the faerie spoke over her.

No. That wasn't quite right. He didn't speak any louder. If anything, his voice was softer. But, somehow, his words cut right across hers with an almost physical impact.

"Enough," he said. "I will tolerate no more of your insolence. Return to that dining room, sit and await me. Fatima, provide the ambassador whatever he requires."

The sergeant turned and started walking, all the while shaking her head as though to clear it.

Behind the front desk, Fatima immediately linked for a runner.

The faerie in red turned to Edik and bowed.

"On behalf of the Fae Courts of Winter and Summer, I bid you good evening, Ambassador Barshai."

He spun on his heels and began to stroll soundlessly back toward the dining room. Or maybe that hallway near it. Edik wasn't sure. Either way, he had a more pressing question.

"Dola? Did you sense him using magic? 'Cause I didn't."

Dola shook his head. "I'm not sure he did."

"Do you know who he is?"

"I'm pretty sure that's an inquisitor. Possibly *the* inquisitor. I don't know if the Fae Courts keep more than one."

Edik had to close his eyes to ask his next question.

"Do I want to know why his eyes look like yours?"

"I'm not sure *I* want to know."

"Ambassador Captain Barshai?" Fatima said. "Your runner is waiting out front."

"Thank you," Edik said, and quickly led Dola out the front doors of the Zanzibar.

———

Large, antique glass double doors opened for Fionn, before Donal and Rowan even reached them. Unusual. Most doors, even those spelled to open for humans, wouldn't notice or open for a familiar.

Another time, Donal might've stopped to inspect the spellwork. Right now, he didn't have time.

He and Rowan stepped out into the cool evening air and onto the dark red and umber bricks of a patio large enough to host a party for two hundred. Donal felt a fleeting flicker of amusement that the Zanzibar could, indeed, host a conference dinner out here, before returning his attention to his surroundings.

The sun was down, though traces of it could be seen still purpling the sky above the mountains to the west. The air was mild, rather than the dry of the spaceport, and just cool enough to be noticeable.

The patio near Donal, Fionn, and Rowan was bare of furniture, which struck Donal as odd. Though he could see the usual sorts of hotel furniture surrounding the immense swimming pool, ahead and just to the right.

Off far to the right looked to be a separate building, likely housing the hotel's stables and runners. And likely those of its guests, as well. Certainly it was large enough, and its design was too simple to draw the attention of hotel guests. Rectangular. Spare. Little more than a nod to decoration in the paint job.

Unlike what appeared to a pool house and recreation facility, just past the pool. That building had been designed as a miniature version of the Zanzibar itself, done to maybe a quarter scale...

"Donal," Rowan said. "The gardens and fountains are this way."

She gestured to indicate the nearby, ornate fountains — as though the sound of their trickling water were inobvious — and the orchards and gardens surrounding them in an arc, sweeping from just left of straight ahead to the far left.

"Fionn," Donal said, "have you already checked out the orchards and gardens?"

"Yes," he said. "Unoccupied as of seven minutes, twenty seconds ago."

"Did you investigate that?" Donal pointed to the "pool house."

"I didn't detect any people in it," Fionn said. "What do you ... oh. No. I would've detected the latent magics. Also, the scale is imperfect."

"What?" Rowan asked.

"Sympathetic magic," Donal said, then shook his head. "I'm starting to see enemies everywhere, and that's not useful."

"If they built one replica," Fionn said, "they could build another, more effectively."

"What would be the purpose?" Rowan asked. "If it's spying, then they either they aren't very good at it, or they allowed their own man to be taken captive. As well as allowing an assassination attempt."

"We have only the sergeant's word about Ahmed," Donal said, but before he could continue, another voice chimed in.

"Ahmed has a concussion," the *sidhe* inquisitor said, stepping out of the shadows. "and no scrying was in use anywhere on the ground floor of the hotel this evening. But if you suspect they're using a likeness spell, there's a simple enough way to foil it."

The inquisitor drew his sword, and the magics on that blade were strong enough that, unsheathed, it immediately gave Donal a headache.

Rowan grimaced and stepped behind Donal, fingers rubbing her temples.

"That is a *deighilteoir*," Fionn hissed, his hackles up and teeth bared. "Sheath it, at once."

A separator? If that meant what Donal thought it meant, even the notion was enough to send a chill down his spine.

"The ambassador has raised a valid concern," the inquisitor said. "This is the fastest way to address it. I need but remove a small section of wall—"

"Not much for subtlety, are you?" Morna asked, stepping out of another shadow. She was clad in moonlight and gossamer again, with her long silver hair flowing down behind her.

"Stop it," Donal said, "all of you."

Morna curtsied, and came to stand beside Donal, opposite Fionn, who eased down his hackles and sat back, regarding his master.

The inquisitor merely looked at Donal, as though undecided on his course of action.

Or perhaps unwilling to be seen as taking an order...

"Inquisitor," Donal said politely, "I request that you sheathe your blade for the time being. While I have no doubt it would accomplish the task you have in mind, it would also dismantle any wards keyed through the walls of the hotel, would it not?"

"Of course."

"I would consider that excessive, under the circumstances," Donal said. "Technically, Venus is under Earth jurisdiction, and therefore the ally of the Courts. The Zanzibar is regarded as the gem of Venus. Destroying its wards without clear and present provocation would be an act ill befitting an ally."

"As you say, ambassador," the inquisitor said, and returned his sword — his *deighilteoir*, which Donal wanted to ask Fionn about later — to its scabbard.

"Now," Donal said, addressing everyone in his little group. "Let's find a spot in the orchard where we can talk privately."

THE RUNNER WAS ONE OF THOSE OVERLY LONG TYPES. AS THOUGH EDIK couldn't possibly be comfortable unless there were enough leather seats in the back to sleep a family of twelve.

A little luxury was one thing. Food, for example. Anna had a point about improving the quality of Edik's ingredients, and maybe even his eating someone else's cooking once in a while.

But all this? To take one human and one familiar to the spaceport?

It just seemed silly.

It did the job though, carrying Edik and Dola rapidly through the dusty yellow streets of Gilgamesh by starlight.

And it was by starlight. The sun was down, and it seemed the locals didn't bother lighting the streets in the "downtown" area. What few horse riders there were carried their own lights. The two other runners Edik saw along the way emitted a ghostly, blue-white glow to light their way. Much like the one he rode in.

Fortunately, it was not a long trip. Edik had hardly had time to grouse about any of this verbally to Dola before the runner came to a stop alongside Edik's beloved *Third Son*, ringed by red light, to mark his assigned landing circle.

Edik flung the door open and hopped out of the runner and into the shadows of a cool, early evening, Dola right behind him.

He was immediately met by the scent of the air — citrus, and something green and grassy. The Zanzibar must've filtered out that smell without Edik's even realizing it, because it wasn't a strong odor, but he couldn't stop noticing it.

He turned to the driver, a heavy man, somewhere in middle age, who stood there staring and Edik. Perhaps surprised that Edik hadn't waited for him to open the door.

"Would you..." Edik shook his head. "Excuse me. I didn't get your name."

"Jamal, sir."

"Would you mind waiting for me, Jamal? I might be as long as half an hour."

"Of course, sir. I'll just head over to the port cafeteria for a snack, so you can have some privacy. I'll check on you soon."

Privacy?

Dola cleared his throat, pitching the sound just for Edik.

Edik spun around, hand on the hilt of his saber.

It was Pajari's blonde serving girl. Dressed for the temperature, at least, in jeans and a properly buttoned-up, long-sleeved felt shirt of dark blue.

She had her hands in the air, and was staring wide-eyed as Edik's sword hand.

Edik eased his hand away from his hilt, and raised his hands to show that they were empty.

"Can I trust you?" she asked, and her voice was deeper than Edik expected. Smoky, was the word that came to mind.

"I was just wondering the same thing, and I don't even know your name."

"Samantha," she said. "Samantha Lawrence."

"Well, Ms. Lawrence," Edik said, "I'm not sure how—"

"Can we talk aboard your ship?"

"I'll keep an eye on her, Edik," Dola said, keeping his words for Edik's ears only.

"All right," he said, and had Dola distract her while Edik unlocked the hatch and opened it. No reason for her to know the passcode, or the proper spot to place her hand. She didn't appear to be trained in magic, and likely couldn't overcome his wards to make the hatch open without his permission, but she could always pass the information along to another...

He led Lawrence inside, with Dola following. He offered her her choice of the passenger seats in the main cabin. She took the first chair, starboard side. The large brown leather chair almost seemed to engulf her.

Odd, that. She was almost exactly Anna's size, but Anna never seemed too small for those chairs...

Edik closed the hatch, but didn't lock it.

"Nixia," he said, "lights, if you would."

Nixia didn't make an appearance. Just told the fire elementals to light the cabin, and they did, with golden light shining down from the red tail feather mural, dominating the gold ceiling.

Lawrence looked about, fascinated most by the mural and the comfort of her chair, which seemed to surprise her.

"If what you need is a job," Edik said, "I can—"

"We can talk about that later, maybe," she said, then drew a deep breath and let it out in a long sigh. She shook her head as though unsure about what she was about to do. "I need to trust someone, and you're all I've got. I..."

"What's going on?" Edik asked, sitting in a chair across from her, and leaning forward, but not too close.

"My job for Pajari was a cover," she said. "I've actually been working for Natalia Romanova for the last five years."

Edik frowned, unsure whether or not this really surprised him. On the one hand, he'd never even considered the possibility. On the other, planting a woman like her in Pajari's employ sounded exactly like something Romanova would do.

Even more surprising was the length of time. Edik had been certain she couldn't have been older than eighteen or so, but clearly she just looked young for her age.

She didn't wait for Edik to comment on any of this.

"Obviously I've been spying for her. Feeding her whatever I've been able to learn about Pajari's plans." She sighed again and shook her head. "Not as much as I'd hoped. For a man who acts as though he doesn't notice his servants, he's surprisingly tight-lipped a lot of the time, and careful with his paperwork."

"Even when he's drinking?"

"Especially when he's drinking. Makes him a little paranoid." She cleared her throat. "Anyway, even with everything going on about the Du Mak and the move for Lunar independence, Romanova didn't care about any of that."

"At all?" Dola asked.

"Well," Lawrence equivocated, "it wasn't that she didn't want to hear about those things. It was more that she kept pushing for information about what he was doing on the corporate front. What his businesses and business contacts were up to."

Edik frowned. "Why would—"

"I don't know," she said. "Maybe she thinks it's a clue to his real intentions, since those are the things that affect his money."

She shrugged.

"Maybe," Edik started, but Lawrence spoke over him.

"Maybe she doesn't care about the rest of it, but I care. I'm worried that humans are going to get caught in the crossfire between all these ancient powers."

She reached out and grabbed Edik's hand.

"That's why I had to come to you. You're another ambassador for the Du Mak, right? You can affect all this, right?"

Edik scoffed without thinking. Yeah, he was an ambassador, but this sounded way above his weight class.

"I'm mostly trying to help the Du Mak—"

"Find a homeworld, right? Negotiate with Venus, along with Pajari?"

Edik nodded.

"If he wants to negotiate with Venus, then why has he left planet?"

"What?" Edik was on his feet before he knew it. "Dola."

"On it," Dola said and darted out through the hull.

"He left fifteen minutes ago. I'm supposed to be on the ship with him, but I found an excuse to head to the ship early. To 'help prepare.' I talked the flight plan out of the pilot, and cut and run. Didn't even take time to pack a bag."

"How did you know to wait for me here?"

"I didn't. I've been hiding in the shadow of your ship until I was sure Pajari was gone. I was about to go hire a runner when yours came up."

Dola came back in through the hull. "He lifted off ten minutes ago. Had to assert ambassadorial privilege to do it. Officially he's head back to Luna."

"He's not," Lawrence said. "But I know where he's going."

"Nixia," Edik said, "prep the ship for liftoff, and inform the port that we, too, are asserting ambassadorial privilege on behalf of the Du Mak."

Nixia swirled past in a whorl of yellow. "At once, Edik."

"Dola, go tell Jamal I won't be needing a lift back. Ask him to have the front desk pack my things and hold them for me."

"Will do," Dola said, and zipped out again through the hull.

Edik turned to Lawrence. "I need those coordinates. You can stay—"

"You're taking me with you," she said, fire in her eyes now. "That's the deal. Just coming to you I've burnt my bridges with Pajari *and* Romanova. I'll need help when all this is over, and right now the safest place for me is on a moving helioship."

Edik frowned, uncertain how far he could trust her. Dola came back in.

"Handled," he said. Then looked back and forth between Edik and Lawrence.

Edik nodded.

"Come on, then," he said, leading Dola and her onto the bridge. While Edik assumed his captain's station, Dola directed her to the guest chair.

Nixia was waiting above the controls, ten-centimeters of yellow excitement, with orange eyes.

"Port authority has sent your safe route out of the reef," she said. "The ship is ready for liftoff, and Xincapph will be ready for speed by the time we clear the atmosphere."

"Thank you, Nixia," Edik said, reaching for the controls to lift off. Frowning, he shook his head.

"Take her up," he said to Nixia, then selected the right strand of blue light from the communications web to link the Zanzibar.

Only a moment later, Fatima's head appeared in the air above those blue, glowing strands.

"Yes, Ambassador Captain Barshai? How may I be of assistance?"

"Please give a message to Anna Lukyanova for me."

"Of course, sir. What's the message?"

"Ivan Tsarevich will return."

"Sir?"

"She'll understand. Thank you, Fatima."

Edik cut the link and turned to Lawrence. "I need those coordinates now."

She gave them. Edik plotted the course. It sounded closer than he expected. Only a dozen decans from Venus. In fact, it sounded...

Edik looked at the phantasmal display of star charts showing his route, and paled.

Pajari was leading them straight into the middle of the zuglodon hunting grounds.

DONAL QUICKLY FOUND A SPOT AMONG THE BLOSSOMING CHERRY TREES and brought his little party to a halt. A cool breeze had kicked up, almost wet from the many nearby fountains.

The absence of a moon in the sky felt wrong to Donal. Unnatural, even though he knew well that Venus had no moon. At least, there was more than enough ghostly, blue-white light from nearby globes staked into the ground along the path, and warmer light from the Zanzibar itself, scarcely a hundred meters away.

The inquisitor snapped his fingers, and a ring of toadstools sprang up, surrounding the five of them: Donal, Fionn, Rowan, Morna and the inquisitor.

"You may speak freely within the ring, and none this side of the mounds will hear your words."

Of course, that also meant that there would be listeners in Faerie, but anything he said around the inquisitor would likely be reported to the queens anyway.

Donal's first question was almost for Morna, but he realized she hadn't done any teasing or flirting since her arrival. She hadn't even leaned toward him, or tried to touch him.

That ... felt like a message. A way of telling Donal she knew something, but was being wary around the inquisitor.

So Donal started with him.

"You said that Ahmed has a concussion," Donal said. "What else have you learned about the assassination attempts?"

The inquisitor frowned, as though uncertain he should answer. Or perhaps merely uncertain he answered to Donal.

How could he explain this in terms the inquisitor would accept?

"I am the one under attack," Donal said. "Not the queens. Not the peers. Me. And I will not stand for it, nor stand by while others fight for me. So either tell me what you know or be on your way."

The inquisitor nodded.

"The local authorities are short-sighted and inept," he said. "Much as the local human authorities are everywhere this investigation has taken me. But they are humans, and this is to be expected."

Donal bit the inside of his cheek to resist rising to the slight on himself and his fellow humans. In fact, he slipped his mind into light meditation, only just enough to increase his focus. He couldn't afford a slipup. Not now. Not with half of him still reeling from the death of that big, blonde assassin.

A death at Donal's hands.

The inquisitor seemed to notice what Donal had done, and nodded approval. One eyebrow even rose, as though reassessing Donal.

"The assassins had been on planet for a week, posing as Terran Naval spacemen, assigned to dock work for the coming six weeks."

"Why would... Supply runs for the colonists?"

"Just so," the inquisitor said. "Their orders were forged, of course."

"But authentication would..." Donal started, then snorted. "Let me guess. Since Gilgamesh doesn't have their own authentication set up, they haven't budgeted for authenticators."

"Just so," the inquisitor said again, and he seemed to improve his assessment of Donal. "But a simple matter for me to determine."

"Wait," Donal said. "Who's in charge of naval personnel here in Gilgamesh? They've got to be in on it."

"Lieutenant Orson Dench," Morna said, "assigned this post as a punishment for 'administrative errors' while serving in the Mars supply chain."

"Have either of you reported him to his superiors?" Donal asked.

The inquisitor shook his head once, with a droll expression. As though of course human concerns were beneath him.

"I wished to inform you first, master," Morna said, sounding a touch more like herself. But her body language made it clear that she was still restraining herself around the inquisitor.

Why was that?

And why was Morna not dressed in her stealthy garb, as she'd been before?

A glance told Donal that Fionn had noticed the same things.

"The assassins came from Earth?" Rowan asked

"Directly," the inquisitor said. "Which is where I am bound now. I believe I shall have all the necessary answers and be ready to take action by sunset tomorrow."

He looked at Donal. Raised one eyebrow. "I am not, of course, required to issue a report to you, nor seek your permission to carry out judgment."

Donal gave the notion a dismissive wave. He never expected otherwise.

The inquisitor nodded, once, decisively. "However. I respect your position on the matter. If the queens permit it, and I expect they will, I will allow you to be present when judgment is carried out."

"I look forward to justice being done, inquisitor," Donal said with a respectful bow.

The inquisitor vanished into the ground beneath him, taking the ring of toadstools with him.

"Fionn, check the wards on my room, if you would," Donal said.

"Of course, master," Fionn said, and darted away through the air.

"You handled him well," Rowan said. "But I'm surprised he didn't stay to ask any questions of his own."

"He doesn't think you could find out anything that he doesn't already know," Morna said, giving Donal a smile. "But he underestimates your resources."

Donal had to chuckle at that, since, on this matter, Morna herself was Donal's best resource. No wonder she was not dressed as an investigator.

"Intact and untested, master," Fionn said. "Shall we adjourn into their safety?"

Donal led the way back into the Zanzibar, up the bubble and into the ridiculously oversized master bath in his suite.

Morna immediately began to disrobe.

"No need for that," Donal said quickly, before she'd managed to uncover more than a shoulder. Not that her outfit left much to the imagination.

"We're going to let that magnificent tub go to waste?" Morna lamented. "It has over a *hundred jets*."

Rowan rolled her eyes.

"We're in this room," Donal said, "because it's the only room without even a slap-pad for a link. Most secure place to have a conversation."

"But slap-pads have to be activated," Rowan said.

"Which keeps their link from crossing wards unless triggered from the inside," Donal said, impressed that she knew what that meant for wards. "Normally. But the magic here on Venus is a little strange, and I haven't taken time to investigate the spells on the slap-pad to see what they've done differently to account for local factors. They might have slipped something else in."

This room has a mirror, Fionn said, directly to Donal's mind.

"Wait," Donal said. "I want to get out of these clothes. They still feel like death. We can discuss this while I change."

Morna was practically bouncing as she, Rowan, and Fionn

followed Donal back into the bedroom, and from there into the over-sized walk-in closet.

Donal'd only used a handful of its dozens of hangers. He hadn't used the large, oaken chest of drawers at all.

But even the closet had a mirror, full-length, affixed to the inside of the closet door.

Donal sighed as he noticed it.

"Oh," Rowan and Morna said at once.

They looked at each other, and for a moment Donal thought they could talk mind-to-mind as easily as he and Fionn could.

"No cheating and looking in the mirror," Morna said. "You agreed to let us dress you."

"It's for the best," Rowan said. "The opinions of two women are worth much more than one mirror."

"I'll just remove it, so you won't be tempted to sneak a peek," Morna said, and with a bare fillip of fae magic she removed the mirror. "We know best."

She placed the mirror in the bedroom, leaning against the far wall, then returned to the closet, closing the door behind her.

"Thank you, Morna," Donal said. "And now I'm quite eager to hear what you've learned."

Morna brightened immediately, and knelt on the soft carpet before Donal, tilting her head slightly forward so she could look up at him with just her eyes.

"Master," she said, emphasizing the word more than Donal liked, "I am pleased to report that the inquisitor is following the wrong lead. I estimate he will require three days to find the culprits, rather than the one day he expects."

"Don't underestimate him," Fionn warned.

"Why does that please you?" Rowan asked, her posture teeming with irritation at the *leannan sidhe's* ... blatancy.

Morna never turned her eyes from Donal.

"Because I already have the answers he seeks." She gave Donal a smile as though they were sharing a secret. "The thread the inquisitor traces will lead him to Robert Drake, a regional manager for Aetheric Dynamics, whose territory includes all of Earth."

"He's one of the four you mentioned before?"

"He is," Morna said, sounding pleased that Donal remembered her previous report. "He is also one of two highly placed members of Aetheric Dynamics who are also members of the organization known to us as the Consortium."

"The Consortium *is* behind the assassinations then?"

"They are. Robert Drake ordered the attempts here and in Washington D.C."

"So he's the one we want?"

"I agree he must be punished," Morna said, "but he was following the orders of another. One of the three founding and ruling members of the Consortium."

"Not dramatic enough if she just comes out and says it, I suppose," Rowan muttered.

"Rasputin Pajari," Morna said, ignoring Rowan.

"Who are the other two founding members?" Fionn asked, while Donal considered the implications of the revelation.

"One is Felix Klemperer, whose family provided a great deal of the funding for the settlements here on Venus. The other is Lars Nicholson, of Zeus Industries."

"Zeus Industries," Donal said with a frown. "There was a Nicholson from Zeus Industries on Ganymede."

"That was him," Morna said with another smile. "He does not speak fondly of you, I should add."

"And Felix Klemperer..." Donal added. "I know that name..."

"Donatello Mancuso," Fionn said, "has complained about Felix Klemperer several times. They seem to have a history."

"Klemperer does not know or care about you," Morna said, "save that you are important to Donatello Mancuso, whom he hates. Klemperer was the one who wanted you to kill Mancuso aboard the *Horizon Cusp*."

"So he sent that assassin after me? In San Francisco?"

"The assignment was to punish you. Your death was optional."

"Kind of him," Rowan muttered darkly.

"After you outmaneuvered Nicholson on Ganymede, he wanted you assassinated. He was outvoted. But after the meeting where the *Fomhóraigh* revealed themselves, Pajari reconsidered. He recently changed his vote, and gave the go ahead to Drake."

"So Pajari started moving directly against me *after* taking up the post of ambassador for the Du Mak?"

"That's correct, master," Morna said. "May I kill the three of them for their insolence? Or shall I leave Drake for the inquisitor and deal with the other two myself?"

Morna's tone as she said that was disturbingly close to the tone she used when trying to seduce Donal.

"Remember, master," Fionn advised, in words pitched only for Donal's ears, "the queens will insist on the deaths of all three. And don't think that the inquisitor will miss any of them, given time."

Unbelievable. Donal had already caused the death of one person tonight. In self-defense, true, but still. And now he was being asked to sanction the deaths of three others.

"I'm not sure I'm cut out for this," Donal said. He felt numb as he leaned back against the wide, oak bureau at the back of the closet. "Negotiations are one thing. But this..."

"Is necessary," Morna said.

"I hate to agree with her," Rowan said, "but they're not going to stop until you make them."

"If you allow your enemies to strike with impunity," Morna said, her tone imploring now without even a hint of sexuality, "eventually they will find their mark."

It was close tonight, Fionn said, directly to Donal's mind. *You are brilliant, and you are good, but if there were a third assassin, you would be dead.*

"Everybody stop," Donal said, hands coming up. He sighed. His mother had warned him that there would be a price for working with the fae. He'd thought only in terms of deals and debts.

He'd thought he was so clever. He'd actually believed he could spend a year and a day working for the Fae Courts, and emerge unscathed.

"I've been a fool," Donal muttered.

"No," Fionn insisted, in words all present could understand. "You are a good man, seeking a path among evil choices while trying to bring good to all sides."

"You could let the inquisitor handle it," Rowan said softly. "It's his job. Not yours."

"And how will it be taken by the Courts," Donal asked, wearily, "if I take no action myself?"

Fionn let his ears droop.

"It will be taken as weakness," he admitted.

"The peers will move to control you," Morna added. "And the queens will likely let them."

Rowan turned away, her eyes shining with tears.

"Rowan," Donal said softly.

"I'm sorry," she said, still looking away. "I got you into this."

"You did what you had to," Donal said, then sighed deeply. "And so will I."

"Then I may kill them?" Morna asked, gleefully.

"This is my decision," Donal said, rubbing a spot between his eyebrows that ached profoundly at the choices he was making.

Even Rowan turned back to see what Donal would do. Tears lined her cheeks.

"Nicholson has clearly wanted me dead for a long time. And he's going to keep coming." Donal reached out and stroked Morna's cheek. "When you leave here, you are to kill him."

"Thank you, master!" Morna said, shivering with pleasure.

"Do it quickly. Do not torture him first. But there should be no doubt that he was murdered, and I don't mind if it's obvious that he was killed by a representative of the Courts."

"Are you sure?" Fionn asked.

"Yes," Donal said. "The queens will need to know I was behind his death, and the politics ... we'll have to sort that out later."

He turned back to Morna.

"When you are done with Nicholson, you are to intercept the inquisitor. Explain Drake's role and the roles of Nicholson and Pajari. Tell him that, at my instruction, you have already handled Nicholson, but that Drake's life is a gift from me to the queens. "

"And Pajari?" Morna asked.

"You will tell the inquisitor that I require time to determine whether Pajari acted on his own, or at the instruction of Hrissapkuss of the Du Mak."

Donal shook his head. "If the latter, then this is a declaration of war against the Courts."

RIDING WAS SUCH A JOY THAT ANNA ALMOST FORGOT ABOUT PAJARI AND his slights. The night was glorious. Chilly, but not cold. Not with her wearing a mimic of Edik's spacer garb. Black pants with many pockets, tall black boots, and a strong, black cotton blouse.

Her father would've been scandalized, to see her riding without proper riding clothes. But at least he would've approved of the horse. A beautiful, speckled gray Arabian gelding named Stormcloud.

Very responsive. Especially after Anna had applied the salve Nalacha gave her, between Stormcloud's eyes. Nalacha had said only that it would aid the horse in seeing, regardless of extant light, but Anna wondered if there was also a calming agent.

The horse might've been able to see as though it were daytime, but the horse was still out riding at night, with a stranger. He'd seemed less certain about that before she'd applied the salve, back outside the Zanzibar.

After she'd applied the salve, though, he'd been more than ready to follow Anna's lead down the long driveway, and then to the north.

They'd left the road immediately, riding instead across hard-packed yellow dirt whose dust would no doubt cling to her pants later. But there was a time and a place to get dirty. And she wasn't expecting to meet anyone who'd care about the state of her clothes.

Gilgamesh proper ended just shy of the Zanzibar, so when Anna and Stormcloud turned to the north, all the alchemiblock buildings were off to her right.

The citrus and clover taste to the air was stronger again, without the Zanzibar's influence to mitigate it, but that just added to the joy of the ride. As though Anna were riding among green hills after a refreshing taste of lemonade, rather than slightly dry-mouthed among the low foothills of Venus.

Strangely enough, this was all inside of Gilgamesh's barrier. Kilometers outside of the settlement. She'd have to remember to ask later, if they set the Barrier so far back to prepare they way for expansion.

She leaned forward in the saddle, pulse racing nearly as fast as the drumming of Stormcloud's hooves. The night was dark, but she dare not raise a light too soon. She couldn't risk anyone following her.

There'd been members of Gilgamesh Port Security milling about when she left. But they'd had the sense to bow to her authority, and she was fairly certain none were following her.

But it was too soon to test that theory.

Besides. Her eyes were adjusting to the gloom. Enough that she was thinking she'd soon reach the point of her first turn. She was told to turn when she saw the larger hill with the great, jagged rock.

Was that it?

Stormcloud began turning. Before Anna signaled with the reins.

Disquiet creeped up the back of her neck. She tried to turn the horse back toward that larger hill. She wanted to make sure that this was the jagged rock Nalacha had described to her.

Stormcloud ignored her command.

She tried again. Then tried turning him right.

Nothing.

She jerked the reins hard enough that he shouldn't just have halted. He should've reared, whinnying complaints.

Stormcloud only snorted and sped up.

The salve. Nalacha hadn't trusted Anna to even follow his directions. His salve was leading Stormcloud to where he wanted Anna.

This was not the first time that Anna faced the notion that Nalacha didn't want a competent ambassador. He wanted a puppet.

And yet, without her help back on Luna, back when the *Fomhóraigh* still hid themselves as the rocklike Rhian, they would have fallen prey to one of the great families. Or to the government. Or possibly to university experiments.

And this was the gratitude they showed her? To not trust her so far as she could *ride a horse*?

This was too much. She'd felt responsible for them for too long, and they'd been taking blatant advantage of her.

Nalacha would answer for this, or he would see how well he fared without an ambassador.

Anna forced herself to relax in the saddle. She stopped worrying about directions and landmarks. Clearly the horse knew where he was going.

And if things went badly when she got there, if she had to find her way back on her own, well, she would manage. After all, the Zanzibar lit up the night like a tiny moon. How hard could it be to find?

And she wore good boots for a long hike. If necessary.

She rode on through the hills for a time, before Stormcloud turned sharply to east by northeast.

Overcome by curiosity, Anna pulled out her small lantern. She'd mixed the reagents herself, and smiled when she shook the lantern to break the separator. The formula mixed in the glass bell of the lantern, and light shined out brightly ahead of her.

The sloping hillside was bathed in blue-white radiance.

Ahead of her she saw the landmark she'd expected for her destination — a wide, flat, red-orange rock surrounded by three smaller, rounder cousins.

But Nalacha had said nothing of that small forest behind it.

She could not see them clearly, but they had to be that new breed of trees. Acacias, mixed with Greek strawberry, and something else. Willow, perhaps, since she thought the were reaching for the ground, as willows did.

What did they call those trees?

Oh, yes. Huluppu.

But then Anna saw something she didn't expect.

Movement among the shadows.

Someone was waiting for her.

MEDITATION. ONE THING DONAL HAD BEEN LEARNING AS HE GOT further in his study of thaumaturgy, was that meditation took on many forms.

It didn't serve only to clear the mind, or to prepare the way for shifts of awareness, or even to facilitate magic.

The meditation skills Donal had developed were all that kept him together and moving at a time when all he really wanted to do was collapse.

Too much had happened tonight.

The assassination attempt. His killing of the one assassin. And now his direct ordering of the death of another human being.

Yes, it was a man who had tried to have Donal killed before, and would do so again.

Yes, it was a man whose death would be mandated by the queens.

Yes, if he did not order Morna to kill that man, Donal would end up fighting a two-front war, with one front being the very courts he'd agreed to serve.

He had still ordered the death of another human being. And he would need to deal with that.

Lars Nicholson. Donal would remember that name.

But he could not afford to get caught up in such thoughts. Not now.

"All right," Donal said, leading Fionn and Rowan toward the closet door.

Rowan put her hand on the door to keep Donal from opening it.

"You said you were changing your clothes," she reminded him.

"What does that matter now?" Donal asked.

"She's right," Fionn said, his fur disgruntled with concern. "If you don't change them now, her grace will see you from another mirror and know with certainty that you deliberately hid information from her. It may change her approach."

"Very well," Donal said. He turned to his hangers.

"Ah, ah," Rowan said, with a sad smile. "You said you'd let Morna and me select your outfit."

She looked over Donal's selection and quickly said, "The kilt."

"You're joking," Donal said, but she wasn't. Rowan took down the full kilt made for Donal by Morna, in a blue and black tartan pattern she designed for him herself.

Rowan handed it to him.

"Wear it over that pale blue airsilk shirt you're fond of. Black socks. Skip the tam though."

Well, at least she didn't want him to wear the hat. But still...

"Why—"

"Donal," Rowan said, looking every bit as serious as he'd ever seen her, "your enemies have attacked you tonight. If we're going to confront them, you need to dress for power. For confidence."

"Morna would agree with the choice," Fionn said, "and I suspect for much the same reason."

"Morna would add something about the way my legs look in a kilt," Donal said, with a sigh.

"And she'd be right," Rowan said, sad smile back in place. "But that's not why you should wear it."

Rowan turned her back so Donal could have something like privacy to change. He'd worn a full kilt enough times over the years that he didn't need long.

He refused to admit it aloud, but he did feel more confident and powerful dressed this way.

As he opened the door, Rowan called over her shoulder, "Ta, Morna. Don't have too much fun now."

Donal led Rowan and Fionn out of the master closet and bedroom in silence.

"All right," he said again, as they passed through the mirrorless meeting room. "We need to talk to Edik, and then Pajari. And we may need to talk to Anna Lukyanova, too. Rowan, do you want to stick with me? Or maybe you should go talk to Anna Lukyanova while I handle—"

"I don't think we should split up right now," she said. "If they make another attempt tonight..."

"Fair enough," Donal said, as they passed through the lounge. "Fionn, much as I'd love to have you track Edik down, I think I need to keep you by my side for the same reason."

"Agreed," Fionn said. He stopped walking. His ears twitched. "There is someone approaching the door."

Donal slipped his tuning fork from up his sleeve and into his right hand. He'd had a little time to think about how he'd mishandled that fight with the assassin, and had ideas about what he should've done differently.

Rowan stepped to one side, and glamour began to sparkle in the air about her.

With his left hand, Donal clasped the doorknob.

"Ready," Rowan whispered.

He whipped open the door.

Ezekiel Collins stood in the doorway, fist raised to knock.

"Oh!" he said, and stumbled back a step, his hands coming up quickly as though to surrender. "If you're looking for trouble, I'm not your guy. I swear."

Mr. Collins was dressed in the same casual outfit he'd worn at dinner, though he looked rumpled and tired now.

"What can I do for you, Mr. Collins?" Donal asked warily.

"Not Mr. Collins," he said. "Please. Let me be Ezekiel for at least a few more minutes."

Another informal visit?

Donal frowned, but nodded, then took Ezekiel's hand and led him in through the wards.

Ezekiel took in Fionn's guard dog stance, and Rowan's ready posture. The air no longer sparkled about her, but Donal could feel her magics ready all the same.

"Would you care to sit, Ezekiel?" Donal asked, not yet ready to put his tuning fork away.

"No," Ezekiel said, shaking his head. He sighed. "Look. I don't know exactly what's going on. But before we go any further, I want you to know that I had nothing to do with those killers tonight."

"I know," Donal said.

"Good," Ezekiel said with a small smile, "because that's not exactly something easy to prove." He shifted as though his shoulders unknotted a little. "I'm not here in any official capacity, because officially I'm not sure I should say anything. But personally, I like you guys."

"Say anything about what?" Rowan asked.

"When port security *finally* let me go, I went back to my suite." He looked about. "It's not as nice as yours, but it does have ... that."

Ezekiel pointed to the divan positioned before the scrying window.

"You saw something through the scrying window?"

Ezekiel nodded. "And it's something you need to see."

7

OF EDIK'S MANY SOURCES OF FRUSTRATION, SOMEHOW ROGER NORTH managed to continue to keep himself at the top of the list.

Even now, while Edik flew into the dangerous space of a known zugoldon hunting ground, North was haranguing him from the link, instead of answering even the simplest of questions.

"...*and that means you left her alone on* Venus, *ya damned fool! What the hell were you thinking? I should—*"

"SHUT UP!" Edik roared, turning from his golden controls for pitch, roll and yaw to focus for a moment on North's ugly, craggy face, with his stupid bushy black beard and hair.

"I have never met a woman more capable of handling herself than Anna," Edik said, before honesty squeezed an objectionable truth past his lips, "except maybe Romanova."

"And Romanova's on Venus for all you know."

"*That's what I've been trying to find out, you stupid, pathetic excuse for an airship skipper!*"

"*I'm a captain and you know it!*"

"Edik!" Edmund's voice, like a drop of sanity in an ocean of madness. Edmund couldn't get in front of the link to show his face, but he must've been close enough to participate in the ... well, *conversation* was something of an exaggeration.

"Natalia Romanova hasn't been seen—"

"All right," North said, speaking over Edmund. "Guess my point's made. I'll tell ya."

Nothing more from Edmund. Must've wisely retreated.

"Romanova's gone to ground or something. Some say she's off on Mars. Others say Venus. I was hoping you knew."

"Haven't so much as seen one of her ships," Edik said, grimacing as he glanced back at his phantasmal scanner displays. The space near him still looked free of zuglodons. And everything else, for that matter.

Though that might be a tiny blue swirl of a nebula, ten degrees off course to starboard. Nothing to worry about yet.

"'Course," Edik continued, "wouldn't put it past her to get dropped off by a landing shuttle, and have her ship hide on the far side of Venus."

"Does sound like her style," North grumbled. "You're sure Anna's all right?"

"Pretty sure it's just her pride that's been hurt."

"I'll kill that son of a bitch Pajari," North said, and though Edik couldn't see below the man's shoulders, he suspected that North had drawn his cutlass.

"Any word from Carl?"

"Not since he got to Mars."

"So, that's a yes," Edik said. "What's the latest?"

"You know Jones," North grumbled. "Just that he's alive."

"That's something. What's on the news front?"

"Something big," North said, "but the anchors aren't doing more than dropping hints. Maybe Earth will ratify our independence. Lukyanov's certainly all over the shadowcasts."

"What about Mars?" Romanova was up to something. She always was. And if she was letting Lukyanov have this much slack on Luna, then she had to be focusing all her efforts right now either on Mars or Venus.

"It's a shooting war again. Some hoity-toity Martian Hierophant figured out how to use carterite in those alchemical fireballs. S'posed to be pretty nasty."

"Romanova's probably on Venus, then," Edik said, shaking his head. "A dogfight among a few ships is one thing. A major battle's another. Doubt she'd want to be anywhere near that."

"So she's on Venus," North said, voice full of accusation. Again. "And you've left Anna to deal with her. Alone."

"All right," Edik said, cutting across North's storm front before his winds could build up speed again. "I need to focus on flying. Say hi to Edmund for me. And Carl, if you talk to him."

"All right," North grumbled. "Keep flying, ya pirate."

"You too," Edik said and cut the link.

"What was that?" Lawrence asked, from the passenger seat.

"That was *Skipper* Roger North," Edik said. "My business partner and primary source of irritation."

"Honestly," Dola added, from the deck near Edik's boots, "that was as close to a civil conversation as those two ever really come."

"The other voice you heard," Edik said, "was Edmund McCutcheon, who manages to keep our business together despite us."

"Hope you pay him well," Lawrence said, shaking her head.

"Probably not as well as I should."

"About that job you mentioned…"

"Wouldn't be with us," Edik assured her, throwing a smile over his shoulder. "Wouldn't do that to you. You just left the employ of one lech. Wouldn't sic North on you."

"Thank Christ," she said softly, making Edik chuckle as he turned back to his scanners.

There. A ship shaped like a double-headed eagle. And the scanners read the ship's name…

"Well," Edik said with a smile, "knew we had to be faster than anything as bloated as one of Pajari's cruisers. There's the *Boyar* now. His personal ship."

"If he's in your scanner range," Dola cautioned, "you're likely in his."

"Good point. Get them on the link, would you?"

Dola jumped onto the white ceramic counter beside the communications web and began manipulating links with his paws.

Lawrence cooed, as though she were watching a real cat play with a tangle of yarn.

Edik, in the meantime, pulled his phantasmal red lever from full ahead back to three-quarters speed, matching the pace of the *Boyar*.

"They're refusing the link," Dola said. "Why would they refuse the link?"

"Too late to deny it's them," Edik said, thinking quickly. "Must be on the link with whoever they're meeting..."

The *Boyar* slowed.

"I don't like this, Edik," Dola said.

"Me either," Edik said, slowing to match.

Three more shapes appeared on Edik's scanners. All of them double-headed eagles.

They had Edik surrounded.

ANNA TRIED SLOWING STORMCLOUD AS THEY CAME DOWN THE INCLINE toward the very large, flat, red-orange rock, surrounded by three smaller, rounder cousins.

But Stormcloud took orders only from Nalacha's salve.

At least the horse handled slopes well. He was a good horse. Honestly, Anna would be enjoying the ride more, if she weren't feeling used.

Whoever was waiting for her at the bottom managed to stay out of the blue-white light of her little alchemical lantern, and the light of the stars above wasn't nearly enough to make up the difference. The glimpse she'd gotten before made her think tall and lean. Or maybe slender?

Why stick to the shadows, though?

Probably someone who wanted to make a dramatic entrance.

Or...

Was her mission a lie? Could it be that Nalacha had led her all this way to have her killed? Someone had made an attempt on the lives of Donal Cuthbert and Rowan MacPherson already tonight. Was she next? Was Edik?

She couldn't rule out the possibility. She should've thought to wear a sword.

Stormcloud finally trotted to a halt beside the flat, red-orange rock. Anna could see now that it must've measured a dozen meters long, and half that wide.

She stood on her saddle and stepped directly onto the flat rock. At least she would have the advantage of height, if she could figure out how to use it.

"Ah," a familiar voice said. "I see my little messenger girl comes at last."

Anna's shoulder's clenched, and it was all she could do to keep her fists from doing likewise as she stepped to the edge and looked down on the speaker.

Rasputin Pajari.

He grinned at her like a *vodianoy* in the blue-white light of her lantern.

"I take it I will be receiving no apology from you?" Anna asked while glancing about. He wasn't tall enough or lean enough to have cast the shadow she saw earlier.

"Did you really expect one?" Pajari asked, while looking her over. Anna found herself wishing she'd brought a hooded lantern, so she could be safe from his lecherous gaze. He tutted at her. "Hardly an outfit becoming one so beautiful."

"What are you doing here, Pajari?"

"Awaiting you, of course." He chuckled. "No easy thing it was, to get a message to your Nalacha without involving you. But obviously he received it, and has agreed to meet with us."

"Us?" Anna said, though she knew it was a weak attempt to play for time. "Us" could only include one other.

"*Da*," Pajari said, and he pulled something from his coat. He kept it concealed within his hand, but Anna knew what it was.

It was a rock, given him by Hrissapkuss of the Du Mak. She had a similar rock, given her by Nalacha, when he was still masquerading as Oolaut, of the so-called Rhian people.

Anna had never gotten a straight answer out of Nalacha about why the *Fomhóraigh* had masqueraded as the Rhian. Or, for that matter, what the term "Rhian" meant to the *Fomhóraigh*.

But then, Nalacha had withheld a great many things from Anna.

This, though. This was one step too far.

"You will call your Nalacha," Pajari said, as though it were the most obvious thing in the world, and she was slow for not having done so already. "Then I will call Hrissapkuss. And then, we shall discuss a plan that will be to all our benefits."

"What plan?" she asked, and spared a glance for Stormcloud. The horse seemed dazed, and confused about why he was out here, in the middle of nowhere, instead of in his nice, comfortable stall back at the Zanzibar.

But that meant that the influence of Nalacha's salve had faded. And that could only be to Anna's advantage.

Pajari tutted at her again.

"Please, Anya ... may I call you Anya?"

"You may not," Anna said in her iciest tones, which had been known to frost unwanted suitors at ten paces.

Pajari only gave a considering frown and said, "Too soon. I understand."

Anna was about to say more about why she would never permit a jumped-up thug like Pajari to address her by any kind of affectionate nickname — no matter how traditionally Russian it might be — but she didn't want to get distracted from her main point.

"What is the plan?"

"The plan is not for your ears alone. You ... are too young to appreciate the subtleties of—"

"What would you know of subtlety?"

Pajari gave her a smile that looked more knowing than she liked.

"You might find yourself very surprised, to learn what I know about subtlety," he said. "But to my point, you ... would not appreciate the plan so much as Nalacha would, I believe. I would prefer to voice it for his ears. Not yours."

"You may wish that with all of your black heart," Anna said, "but *I* am the *Fomhóraigh* ambassador. *I* hold the key to summoning them. And *I*, not you, will decide what is worth bringing to them and what is not."

"Unless I am greatly mistaken," Pajari said, apparently untroubled by Anna's tone or opinion of him, "your Nalacha gave you instructions to come to this spot after dinner tonight, and then summon him. Did he not?"

That was exactly what Anna had been told to do. And the fact that Pajari knew it lent credence to the idea that Nalacha was expecting to come here and talk with Hrissapkuss directly.

But Anna saw no reason to admit that to Pajari.

"My instructions included coming here after dinner," Anna said, "but you underestimate the freedom I have to exercise my own discretion. I will hear your plan, and then — and *only* then — will I decide whether or not it is worth bringing to Nalacha."

"The truly beautiful should never be given important diplomatic tasks," Pajari said, shaking his head. "Their beauty enthralls so many that they do not develop their skills properly."

Pajari smiled at her. "That you are lying is only too obvious, to one such as I, who has a great deal more experience, and none of your unfortunate beauty."

"You are—"

"I am *not finished*," Pajari snapped at her. "We both know you are lying. We both know you were instructed to come here and summon Nalacha. And I believe we both know that he will likely kill you painfully if you fail him in a task of this importance."

Anna started to say something else, but Pajari raised a tired hand.

"If you do not know beyond doubt that Nalacha will kill you without hesitation if you fail him, then you are even more naïve than I already think you."

Anna gritted her teeth. He was right, and she knew it. If Anna denied Nalacha the opportunity to negotiate directly with the Du Mak — any faction of the Du Mak — he would kill her and find another who would prove more pliable.

She reached into her pocket for the stone Nalacha once gave her. It was the greenish-gray of the native rock outside the Barrier at Kennedy, back on Luna.

Nalacha had seemed so different then. Poor, desperate Oolaut. In need of her protection. Her advocacy. In need of her.

But since revealing his true self, he'd been only arrogant and presumptive. He'd shown her no respect, nor even consideration.

And now. To reduce her to nothing but a messenger girl. Her. *Anna Lukyanova.*

She would not stand for it.

"Call your master," Pajari said, "and let's get on with this."

Anna gave Pajari a smile filled with all the confidence she'd earned through years of defying her father, her brothers, and everyone who ever tried to tell her what she could and could not do.

"I have no master," she said.

Event the lingering scent of borscht on Edik's bridge failed to bring him comfort right now. Though a bowl would've done him good, after skipping Pajari's dinner.

Not that he had time to eat.

The double-headed eagles might've been slower than the *Third Son*, but there were four of those helioships to his one. And they were coordinating their chase.

Plus, they were armed.

Another great, green fireball soared past the *Third Son*. This one almost close enough to singe the wings.

"Mayday, mayday," Dola called on the general distress link. "This is the *Third Son* calling all ships. We are a diplomatic ship under attack. Repeat. We are a diplomatic ship under attack."

Dola sounded far calmer delivering and repeating that message than Edik would've been. But then, Edik didn't have attention to spare for the link. He was too busy bobbing and weaving his ship, trying desperately to force each one of those double-headed eagles to risk shooting at his fellows, in order to take a shot.

Problem was, they must've fought together before. Or at least they were well-trained. They seemed to be experts at staying just too high or too low to cross each other's lines of fire.

"Damn Pajari anyway," Edik muttered through gritted teeth.

"Is there anything I can do to help?" Lawrence asked from the passenger chair.

"Pray?" Edik asked, diving in a swirling pattern.

Which was closer? Venus? The Terran Naval no fly zone? Either should draw attention from the Terran Navy...

What did it matter? All this action would soon be attracting...

There. Four hundred klicks aft and to port.

A zuglodon. And it wasn't alone. Already two others trickled into scanner range.

Edik's heart, already racing, threatened to rebel. His mouth dried. Fear washed over him.

Zuglodons. The dragons of space. He'd run from a few, on that flight out to Ganymede, with Donal. So he knew what to expect.

Translucent gray, they were, and long. Longer than any ship ever made. Skinny as worms, but bloated in the middle.

And the tentacles. Those horrible tentacles at the head end. Tentacles that could enwrap a ship four times the size of the *Third Son*. Tentacles that could spark with power enough to rip through any wards...

Whatever it was that flared in Edik's chest felt too weak to be hope. But it was definitely an idea. Or at least, as close as he could come to one right now.

"You're not doing what I think you are, are you?" Lawrence asked.

Edik didn't bother answering. He just steered toward the zuglodons and kicked up his speed to full-ahead.

"Aren't those *zuglodons*?" Lawrence asked, disbelief all through her voice. Hell, even Dola's voice almost stumbled as he continued his mayday mantra.

"Yep," Edik said.

The four double-headed eagle ships were moving to pursue, but they took a break from firing.

Edik grinned. He'd read his angles right, spinning his ship along a route that — when their fireballs missed — they'd risk hitting the zuglodons.

"They'll rip us apart," Lawrence said. Her voice sounded weak, as though she was going into shock.

She was the lucky one. Edik was sweating a waterfall while going through most of his body's supply of adrenaline.

But his focus sharpened more than he expected. His entire world narrowed down to those double-headed eagles and the zuglodons. His hands worked the controls as though the ship were an extension of his fingers.

Pajari wanted to kill him? Then Pajari could damn well follow Edik out of the frying pan and into the fire.

Pajari's laughter rang out into the dark, Venusian night, as Anna turned and hustled back across the wide, red-orange rock toward Stormcloud.

If the horse was free of Nalacha's influence, he should respond to her commands again. And though he wouldn't like riding in the dark, her alchemical lantern was good for at least another hour. It would provide more than enough light to ride by...

Just as Anna reached the edge of the rock, Funar — the serving man who'd picked up Anna and Edik at the spaceport — took Stormcloud by the reins and led him out of easy jumping range.

"Funar," Pajari taunted in a loud voice, "our messenger girl thinks she can escape us."

Funar drew his cavalry saber.

Anna drew shallow, citrus and clover breaths.

It was now or nothing.

She drew a small, fragile glass bottle from one of the many pockets in her black, spacer pants and threw it at Funar.

He moved his sword to parry, but wasn't fast enough. The bottle exploded against his chest.

Pinot noir grape smoke engulfed him.

Her sleeping formula worked! He collapsed to the hard, yellow dirt.

Unfortunately, Stormcloud lay down and went to sleep as well. Neither of them would wake. Not for hours. Not even if shaken.

Anna jumped down. Grabbed Funar's cavalry saber. She wasn't used to fighting with a saber, but it was close enough to a sashka that it shouldn't be too different. Felt a little guard-heavy though.

She turned back toward Pajari. He was a heavy man, and no doubt he never did his own fighting...

"You insulted me at dinner tonight," she said, drawing herself straight and holding her head high. "And you insulted me again here. Yet you have shown no contrition. Offered no apology. I have no choice but to challenge you to a duel."

Pajari laughed. "This is not Luna. Venus—"

"We are members of great families, you and I," Anna said. "We are laws unto ourselves."

"True," Pajari said, "but I will not duel you."

"You admit you fear me?" Anna said with a smile.

"I admit I fear marring your beauty," Pajari said, shaking his head. "But we have dallied enough. Call Nalacha, or I will force your hand."

"I will hear..."

Anna didn't bother finishing the sentence. As soon as Pajari realized he wasn't getting his way, he held up his stone and called Hrissapkuss.

The answer came immediately. Hrissapkuss appeared.

He was humanoid, but more lizardlike than manlike in features. Two legs, but four arms, and standing over two meters tall. His smooth skin had diamond patterns in its browns and grays.

He had three black scars running low across his chest, and his lower left arm had been burnt off at the elbow.

A reddish crest flared behind his head, and he spoke in a high, hissing voice as he addressed Pajari.

"Where issss Nalacha? You promisssed me Nalacha."

Pajari, apparently untroubled, pointed at Anna.

"She holds his summoning stone, but she is young and obstinate."

"Force her."

"I would prefer not to mar her beauty, as we discussed."

As they discussed? Were they planning to *give her to Pajari* like a party favor?

"Must I do everything myself?" Hrissapkuss complained.

Anna threw down a smoke formula, clouding the air behind her as she turned to run. She thought briefly of throwing Nalacha's stone with all her might, but that would do no good. Powerful magicians had proven able to sense the stone, so likely Hrissapkuss could as well.

If she threw it, Hrissapkuss would find it, then Pajari would have both.

Instead she threw her only other smoke formula toward the forest, hoping to misdirect her pursuers. She threw her lantern the same direction. Right now its light would only work against her.

Anna's boots beat hard on the yellow dirt as she made her way up the slope. Stumbling every third step or so. Her night vision had been ruined by her lantern.

But she still had the cavalry saber, and she still had her wits. She would escape them. She had to. And if not, she would fight them.

But if she died, she would die her own woman.

"Mayday, mayday," Dola repeated for what felt like the thousandth time on the general distress link. "This is the *Third Son* calling all ships. We are a diplomatic ship under attack. Repeat. We are a diplomatic ship under attack."

One more bowl of borscht. If Edik was really going to die here today, all he really wanted was one more bowl of borscht.

Well, that wasn't quite true. He wanted to see Anna again. And Carl. And Edmund. And hell, even North.

More than anything, he wanted not to die at all. But that was looking less and less likely.

He was doing everything he could. Diving, rolling, spinning, juking. He was pulling every maneuver he knew, and he was pretty sure he'd come up with a few new ones.

But his enemies seemed to be legion.

All four of Pajari's thrice-damned double-headed eagles were still flying, and still firing. Sometimes at the *Third Son*, and sometimes at the zuglodons.

There were eight of the zuglodons now. All of them with their tentacles sparking on the attack.

The *Third Son* had taken two of those fireballs so far, and been nicked by at least four tentacle attacks.

Edik's wards were almost down. Nixia's tiny yellow form was floating above the control console at Edik's captain station, passing more direct orders from him to the elementals, but even Xincapph couldn't seem to get them out of this one.

Poor Xincapph. Whether the *Third Son* went down to a fireball or a tentacle, Edik had no doubt the zuglodons would be feasting on that poor lacuna before long.

Escape was no longer an option. Enemies in all directions. All Edik could do was keep evading. Buying as much time as he could. Maybe, just maybe, the zuglodons would crack open one of Pajari's helioships first. Maybe the zuglodons would frenzy, the double-headed eagles would focus on defending their fellow, and Edik could slip away during the confusion.

Only problem was, their wards were better than Edik's. And his ship was a lot closer to getting cracked open than any of theirs...

Another blazing green alchemical fireball roared across his bow, only just missing because Edik dove on instinct. He was well past thinking about flying at this point.

"Nixia," he asked, "is there anything our salamanders can do about those fireballs?"

"Sorry, Edik," she answered in her breathy voice. "They're too small to shift more than a fraction of that kind of heat."

"Mayday, mayday..." Dola continued, and now Edik could hear desperation in his familiar's voice.

Edik hated that more than anything else. Bad enough that he would die here today. Samantha Lawrence, just behind him, she'd die too, but she was the reason he was here. Her death wouldn't be on him.

At least, from the sound of her steady mumbling, she'd taken his request for prayer seriously.

But the many elementals on his ship? And Dola? They were all counting on Edik to get them through this.

Edik banked hard to port and pitched up ten degrees, barely avoiding the tentacles of an attacking zuglodon. This one smaller than its fellows, but still five times the size of the *Third Son*.

He rolled and whipped back along the length of its body to avoid its tentacles, and almost flew into the path of another fireball.

What would Ivan Tsarevich do?

Ivan Tsarevich wouldn't have gotten himself into this jam in the first place. Or if he did, he would've pulled out some magic he'd found earlier in the adventure. Something given to him, perhaps, by someone he'd helped along the way.

But even though he was an Initiate with more than his share of space certifications, magic was never really Edik's strong suit. And he couldn't think of anything he could do now except keep flying. Keep trying. Keep—

"*Third Son*, this is the *Magellan*." A woman's voice, coming over the distress link like an angel from heaven. Out of the corner of his eye, Edik saw dark skin and beaded dreadlocks. "Sending you a course now."

The phantasmal workstation pinged.

"Received," Dola said, sounding excited. The route showed up on the scanner display to Edik's left. Looked as though they wanted him to dive straight through the pack of zuglodons.

"Are you mad, *Magellan*?" Edik cried. "That's flying down the dragon's throat!"

"Our magician will clear the path."

"Who the hell is your magician?"

"Bran Cuthbert."

Edik blinked. Donal's brother? The famous one?

"Say when, *Magellan*," Dola said, whiskers twitching in a kitty smile.

"Go!"

Edik whirled his ship through a half-loop to align with the *Magellan's* course and shoved the speed lever full-ahead.

Suddenly, all eight of the zuglodons broke off after the double-headed eagles. The timing was such that none of the helioships could bring their weapons to bear against the zuglodons.

They'd probably escape. They were armed and ready. But Edik didn't care.

He followed the *Magellan* to freedom, and the chance to see another day.

He let loose a sigh so deep he worried for a moment that he'd pass out.

"Nixia," he managed, "turn the flying over to Xincapph, if you would."

"Gladly, Edik."

The *Magellan* was leading them back to Venus, which suited Edik just fine. Turned out his rescuer was only maybe twice the size of the *Third Son*, and built to resemble a purple wyvern.

"Wow," Lawrence said, once they were clear of the fighting. Sounded as though Edik wasn't the only one gasping for air.

"Nice praying back there, Ms. Lawrence," Edik said with a chuckle.

"Call me Sam," she said, sounding stunned. "Anyone I face death with gets to call me Sam."

"All right, Sam," Edik said. "Call me Edik. And this, of course, is Dola."

"Pleased to meet you, Sam," Dola added.

A strand of the link web glowed blue. Edik answered it himself.

The head that appeared above the communications web looked disturbingly familiar, but just a little different.

The man had a stronger chin than Donal, with a cleft. But still, the resemblance was remarkable. His eyes were even the same bright shade of blue.

"You must be Bran Cuthbert," Edik said. "I'm—"

"Captain Edik Barshai," Bran said with a smile. Was his voice deeper than Donal's? "Donal's told me a lot about you and your ship."

"How did you control the zuglodons?"

"I didn't so much control them as take advantage of their hunger," Bran said, sounding too much like Donal for Edik's taste. "There's a trick to it, and it requires knowing the right kinds of deceptions, but it works. When there are other food sources conveniently near."

He held up a hand to forestall whatever Edik would say next.

"Is Donal with you?"

Edik shook his head. "He's still on Venus, last I heard. I think someone tried to kill him tonight."

"Not just tonight," Bran said. "Is your ship fast?"

"Believe it."

"Then let's get moving."

Bran cut the link, and Edik turned his attention to flying.

───────

SWEAT CHILLED ON ANNA'S BROW AND DOWN HER BACK. THIS WAS NO mere sweat of effort, caused by her sudden fleeing. She hadn't gotten far enough for that. Barely a quarter of the way up that long, steep rise.

No. The cause of this sweat was the same as the cause of the desperate way she clutched the hilt of her stolen cavalry saber. The same cause as the adrenaline that kept her legs moving, even after that fifth stumble turned her ankle. That kept her panting that too-fresh-tasting air.

Fear.

She was fleeing in the dark, across the surface of Venus. Well outside of Gilgamesh, though not beyond its Barrier, still a towering yellow presence in the distance.

She could only hope her distraction worked. Bought her time. They likely had horses. Or runners. Or—

A dark shape loomed suddenly before her.

A dark shape with four arms, though one was foreshortened by half.

Hrissapkuss.

His honey cake smell made Anna's empty stomach clench. How unfair was it that he smelled like honey cakes?

"Enough of thissss chasssse," he said, and hefted her with two arms. With his maimed, lower left arm he struck her forearm and forced her to drop her sword.

With his upper right hand he clutched her chin.

"You will ssssummon Nalacha," he said.

"I will not," Anna said, mustering all the prideful defiance she could.

Strangely, being caught calmed her. Not in a reassuring way, but in the sense that the number of variables were now reduced.

If this was to be her death, she would face it properly. Even the painful throbbing of her ankle could not deter her now.

"You will summon Nalacha," Hrissapkuss said, "or I will remove your head, and give your summoning stone to Rasputin Pajari."

"*Nyet!*" Pajari called. From the sound of things, he was closing the distance between them on a horse. And from the increasing pale light, he was carrying her lantern. "She is not to be harmed. You agreed."

"An agreement contingent on her summoning Nalacha," Hrissapkuss said, and as the light grew closer, Anna could see too well into those fiery yellow eyes. "You will correct this. Now."

"I am no mere servant to be ordered about," Anna said. "I am ambassador for the *Fomhóraigh*."

"Just sssso," Hrissapkuss said, leaning closer still until their eyes were only centimeters apart. "But I am no mere ambassssador. Nor will I treat with a lesser. Do your job. Ssssummon my equal."

"Your ambassador insulted me gravely at dinner, and again here, then threatened me with that very blade." She pointed to roughly where she thought the cavalry saber had fallen. "I will not risk summoning Nalacha into a similar trap."

"Nalacha expects this summons."

"Nalacha did not instruct me to summon him here," Anna said, stretching the truth to the breaking point. True, she'd been told to call Nalacha, but that had been while standing on the flat red-orange rock, which was well behind her now.

Hrissapkuss applied pressure to Anna's jaw, stretching her neck, just shy of the point of pain.

"Rasputin Pajari, if you have any influence over this one, exert it. Or I will take her head."

"Anna," Pajari pleaded. "Please. Your death will solve nothing. Nalacha will be summoned regardless."

"Then what, Pajari?" Anna asked, every word painful through the Du Mak's grip. "I am to have my mind warped until I agree to become your plaything?"

"Of course not," he said, but she heard the lie in his voice.

But even if she would be allowed to walk away from this, free and her own person, she would not agree to summon Nalacha.

Nalacha had lied and withheld about what she would be doing here. He had lied and withheld about her work as an ambassador from the beginning.

And there was no reason to lie so consistently, unless whatever he planned was against either her interests, or those of Luna, or perhaps even the those of the entire human race.

Perhaps she couldn't stop those plans. But she would no longer help them.

"Kill me then," she said through gritted teeth, "and be done with it."

Perhaps it was only the fluttering of her frantic heartbeat, but Anna imagined she heard hoofbeats. Though they sounded far too far away to help her now.

Suddenly fairy lights danced about, brightening the darkness of evening to the warmth of late afternoon.

"Hrissapkuss of the Du Mak!" That voice. A man's voice, and it sounded familiar. "I am—"

"I know who you are," Hrissapkuss said, releasing Anna and dropping her to the ground and turning his back on her as he faced the newcomers.

Apparently he would only try to murder her without witnesses.

Anna felt a fleeting desire to grab that fallen saber and stab either Hrissapkuss or Pajari. Or both. She fought that urge as Hrissapkuss continued.

"You are Donal Cuthbert and Rowan MacPherson, ambassadors from the Fae Courts."

Sure enough, there they were, astride black horses with coats that glistened like starlight and eyes that glowed like embers. Loping between them came Donal Cuthbert's emerald green fae deerhound, Fionn.

The two Fae Court ambassadors looked ready for a fight. The MacPherson woman in a riding outfit of forest green that made her red hair seem to blaze all the brighter. And Donal Cuthbert, in that kilt, eyes full of fury and voice full of authority.

Anna suddenly found the cold night a good deal warmer.

"This is a private meeting," Pajari said, "and you were not—"

Donal Cuthbert spoke right over him.

"Your ambassador, Rasputin Pajari, is behind two attempts on my life within the past week. Most recently this very evening, not three hours past."

"Lies!" Pajari said. "I will not—"

"I will provide proof, if required," Donal Cuthbert continued, all his attention on Hrissapkuss. "But more importantly, I would know if he acted alone, or if this deed was sanctioned by your faction of the Du Mak."

Anna held her breath. If the Du Mak were behind those attempts, on top of her own near murder…

"No proof issss necessary," Hrissapkuss said. "I hear the truth in your voice."

"No!" Pajari cried. Hrissapkuss silenced him with a gesture and a pulse of magic, though Pajari attempted, without success, to continue speaking.

"I assure you that he acted alone, and without my knowledge or conssssent. Let alone the knowledge or conssssent of the Du Mak people, who do not sssseek war with the Fae Courts."

"Excellent," Donal Cuthbert said. "For the Fae Courts do not seek war with the Du Mak."

"As a gessssture of goodwill, I offer his life to your queens."

"On behalf of the queens, I accept."

Pajari turned and tried to ride away.

Rowan MacPherson set off in pursuit. She caught him quickly, then blew him a kiss that seemed to put him in a daze.

She returned, leading his horse, with Pajari making moon eyes at her, to her evident disgust.

"You are ssssatisfied?"

"On this matter, yes. But so long as we are both here—"

"We will not aid you in your war against the *Fomhóraigh*, unless—"

"We would not ask you to. It was never the intention of the Fae Courts to seek your aid against our ancient enemy. We defeated them before. We will defeat them again."

That was unexpected enough that Anna almost stumbled on her throbbing ankle.

Hrissapkuss tilted his head. Snapped the fingers of several hands.

"And if we desire an ally against the … the faction of our people led by Artissatass?"

Donal Cuthbert chuckled.

"I doubt you would," he said, though Anna was quite certain that was what Hrissapkuss had been about to ask for. "The Fae Courts are famous for the conflicts between our two factions. Winter and Summer have only ceased their endless wars because of two things."

He held up one finger. "The return of the ancient enemy." He held up a second. "The discovery of a potential cousin."

Hrissapkuss said nothing, though he tapped his fingers on his torso in a strange pattern.

"You enjoy your war with the faction led by Artissatass, do you not?"

Hrissapkuss stopped drumming his fingers. "All wars must end."

"Then the joys of war end, and your people become lesser for it. What would Winter be without Summer, or Summer without Winter?"

"What, then, would you asssssk of us?"

"We would remind you that when your people were imprisoned on Ganymede, it was the Fae Courts, not the *Fomhóraigh*, who sent an envoy to aid you. On behalf of the Courts, I personally faced down governmental, corporate, military and scientific leaders to assist your people, while asking nothing in return. Do you acknowledge this?"

Hrissapkuss emitted a series of clicking sounds, but finally said, "I so acknowledge, though I wonder now at the price tag of your assistance."

"You misunderstand," Donal Cuthbert said. "There is no price tag. The Fae Courts sent me to aid you, because you are the first new thing they have encountered in time out of time. They see kinship in you, and wish the chance to get to know your people."

Hrissapkuss clacked his jaw several times. Anna wondered if this was his form of laughter.

"War is contagiousssss. If our people spend time with yourssss, we will be drawn into your war, or you into ours, whether we sssseek to or not."

"Perhaps we are at an impasse?" Rowan MacPherson asked softly.

Donal Cuthbert shook his head.

"Then withdraw from the field," he said. "Your people walk among the planets easily enough. And I imagine that time means as little to the Du Mak as it does to the Fae Courts. Take your people — all your people — and go off into space for a time. Perhaps you could provide us a means of telling you when the war is over."

Hrissapkuss clacked his jaw again. He turned his head and spoke several words that Anna could not understand. He paused then, as though listening.

He could only have been holding a conversation with someone who was not present. And that conversation did not take long.

"Very well," he said at last. "I have sssspoken with Artissatass, and we both agree with this plan."

Hrissapkuss leaned down and without any apparent effort yanked a section of stone out of the hillside. It had to measure three meters long, and no more than a handful of centimeters in width.

He passed his three hands and one stump along its length once, and it became a spear of yellow stone. He turned and threw the spear into the air.

It came down in the center of the flat, orange-red rock, handle pointing straight up.

"I have put on that sssspear a ... what is your word? *Geas*?" When Donal nodded, Hrissapkuss continued. "It may not be drawn from the rock except by the victor in your coming war with the *Fomhóraigh*. Whoever pulls the sssspear will gain the power to contact us wherever we might be."

"And if we avoid the war?" Donal Cuthbert asked.

"I do not believe you will. But if you do, we will see you next when the stars turn."

And with that Hrissapkuss disappeared.

THE FAE LIGHTS THAT ROWAN HAD CREATED FADED INTO THE VENUSIAN night, but the lantern Pajari carried still shed more than enough blue-white light for Donal to see by.

The night was cool, and getting chillier, and tasted almost as though someone had dropped ground clover into a glass of lemonade.

The taste reminded him that he had yet to enjoy a meal tonight.

Rowan had Pajari handled. He gazed at her as though there were nothing more lovely in the universe, and he was too intimidated to do more than bask in her radiance.

Anna Lukyanova, however, was another matter. He'd never seen her like this, and not just because her outfit was so simple, shirt and slacks instead of a dress, and all of it black. She was sweaty and covered in yellow dirt. Her long, golden hair, disheveled, and her right ankle clearly a source of pain.

She'd also been carrying a naked cavalry saber, which lay on the ground at her feet.

She looked as though her night might even have been rougher than Donal's.

He rode up beside her. Offered her a hand.

"May I help you up, Ms. Lukyanova?"

"Please," she said, taking his hand and mounting the fae horse behind him. "Call me Anna. Or ... Anya ... if you like."

"I'm not sure that's a good idea," Donal said. "I represent the Fae Courts, and you—"

"Represent the *Fomhóraigh* no longer," she said.

"Truly?" Donal looked back at her and saw anger seethe in her eyes. She'd definitely had a hard night.

But all she said in response was, "Truly."

"Then please," he said, "call me Donal."

The saddle instantly adjusted to ride two comfortably. He could get used to riding a horse like this one, though he knew he shouldn't. He didn't know if Rowan had paid a price to call these *capall sidhe* forth.

"And call me Rowan, please," Rowan said. "But if I may ask, who now represents the *Fomhóraigh*?"

"No one at the moment," Anna said, sliding her arms around Donal's waist as she settled on the saddle. "I don't care, to be honest. They've lied to me and used me for the last time."

"Shall we go?" Donal asked.

"Well," Anna said, then hesitated. "Pajari's man Funar is asleep down there, thanks to my alchemical mixture. Unfortunately, one of the hotel's horses, Stormcloud, sleeps there for the same reason. They won't wake for quite some time."

"Have you heard of any natural predators out here?" Donal asked, meaning it as a general question.

"No," Rowan said, while Anna added, "None were warned about in the hotel guide to Gilgamesh."

"Shall I check?" Fionn asked.

"It'd be best," Donal said.

Fionn trotted off to do so.

"What became of the rock they gave you?" Donal asked Anna.

She held it up. It pulsed with a magic similar to that of the fae, but somehow different.

"It's yours," she said, "if you want it."

"I think that would be a colossally bad idea," Rowan said.

"I agree," Donal said. He regarded the stone through shifted awareness, unable to resist examining it more closely, while he could. "It shines too brightly to just toss out here though."

He had only a moment of study before Anna put it away again. But in that moment, Donal was able to determine that *Fomhóraigh* magic and fae magic were built off of different foundations. Their similarities came in the early stages of development, after which they forked apart.

Too much and too many subtleties for him to parse them all here and now.

"I'll find something to do with it," Anna said. "Oh, and since I'm no longer their ambassador—"

"If you're about to share a secret," Rowan said, "I want to ask first — have you formally quit?"

"They were going to turn me into a sex toy for Pajari."

"Sounds quit enough for me," Rowan said with a nod. "Go ahead."

"Do you need any help?" Donal asked.

Anna started to deny him, but stopped and sighed. "I don't know."

"If you do," Donal said, "just say the word."

Anna gave him a squeeze that made Rowan lift an eyebrow.

"Thank you," Anna said. "I want to warn you, and the Fae Courts, that the *Fomhóraigh* have some resource they think will give them an edge even against terran warships. I couldn't find out what, though."

Donal considered that, then felt his eyes widen as cold realization washed over him.

Rowan seemed to reach the same conclusion, and spoke first.

"They were always a sea people, and then they were driven into space."

"Zuglodons," Donal said. "Or at the very least, lacunae. They must have figured out some way to tame the mighty elementals of space..."

"No sign of any predators," Fionn said, trotting back up. His ears flattened when he saw the look on Donal and Rowan's faces. Perhaps the look on Anna's face too, Donal couldn't be sure.

"What have I missed?" Fionn asked.

Donal and Rowan looked at each other. He shook his head.

"Nothing we can do anything about here and now," Donal said. "And you confirmed that the man and horse will be safe enough?"

"Horses, plural," Fionn said. "I found a second horse, hobbled near the tree line. But yes, I am confident they will be safe here through the morning."

"Then let's just leave them for now and tell the hotel where to find them when we get back."

To a general chorus of agreement, Donal turned his fae steed and started back toward the Zanzibar.

8

Donal enjoyed the ride back to the Zanzibar more than he would want to admit. He'd never been all that great on horseback, but his fae steed rode so smoothly he felt like a master horseman.

And so silently, both his and Rowan's, that Pajari's horse sounded clumsy by comparison.

So far as Donal could tell, the *capall sidhe* didn't even kick up dust as they rode.

Did feel eerie to ride under a night sky that lacked a moon. The stars were plentiful, but the majority of their light came from the lantern Anna held aloft with one hand.

She'd offered to have Donal call her "Anya." He was pretty sure that was a Russian thing. An increased level of familiarity. But was it just a friendliness thing? Or were there other implications he needed to be aware of?

Would she be offended if he stuck to "Anna" for now? He'd have to hope not. He'd...

Donal steadied himself through a quick breath. He needed to keep his focus, or risk all the events of the evening showering down on him right here and now.

And this was neither the time nor the place.

So Donal kept to his breathing, and focused on the ride back to Gilgamesh and the Zanzibar. It helped that no one else seemed inclined to try talking. Not even Pajari, though he looked as though he kept starting to say something to Rowan, and changing his mind.

He'd probably be free of that charm by sunrise. Donal and Rowan would have to figure out what to do with him before then. Some way of getting him to the queens, along with an explanation.

Thoughts of having to ride off into Faerie to report to the queens were disturbing enough that Donal's focus came close to shattering.

But suddenly Fionn was there, flying backwards through the air while staring into Donal's eyes. The courage in the *cú sidhe's* emerald green eyes brought Donal back and helped him focus once more.

The ride went easier after that. Before long, they left the yellow hills of Venus behind, for the simple wooden construction and alchemiblock buildings of Gilgamesh.

As they approached the marble street that led between rich, beautiful gardens to the front door of the Zanzibar, Donal noted that two figures stood waiting.

Morna and the inquisitor.

Morna was barely dressed once more in moonlight and gossamer. The inquisitor, though, was dressed like a bloody mirror of Donal. He wore a full kilt with a tartan that echoed Donal's, though instead of the shades of blue and black, the inquisitor's was done mainly in bloodred, with its secondary color seeming to be starlight.

That looked like an outfit for issuing a challenge.

It would seem that Morna underestimated the inquisitor, Fionn said, directly to Donal's mind. Donal only nodded in response.

"I would have words with you, Ambassador Cuthbert," the inquisitor said. And despite his aggressive posture and mode of dress, his tone was simple.

"I suspect these are not words for outsiders," Donal said, "but this woman cannot walk. I should—"

The inquisitor clapped his hands, and fae magic pulsed out from him.

"There," the inquisitor said. "Neither she nor the dead man will hear anything other than a variety of Gaelic beyond their comprehension."

Pajari wasn't dead yet, but Donal didn't dispute the point.

"Very well," Donal said. "Proceed, inquisitor."

"Precisely," the inquisitor said, his rich baritone giving his words almost physical presence. "*I* was assigned the task of investigating this matter for the queens. Not you. And certainly not your *leannan sidhe*."

"True. However *I* was the one who was being attacked. Is it the policy of the Courts to take no action when attacked?"

"An attack on you is an attack on the queens. It was for them to meet the attack."

"An attack on me is an attack on the queens. And thus, any response I make is a response from the queens. I fail to see the difficulty."

"You have stolen a kill that was rightfully mine. Lars Nicholson."

"That life was not yours when Morna took it." Donal glanced at Morna for confirmation. She smiled and curtsied, making even that move suggestive. "However, she could have moved on Robert Drake—"

"She could not," the inquisitor said.

"I could have," Morna disputed.

The inquisitor reached for his sword.

"Wait," Donal said quickly.

The inquisitor kept his hand on his hilt, and his posture facing Morna, but his eyes regarded Donal.

"I had already taken the life of Robert Drake when your *leannan sidhe* arrived at his office. She then had the audacity to pretend that Drake's life was your gift to the queens. Do you confirm?"

"I confirm that I told her to say so" — Donal had to hold both hands up then as the inquisitor turned his barely restrained aggression toward Donal — "however, I wish to make this clear. When I gave that instruction, she expected to arrive days ahead of you. She did not."

The inquisitor did not move, which Donal took as his listening.

"If she had arrived well ahead of you, as we expected, then she could easily have taken Drake's life. Do you confirm?"

The inquisitor nodded. Once.

"She was instructed not to do so, but by her presence indicate that she could have. Drake's life would then have been my gift to the queens. I meant nothing more than that."

"Do you acknowledge that this gift is no longer yours to give?"

Morna frowned, but nodded.

"I so acknowledge," Donal said, "and further confirm the accuracy of your investigative work that led to his execution."

The inquisitor relaxed his posture, and eased his hand away from his hilt.

"I see you have Rasputin Pajari under control," he said.

"Rowan and I received direct confirmation from Hrissapkuss of the Du Mak that Pajari acted without the knowledge and consent of the Du Mak, when he sent assassins after me."

"Pity," the inquisitor said. "War with the Du Mak would be interesting."

"Hrissapkuss offers Pajari's life to the queens, as a gesture of goodwill."

"His gift," the inquisitor said, one eyebrow high, "not yours."

That sounded as though it should've been a question, but Donal didn't think it was one.

"Then I believe this inquiry is complete," the inquisitor said. "I have executed one guilty party, you another, and the third I shall bring home as a gift to the queens from Hrissapkuss of the Du Mak."

"That's how I understand it," Donal said, and Rowan confirmed.

The inquisitor smiled then, and that smile was even creepier than his bloodred kilt.

"The queens will ask me how you acquitted yourself," the inquisitor said. "You have nothing to fear from my report."

"You are kind," Donal said.

"Not at all," the inquisitor replied. "A warning, though. You were fortunate this time, but a *leannan sidhe* is a risky investigator. It is true that, when they find the right path, they find it faster than any.

However, betimes they follow connections and inspirations in entirely the wrong direction. You are warned."

The inquisitor then took the reins of Pajari's horse, and he, Pajari, and the horse all melted down into the ground.

"That," Anna said, "was not a man I ever want to meet again."

Donal knew the feeling.

THE ZANZIBAR HAD A COMPETENT DOCTOR ON CALL TWENTY-FOUR hours, and before long, Anna's ankle was wrapped with the right combination of spells and alchemy that would ensure it was better by morning.

That was, assuming she did nothing to make it worse.

What she was supposed to do, of course, was go back to her room and put her foot up while she ate a room service dinner, then go to bed.

She wasn't supposed to get her foot wet, which meant no bath before morning. A truly criminal thought.

Anna was hungry, tired, sweaty and dirty, and she could only do something proper about the first of these.

She ordered up a lamb dish from room service, that was well-spiced and savory, prepared with a selection of vegetables that served as an excellent counterpoint to the meat.

And she treated herself to some honeyed baklava for dessert.

After eating, she hobbled into the bathroom and did the best she could with a washcloth and soap. Her hair ... her hair would simply have to wait.

This was terrible. She would have to present the proper image when she made the links she needed to make. But it couldn't be helped. She would have to make up in presence what she currently lacked in proper grooming.

She made her way into her suite's office and grimaced in distaste as she sat in one roller chair. She considered putting her ankle up on another, but had visions of the chairs rolling away from each other.

Wheels. On chairs. In a conference room. Idiocy.

Alas, though, the links were a waste of time. She could neither reach her father, nor even confirm his whereabouts.

That was troubling. Even more so after she spoke with Roger North and Edmund back on Luna.

Something big was happening back on Luna. Something her father was clearly in the middle of. And she couldn't reach him.

After perhaps an hour in that little conference room, Anna gave up and hobbled back into the lounge, to sprawl on a divan.

She had given up so much to help the Rhian people. But they were a lie. They were the *Fomhóraigh*, and they'd been using her from the beginning.

What did this mean for her now? She had been building her identity on Luna around being the *Fomhóraigh* ambassador, a position she could no longer stomach.

Should she go back to her father? Take up a role in the family business? Certainly she'd accomplished enough to prove that she should be given an important role...

No. She would not place herself under her father's thumb once more.

She would always be a Lukyanova. She would aid the family as she could, but on her terms. Only in ways that aligned with her principles.

As for the rest, she just didn't know yet.

Perhaps she could go to school for alchemy...

Someone knocked on her door.

Anna sighed. Who could possibly be...

What if it was Donal, checking on her? Would she want that? *Should* she want that?

She contemplated this question as she made her way to the door. It almost had to be Donal. Rowan MacPherson was a possibility, but seemed more remote than the idea of Donal coming to check on her. He seemed the type.

If so, she would thank him, but wouldn't invite him in.

She opened the door.

It wasn't Donal.

Edik looked as exhausted as she felt, and so did Dola, for that matter. Even his tail seemed to droop.

Edik dropped his duffle bag and seized Anna in his arms.

"*Mladshaya sestra*! You're all right!"

Anna quickly kicked the door closed behind him.

Mistake. Wrong ankle.

She cried out in pain. Edik misunderstood and let go immediately. Anna tumbled to the floor.

"Anna?" Edik said, aghast, and scooped her up and carried her to the divan. "Are you all right?"

"Just a sprain," she said. "It should be fine by morning." She pointed to his duffle. "What's—"

"Mind if I crash on your couch? I kind of ... offered my suite to someone else."

Anna smiled. Started laughing. Then Edik was laughing too, and Dola perked up once more.

"I think you'd better tell me all about it," Anna said, when she could talk.

"You first," Edik said, pointing to her wrapped ankle.

"All right," Anna said, "but we'll need some tea."

"As long as we're ordering room service..." Edik said with a hopeful smile.

"Get whatever you want," Anna said, feeling better already and knowing one thing for certain.

Whatever she did next, Anna wanted to be on Edik's side again.

DONAL AND ROWAN STOOD IN THE DOORWAY OF HIS SUITE. FIONN HAD already sauntered inside, and now sat, looking back at them.

Rowan looked as though she wanted to come in. Donal didn't want the company. Not just then. He needed time to finally deal with the events of the evening.

Especially the assassin he'd killed, and the death he'd ordered.

Lars Nicholson.

Donal was about to try to explain, but Rowan's body language shifted. Instead of looking as though she wanted to come in, she looked ready to say goodnight.

Could she read his body language as clearly as she expressed thoughts the same way? If so, what else had she learned without his trying to tell her?

"One thing," she said, as though they'd been having a conversation, even though they'd been silent as they'd moved through the hotel.

Donal raised his eyebrows in question.

She switched to Gaelic.

"The queens may not take it well that you sent the Du Mak away."

"'Sent' is a strong word."

"Suggested, then. The politics might be slightly different, but the effect is the same. As, I suspect, will be the opinions of the queens."

"It was the best solution I could think of. Besides." Donal smiled. *"Think of all the time they and the peers will have for preparatory scheming."*

Rowan laughed. She kissed Donal on the cheek.

"Good night," she said. "Join me for breakfast tomorrow?"

"Certainly," Donal said. "Sleep well."

Then, still feeling the touch of her lips on his cheek, he stepped into his suite and closed the door behind him.

He let out a long sigh. Alone at—

"Master," Morna said. She abased herself before him, dropping to her knees, clutching his shoes, and refusing to look at him as she spoke. "I'm so sorry I failed you. Punish me as you see fit, only please, please don't send me away."

Donal frowned a glance at Fionn, whose ears flipped in a canine shrug.

"In what way could I possibly think you failed me?"

"I underestimated the inquisitor. I failed to reach Robert Drake in time to enact your plan. I angered the inquisitor in your name. I am sorry, master. I am an unworthy slave and—"

"Morna," Donal said, and her words halted the moment he spoke, but she remained clutching his shoes and looking down. "Look at me."

She slowly raised her head. Fear filled her eyes and silvery tears lined her cheeks.

"Morna, in no way did you fail me."

"But—"

"I am speaking," Donal said, hating that he was playing into the master role, even though he knew she needed it.

It worked. She stopped speaking again.

"Morna," Donal said, and now he crouched down to look her in the eyes. "You solved the mystery of those assassins faster than even the inquisitor of the queens themselves."

Donal's mouth dried at what he had to say next, and the words caught in his throat, but this was a matter of the Fae Courts, and he had no choice.

"You br... brought justice in my name on the head of one responsible. You identified another in time for me to prevent a war between the Fae Courts and the Du Mak."

His voice gained certainty as he felt on steadier ground now. "Because make no mistake. Their third attempt would likely have succeeded. And even if the inquisitor learned the truth while I yet lived, he would have concluded that the Du Mak were behind it. Not Pajari."

"He's right," Fionn said softly. "The inquisitor would not consider Pajari anything more than a tool of Hrissapkuss."

"You see?" Donal said. He reached out and wiped the tears from her cheeks.

Morna shuddered as he did, and Donal took that as a good sign.

"You have served me very well in this, and I am grateful." Donal smiled and stood, taking her hand and helping her to her feet. "So let us have no more talk of punishment."

"Master," Morna said, teasing with her voice once more so that little chills traveled along Donal's spine as she spoke, "if you are best pleased with me, might I ask a reward?"

"I will not have sex with you tonight, Morna."

Donal didn't like including the word "tonight" in that sentence. But Fionn had warned him several times not to take away all hope from her. That doing so might cause her to fight against her very nature and damage her at her core.

"Perhaps I could massage you before bed?" she asked, voice teeming with hope. Hope, and likely the knowledge that Donal loved massages.

"Can you do so without trying to seduce me?"

Morna frowned and looked away.

"What about this?" Donal asked, and waited until she was looking at him again, out of the corner of her eye, before continuing, "I want to try to invent a new technique for long-distance communication. I have an idea based off the spells used to create memory circles, but it'll take a lot of work."

Her eyes widened, brimming with excitement as she turned to face Donal again.

"Oh, master, I could—"

Donal held up a hand. "I would ask you to aid me in this. To help me brainstorm, to be present as I experiment, and to work through it with me from start to finish. Would you consider that a reward?"

"Thank you, master! Thank you!" Morna kissed his hand three times. "When shall we begin?"

"Not until I'm home again," he said. "But if you have any ideas about reagents, you could have them waiting for me when I arrive."

"I go at once," she said with a suggestive curtsey. "Thank you, master."

She turned into the shadows and was gone. The very air seemed stiller without her presence.

"I would swear she's part whirlwind," Donal said.

"Whereas you look dead on your feet," Fionn said. "Food, and sleep, in that order."

"I agree." He rolled tight shoulders. "Do you think they have—"

Someone knocked on his door, rapid. Almost frantic.

Not more trouble.

Rowan?

Donal moved to the door as quickly as his exhausted limbs could carry him. He yanked it open.

Standing there, ready to knock again, stood his brother. His hair was a mess. His airsilks looked as though he'd slept in them for days. But unmistakably his brother.

"Bran?"

"Thank Brigid!" Bran said, and grabbed Donal in a crushing hug. "There are assassins after you. I sent Res—"

"I know," Donal said, pulling back to close the door. "I got Res' warning. Our old wards code." Donal managed a ghost of a smile. "The assassins ... have been dealt with."

Bran managed a smile that looked as tired as Donal's. He chuckled softly.

"I raced here from halfway to Ganymede. Set our mission back a month. And you didn't need me at all, did—"

Donal grabbed his brother in the tightest hug he could manage. Tears flowed and great sobs wracked him.

And there, in his brother's arms, Donal let it all come pouring out. The stresses, the fears and doubts, and most of all what he'd done and what he'd ordered.

He didn't hold anything back. And if Bran ever judged him about any of it, Donal never found out.

EPILOGUE

EDIK SAT ONCE MORE IN HIS FAVORITE PLACE IN THE UNIVERSE — THE captain's chair on the bridge of his beloved *Third Son*. He had a still half-full bowl of borscht in his hands, and no doubt some of it in his Van Dyke.

He even allowed himself the rare pleasure of putting his feet up on the ceramics of his workstation.

Xincapph was handling the flying, along the route provided by their escorts, a pair of Terran Naval gunboats, which would see them well past the zuglodon hunting grounds.

And so far as Edik was concerned, if he never saw another zuglodon, it would be too soon.

Dola sat curled up on the deck beside his chair, contented, and possibly snoozing.

Behind him, from the back of the main cabin, he could hear Anna talking with Sam in low voices. They needn't have bothered. If Edik wanted to know what they were saying, Nixia would tell him.

He didn't want to know. If those two were cooking something up, he'd probably find out all too much. And all too soon.

One of the strands of his communications web flared bright blue. A link coming in.

Well, on the one hand, it might be his escort. If so, Edik could choose to ignore it, secure in the knowledge that if it were important, they'd override his ignoring them and send it to his slap-pad.

Military vessels had that kind of priority link override, when they wanted to use it.

On the other hand, it might be the *Magellan*, flying just off the *Third Son's* port bow. Like a purple wyvern flying second escort.

If so, it might be Donal, and it would be good to talk to Donal.

"Would you?" Edik asked Dola, who admitted he was awake and jumped up to activate the link.

The head that appeared above the link web was not Donal's, but the black hair and widow's peak of an angry-looking Maximilian Pajari.

"Barshai," Pajari snapped, "where is my father?"

"Don't know, don't care," Edik lied idly, then frowned. "Actually, I kind of hope he's zuglodon chow." He turned an angry look on Pajari's eldest son. "He tried to kill me."

"Ridiculous. You aren't important enough to kill."

"Dola," Edik said, and Dola cut the link.

"The house of Pajari is now in that punk's hands," Edik said.

"Think he's really dead then?" Dola asked.

"The father? Dead if he's lucky. Anna said Donal gave him to the fairy queens."

"Politics is an ugly business."

"One I am happily out of." Edik smiled and indulged himself in one more spoonful of borscht, even though he felt full. "Good of Artissatass to thank me, before disenchanting my stone."

"What are you going to do with it?"

"Keep it as a memento." Edik shrugged.

"And what about Anna's?"

"Oh, good point. We should be in a safe spot by now. Nixia?"

Nixia swirled into presence before Edik, this time a half-meter tall and seemingly dressed in a lightweight summer gown, with her hair flowing wild around her.

"Yes, Edik?"

"Please ask Magom to release that rock now."

Magom, the earth elemental that handled Edik's hull maintenance had been holding that stone to the bottom of the hull since before takeoff.

"At once, Edik."

"Thank you."

She vanished if a puff of yellow smoke that dissipated at once.

Dola's whiskers twitched uncertainly.

"Zuglodon hunting ground would've been a safer place to dump it."

"I'm not so sure," Edik said. "Anna said something about the *Fomhóraigh* maybe working with zuglodons. And anyway, it's not as though anyone will know to go looking for it out here."

"Fair enough." Dola glanced back into the main cabin, then back at Edik. "Think Anna will be able to help Sam? With a job, I mean?"

"If not her, then either Donal or Carl," Edik said with a shrug. "But right now, we have space before us and time to fly. Let's just enjoy it."

DONAL'S CABIN ABOARD THE *MAGELLAN* WASN'T MUCH BIGGER THAN what he'd had aboard that Terran Naval ship on the way out here. But it felt infinitely more comfortable.

A bed and a desk that could be used at the same time. A toilet in its own, if tiny, room.

Plus, the air smelled clean, not of oil and steel.

A vastly superior way to travel, even if this wasn't the ideal location for a meeting.

Donal sat at one end of his bed, with Fionn on the deck bedside him. Bran sat at the other end, with Res perched on his shoulder. Both brothers were dressed in airsilks, though Donal expected that Bran's were a little better made, from the way they fit him.

Rowan, in a casual, green summer dress, sat on the desk's chair.

And Morna wore her usual gossamer and moonlight as she sprawled on the desk.

"And I think we're all up to speed now," Donal finished.

Bran sighed, "You do find yourself some deep messes."

"This one isn't necessary," Morna said. "It is right for us to battle the ancient enemy. I don't see why you wish to prevent it."

"Enough blood has been spilled," Donal said. "If I can stop this war, I will."

"But you've made the return of the Du Mak contingent on a war and a victor," Bran said. "At least, if their return is going to be within the next several lifetimes."

"I've been thinking about that," Donal said. "Hrissapkuss said only the victor could pull the spear."

"Please don't call it Excalibur," Bran muttered.

"Wouldn't dream of it," Donal said, then continued, "if I manage to prevent the war, doesn't that make me the victor?"

"That depends on how the Du Mak view war and victory," Fionn said, and not for the first time.

"Look," Donal said, "it's the best I've got. And it's a shot I've got to take."

"All right," Bran said. "But finding Fintan mac Bóchra. That's a pretty tall order."

"And possibly impossible," Donal said, "if he doesn't want to be found. With that in mind, will you help me?"

"Of course, master," Morna said before anyone else could speak.

Rowan looked as though she wanted to say something unpleasant to Morna, but swallowed the words.

"Of course I'll help," Bran said. "I do have to make one more trip out to Ganymede first, though. Lives are at stake, and I've pushed things already with this side-venture."

"You know you can count on me, Donal," Rowan said.

"Good," Donal said, and he looked around at all of them. Bran and Res. Rowan. Morna. Fionn.

They would make a good team.

Donal could only hope they were good enough to stop a war.

SIGN UP FOR STEFON'S NEWSLETTER

Stefon loves to keep in touch with his readers, and loves to keep you reading. The best way for him to do both is for you to sign up for his newsletter.

Sign up at http://www.stefonmears.com/join

If you sign up for Stefon's newsletter, you get...

- Monthly updates about his publishing and travel schedules
- His latest news, in brief, and answers to reader questions
- A free short story for signing up
- List-only offers and occasional specials
- Plus a free short story every month!

ABOUT THE AUTHOR

Stefon Mears avoids striking bargains with the Fae. Stefon has more than thirty books to his credit, and he never stops writing. He earned his M.F.A. in Creative Writing from N.I.L.A., and his B.A. in Religious Studies (double emphasis in Ritual and Mythology) from U.C. Berkeley. He's a lifelong gamer and fantasy fan. Stefon lives in Portland, Oregon, with his wife and three cats.

Look for Stefon online:
www.stefonmears.com
himself@stefonmears.com

www.ingramcontent.com/pod-product-compliance
Lightning Source LLC
Chambersburg PA
CBHW050348190726
48284CB00007BB/2202